# The Oedipus Murders

## Casey Dorman

Black Rose Writing | Texas

The author grants the final approval for this literary material.

First printing

This is a work of fiction. Names, characters, businesses, places, events, and incidents are either the products of the author's imagination or used in a fictitious manner. Any resemblance to actual persons, living or dead, or actual events is purely coincidental.

ISBN: 978-1-68433-331-8
PUBLISHED BY BLACK ROSE WRITING
www.blackrosewriting.com

Printed in the United States of America
Suggested Retail Price (SRP) $18.95

*The Oedipus Murders* is printed in Calluna

To Lai, Andrea and Eric

# The Oedipus Murders

"He that has eyes to see and ears to hear may convince himself that no mortal can keep a secret. If his lips are silent, he chatters with his fingertips; betrayal oozes out of him at every pore."

~Sigmund Freud
*Dora: An Analysis of a Case of Hysteria*

# Chapter 1

Descending through the gray curtain of fog, Regina Bonaventure navigated her white Mercedes down the tortuous curves of the narrow streets of Pelican Hill, guided only by the haloed porch lights softly visible on either side of the road. At the bottom of the hill she turned left into the parking lot of a shopping center, the wet pavement shimmering in the mist-muted glow of the metal halide lights perched atop their tall poles. The high-end mall, which fronted on the Pacific Coast Highway, was home to a collection of women's and children's boutiques, a hardware store, a supermarket, and three restaurants.

It was nine at night and the stores were dark, their long low line of attached buildings appearing as black shadows against the hillside. Only the lights from the supermarket and restaurants shone through the fog. Regina was badly in need of a drink.

She and Lucas were regulars at two of the restaurants: the expensive steakhouse and the Southwestern style cantina. She'd never entered the Asian restaurant because Lucas didn't like Asian food. From what her friends told her, it was a generic, Far Eastern dining spot. They'd also said that the restaurant had an elegant bar, which served a variety of cocktails, including exotic oriental drinks and, of course, wine, which was what she so badly needed at this moment. She parked along the side of the restaurant in the shadows near the back, hoping that no one she knew would see her car. She prayed that none of her friends were inside.

The bar was almost empty, and she ordered a glass of chardonnay. She'd had three glasses before leaving the house. The wine had probably contributed to her argument with Lucas—her wine and his whiskeys. It wasn't the first time that she had left after one of their alcohol-infused fights. She usually fled to the house of a friend. Lately, though, she had been going to bars, places such as this one, but farther away from home, places where she was not likely to be recognized. Although her visits to bars were driven by fear, she also felt a thrill, entering a strange setting, knowing no one… or usually no one.

She remembered the night she had run into an old friend, someone she hadn't seen for years. It had been a strange encounter. The man, whom she had known since childhood—a relationship she remembered with some pain—apparently hadn't recognized her, although she was sure it was him, despite his portly shape and the well-trimmed beard that he now wore. Later, she found him looking at her, staring, until he finally came over to the bar and sat down next to her, but when she addressed him by his name, he seemed confused. Then, as abruptly as he had come, he left without a word.

That was months ago. She never thought about it again except when she entered a bar by herself, as she had tonight. A quick look around told her that there was no one here whom she recognized. She breathed more easily and thought about why she was here.

Lucas was a bully. But he had been her father's choice and Regina had always done what her father had wanted her to do. Bertram Knowles, her father, whose oil company, with its platforms dotting the Santa Barbara coastline and stretching all the way to Huntington Beach, had sold his self-built business to Exxon Mobile for billions, retiring at the age of forty-two. He'd raised his only child as a princess, especially after her mother died when she was thirteen. At college she'd lived the protected life of a sorority girl, majoring in Romance Languages with vague thoughts of a career in international journalism or fashion advertising. She expected something to materialize through her father's connections. But when she graduated, her father told her that it was time for her to marry; time to give him a grandchild.

She and Lucas had never had a child. Her doctors told her that she was fertile. Lucas refused to submit to an examination.

She signaled the waiter to bring her a second chardonnay.

"The man at the end of the bar would like to pay for your drink," the tall Eurasian bartender said, nodding toward her left.

She looked down the bar. An early-thirties blonde-haired man smiled at her, then winked. He wasn't bad looking, she thought, well dressed in a light blue sport coat, open-necked shirt, and dark slacks. He looked well built and younger than her. He could be a businessman or a golfer, topping off a day at the office or at the nearby country club with a drink before heading home, someone hoping for a little action to spice up a dreary life. He caught her eye then raised his glass in her direction. He was drinking what appeared to be whiskey. She smiled back but shook her head. "I'll pay for my own," she told the bartender, "but thank him." She wasn't about to be picked up in a bar, not this close to home, not by someone who winked at her. She shuddered.

Was it time to return home? If she drank many more glasses of wine, she might have difficulty driving, especially in this fog. She'd have one more drink. She downed the rest of her glass in one gulp, then signaled the bartender for another. The man at the end of the bar held up his glass and raised his eyebrows as if in question. She ignored him. Even a second glass of wine had not heightened his appeal.

She sipped the third glass more slowly. Maybe Lucas would have gone to bed. He often retired early when he'd had too many whiskeys, and she was sure that he'd kept drinking after she'd left. But now she needed to use the restroom. Better do it before heading home, she thought. She left her drink half finished and headed for the restroom at the back of the restaurant.

When she returned, she noticed that the man at the end of the bar had gone. She relaxed a little. He looked harmless, but his friendliness had made her uncomfortable.

In the near blackness outside the restaurant, she fumbled with her key, almost dropping her purse. She hadn't realized how drunk she was. Finally opening the car door, she sat behind the wheel and, with some unsteadiness in her aim, touched a finger to the starter button. The car purred to life, the lights blinking on automatically. She sat for a moment to steady her head. Was she really OK to drive? Startled by a sound behind her, she turned. She stiffened in terror at the face looming at her from the back seat, the hand raised in a closed fist. Before she could utter a cry, the fist slammed into her cheek, knocking her unconscious.

Her assailant climbed out of the car. He pulled the unconscious woman from the driver's seat, then opened the back door and thrust her limp body onto the back seat. Closing the rear door, he got behind the wheel and backed away from the building and then headed out onto the fog-shrouded ribbon of the Pacific Coast Highway.

# Chapter 2

Doctor George Farquhar rested an elbow on his desk, his bearded chin cupped in his hand, a look of bewilderment on his round, middle-aged face as he stared apprehensively at his office door. He felt a disconcerting sensation of butterflies in his stomach, as if an unknown disaster were impending. He didn't know who was going to walk through his polished Oak door, and it bothered him not to know.

George's life followed a strict routine: out of bed by seven-thirty in the morning, coffee and toast while reading articles from the newspaper or one of his psychoanalytic journals, off to the office for his first patient at ten, lunch at twelve, a break to answer phone messages and complete other housekeeping chores until two, then three more patients before more catching up on messages and notes at five, and finally home, only ten minutes from his office, for cocktails with his wife before dinner. His world was deliberately circumscribed, both in his thinking and in his actions... except when he had lapses. And yesterday George had a lapse.

His secretary had called in sick, a rarity in the woman's ten years of employment for the three psychiatrists who shared her services on George's floor. George had allowed his answering service to take his calls during sessions, returning them in the breaks between clients. Everything had run smoothly until the exit of his two o'clock patient. For the next hour, one that was open due to a vacationing client, George's recollection was completely blank. His appointment book, however, had been diligently filled in with the name and telephone number of a new client, including the note *anxious and desperate,* but no other identifying information. The note was in his handwriting, but he couldn't remember writing anything. He had given the new client an appointment for today at three p.m. The thought that he had no memory of having received a call or booked a client spiked his anxiety. Pools of sweat, like telltale signs of his lapse, formed in his armpits.

From his late teens through his early adult years George had been plagued by such bizarre *fugue* states: periods of time, from minutes to several hours, for which he had no recollection. Each time he became aware of his excursions only later when he "woke up" in unfamiliar surroundings without any memory of how he had gotten there, haunted by a crushing feeling of guilt that he had committed an act too terrible to face.

George's recurrent amnesiac condition, which he later found was termed a *temporary dissociative state*, was the reason he had chosen psychiatry as his medical specialty and beyond that, further training in psychoanalysis, which had included his own 600-hour personal training analysis. His analysis had not only rid him of his dissociative symptoms, but taught him that his mysterious *absences* were a defense against the intrusion of wishes from his unconscious, as if his mind were burying itself in sand in order to refuse the entrance of disturbing and perhaps seductive thoughts, and that the guilt he always felt afterwards was related to the sexual nature of those thoughts. His analyst had reassured him that his behavior during such periods had surely been harmless.

But now, ominously, after a twenty-year respite, his fugues, like a disturbing object placed out of sight but not disposed of, had reappeared. Twice in the last two months he had found himself driving alone, near midnight, headed toward his home, with no memory of his actions for the previous several hours. In each case, his last recollection was of sitting alone in his house drinking a gin and tonic, usually his third or fourth. To quell his terrifying fear, he reassured himself that the episodes were related to his alcohol consumption; an alcoholic "blackout," not without worry in itself, but surely not a return of his dissociative symptoms. But now, for the first time, George had experienced one of his fugue episodes during the workday, without any prompting from alcohol. And as a consequence of its return, he had a new client, one who was anxious and desperate, according to George's notes, but otherwise a mystery to him.

—— —— ——

Lucas Bonaventure was dressed impeccably: dark suit, jacket open to reveal a vest across his flat midriff, neatly pressed pants, highly polished wingtips. He was over six feet tall and appeared to be in his late forties, with a clean-shaven face and neatly trimmed black hair, the stereotype of a successful businessman. He occupied the leather armchair in front of George's desk proprietarily, while exhibiting a mild frown as his eyes darted from the analyst's face to the circular French clock on the wall, seeming to be impatient for their conversation, which had barely begun, to be over. It was only when the man began to speak that George noticed the quaver in his voice, the nervous twitch of his eyelid.

"I really don't know if talking to you is going to do any good," Lucas said. He gazed at George with an aggressive stare, as if challenging him to disagree.

"I don't either," George answered. When Bonaventure had entered his office, George had been seized by the thought that he knew the man from somewhere, but he couldn't place him, and he was almost sure that they had never been introduced.

Lucas looked around the office as if he were noticing it—the framed degrees and licenses on the wall to his right, the well-worn couch behind him—for the first time. His eyes remained fixed on the couch, a low Mies van der Rohe-designed *Barcelona* couch—actually a daybed, complete with a rolled leather headrest—created in 1930 by the famous German-American architect and furniture designer.

George had paid more than ten thousand dollars for the leather couch fifteen years earlier, another five thousand for the matching chair, which sat slightly behind it, so that neither the therapist nor the client could see each other's eyes. George's training analyst had owned an identical set, and when George sat in the antique chair, listening to the associations of his clients lying on the couch in front of him, he felt the confidence of having achieved the reversal of roles, from *analysand* to *analyst*, awarded to him by his training.

Bonaventure's gaze lingered on the couch, as if drawn by a magnet. George was aware that the low-slung piece of furniture could represent an object of fear to a new client. Its height, a mere eighteen inches off the floor and approximately the same as the height of the seat of the analyst's chair, signified surrender, the helpless vulnerability one felt when lying down on a physician's examining table or leaning back in a dentist's chair. To lie on the couch meant to give up power, something George doubted Lucas Bonaventure was used to doing.

"I'm not in need of anything myself," Lucas said, turning back to George and settling himself in the chair, as if he had decided that, after all, he would stay. "It's a woman. I'm worried about her mental state; I'm hoping you can give me some advice."

"A woman?" George glanced at Lucas' left hand on which a slim gold wedding ring shone.

"An acquaintance... actually, someone who works for me."

"An employee, then."

"Yes, I'm very concerned about her."

"Someone you're close to?" George asked.

"Very." Lucas showed no sign of being self-conscious about his admission.

"You're married?" George wasn't judgmental, an analyst hardly could be, but he wanted to verify his assumptions before continuing.

Lucas' face became slack, as if the muscles supporting his aggressive jaw line, the scowling curve of his mouth, had lost their purchase. He avoided looking directly at George. "I was."

"Was?"

"My wife is missing."

Suddenly George knew why the man had looked familiar. The disappearance of Lucas Bonaventure's wife had been the main topic of the local news for the last two weeks.

# Chapter 3

"I read about your wife's case in the newspaper."

Lucas' gaze drifted around the room, as if he were looking for something upon which to focus. "There's been a lot of media coverage," he said at last. With apparent effort, he drew his attention back to the psychiatrist. "But that's not why I'm here."

"No? It's this other woman you're concerned about?"

His gaze regained its intensity. "As I said, she's behaving oddly." Lucas stared at George as if he'd said all he was going to say on the matter.

"What do you mean she's 'behaving oddly'?" George asked.

Lucas hesitated, as if he were composing his answer. "Provocatively. She's a nice girl, or woman really, well mannered, shy, or at least she had been until now. Now she acts as if she's a prostitute." He spit out the words with venom.

George was surprised by Bonaventure's virulent tone. "She acts like a prostitute?"

Lucas shifted in his chair, casting his gaze around the room, as if he had to swallow his anger before he spoke. "She wears short skirts, low cut blouses," he answered, his face starting to color. "She deliberately walks past our male employees, swaying her hips, or bending over to reach for something. Sometimes she stops to talk to them for no reason, stays late to talk, or lets them walk her to her car."

"And this concerns you."

A flash of anger darkened Lucas' expression. "Of course it concerns me. She's playing with fire. Those men don't value her. They don't know what kind of woman she really is. One of them is going to take her seriously and then she'll be in real trouble."

"Trouble?"

"Of course, trouble. Those guys would like nothing better than to get her in the back room, or into the back seat of one of their cars. She's just asking for it."

"I see." George nodded, doing his best to conceal his skepticism. "And this behavior, this provocative behavior, it's new? She didn't behave this way before?"

"No." Lucas still looked irritated, as if he suspected that George doubted him.

"When did you notice that she'd changed?"

He gazed at the ceiling as if trying to recall. "I don't know, maybe a week and a half ago, two weeks maybe."

About the time his wife had disappeared, George noted. "You said that you and this woman were close. Does she have a name, by the way?"

Lucas looked at him suspiciously. "Why do you want to know her name?"

"I don't really. It just makes it easier to talk about someone if we can refer to her by her name."

Lucas looked down at the floor. "Sherry, her name is Sherry."

"So with this Sherry, things changed about a week and a half or two weeks ago, is that right?"

Lucas nodded. "That's about right. She just started acting differently. I spoke to her about it."

"What did you say to her?"

He screwed up his face, as if making an effort to remember. "I think I asked her why she was acting that way. I might have told her that she was taking a risk."

"How did she react when you told her that?"

Lucas' face hardened. "The first time she thanked me. But it didn't change the way she acted or dressed. The second time she told me that I was being inappropriate, saying the things I said to her."

"What did you say to her?"

He shrugged nonchalantly. "I don't remember exactly. I might have said that she was acting like a whore."

"Does that sound appropriate to you?"

Lucas frowned. "Perhaps not. But I was concerned. I didn't want anything bad to happen to her."

"And since then?"

"I called her at home. I thought maybe I could talk to her as a friend instead of her boss."

"How did that go... when you called her at home?"

"She said I was harassing her. She told me not to call her again."

"And have you?'

"A couple of times. She changed her number, so I stopped." He didn't look embarrassed by his admission.

George leaned back in his chair and took a long look at the man across from him. George's anxiety had dissipated as he became more and more intrigued by what he was hearing from the man. Bonaventure was clearly in denial about the significance of his wife's disappearance. He seemed to have transferred all of his anxiety about his wife to his secretary. "While all this has been going on between you and Sherry, your wife has been missing. Isn't that hard on you?" George asked.

"There's nothing I can do to find my wife. The police are doing it all. I'm just waiting until they find her." He spoke matter-of-factly, as if he were referring to someone else's problem.

"But it must take an emotional toll on you."

Lucas stared back at him with a blank look. "Not really. Like I said, there's nothing I can do. I'm just waiting."

"What do you think happened to your wife?"

"I have no idea." He looked disinterested.

"No suspicions, no theories?"

"She took chances."

"What do you mean?"

"Sometimes she took risks, did dangerous things." He looked blankly at George, but his jaw muscles were working furiously, as if he were stifling a rage.

"Risks? Dangerous things?"

"You know, went out at night, things like that."

"She was having affairs?"

Lucas scowled. "I didn't say that. She just ran around. I warned her."

"Warned her?"

"That she was playing with fire, that something could happen."

"Something like...?"

"I don't know. Like what happened. Now she's missing." He looked at George with suspicion. "Why are you asking me about my wife? That's not what I'm here for."

"And what are you here for?"

Bonaventure sighed. "I told you, I want to find out what's wrong with Sherry; how I can help her. I want to stop her from doing something that could lead to her getting hurt."

George placed both hands on his desk. "I can't really figure out Sherry for you, Mr. Bonaventure. She's not the one who's here, you are. It seems to me that you're very mixed up about how you feel about this Sherry woman. It also sounds to me as if your feelings for Sherry may be related in some way to how you feel about your wife. If you'd like to come back and talk to me more about these things, I'm willing to see you. But we will be learning a lot more about you than about Sherry."

Lucas gazed down at the floor, a glum expression on his face. When he looked up, he seemed to have lost his aggressiveness. "OK, I'll come back and talk some more," he said meekly. Then he straightened, regaining his self-assurance. "But I still intend to help Sherry. Maybe you can teach me something about myself that will help me do that. I feel better now than before I came in here."

George was surprised. He had been certain that Bonaventure would reject his offer. "I'm glad to hear that. Shall we say day after tomorrow at three?"

Lucas pulled out his cell phone and tapped it a few times. "That will work."

# Chapter 4

"I can't believe you're planning to take that man as a patient," Madeline Farquhar said to her husband. "You always make the wrong decisions."

She raised her pencil-thin eyebrows and stared at him, her thin lips pursed in a frown. It was an expression George was used to, but he still felt intimidated by it. By her.

Madeline was a tall, slim woman. With her narrow face and heavy makeup, she had a severe look about her, a look that George felt she had developed, perhaps even cultivated, over the years of their marriage. She was a novelist, an Avant-garde artist, committed to breaking barriers, to creating new icons for the intelligentsia. In the early years of their marriage, she had admired George's status as a physician, his intellectual sophistication represented by his identification with Freudian theory, which had not yet completed its descent from its position of prestige in Western culture. His degrees and his position should have made him feel as if he were her superior, although they never had. In time, she had lost her respect for him and his profession, grown to disparage what she called his "slavish" adherence to psychoanalysis, which she referred to as a "worn-out theory of human behavior." She told him that his continued belief in the methods of psychoanalysis was a symptom of his timidity, his reluctance to try anything new, traits that she claimed characterized his personality.

"But I'm fascinated by the man," George answered, feeling, as usual, as if he were on the defensive. "He seems to have completely denied any emotional attachment to his wife."

"And that's unusual?" Madeline replied. "Physician, examine thyself." Her dark eyes, under her arched eyebrows, were filled with scorn.

"I mean he's displaced all of the emotions he should be feeling toward his wife so they're now focused upon his secretary," George continued, doggedly. "*That's* unusual, especially since his wife may still be alive."

Although his professional ethics forbade it, George often discussed his cases with his wife. Her curiosity, and even more, her insistence, trumped his ethical reservations. The only rule upon which he insisted was that she not use any of his revelations as material for her novels.

"But he's in the news, George," she said. "And so will you be as his psychiatrist." They were in their living room, sitting in matching curved-back Queen Anne chairs, sharing their ritualistic evening gin and tonics, looking out at the sunset over the Pacific Ocean from their house's perch high on the western side of Newport Beach's Spyglass Hill. The sea, in the distance, was a glistening silver in the light of the descending sun. "The press has already convicted the man of his wife's disappearance, and no doubt of her murder. The police haven't said so directly, but the newspapers say the police are treating him as a suspect. And you, you're considering taking this psychopath on as a client. What do you think people will say about you when he's found guilty and it comes out that you began seeing him as a patient *after* he'd murdered his wife? Whatever possessed you to do such a thing?"

"You're jumping to conclusions," he said, feeling the sweat beginning to form under his arms. He couldn't tell her that he hadn't even been aware of giving Bonaventure an appointment. His history of dissociative states and their recent reappearance were something he shared with no one, least of all his wife. "The man hasn't been accused of anything, except by the press and by people like you who can't wait for the police to do their job. Besides, why would me seeing him for therapy get anyone's attention? Why would the papers even mention it?" George knew why Madeline was upset. She was afraid that he would do something foolish to jeopardize their income. It was her chronic fear. His wife had grown up in an impoverished household, her father an alcoholic who was often unemployed. She acted as if the financial success she and her husband enjoyed could be wiped out at a moment's notice. George suspected that it was his earning power as a physician that had attracted her to him, even more than the prestige of his profession, certainly more than his personality, which she rarely hesitated to disparage.

"Are you serious? Why do you think a man suspected of killing his wife would seek psychiatric help and then display symptoms that made his doctor—you—think that he's some kind of psychotic who doesn't know what he is doing; or more pertinently, what he might have done?"

"You think he's trying to set up an insanity plea?"

"Don't you?"

It *had* occurred to him, although he had dismissed the idea. "I don't think that's what's going on. His manner was genuine. I had to drag some things out of him. The indifference he displayed regarding his wife was real, I'm convinced of that. And it's that symptom that points to some kind of neurosis, an unhealthy, even abnormal, reliance upon repression. That would hardly serve as a basis for an insanity plea."

"Sometimes, dear, you intellectualize things so much that you can't see what's right before your eyes. The man is a psychopath. He is a dissimulator. He presents exactly the kind of picture that convinces you that he has some kind of mental illness, and you fall for it hook, line and sinker." Her expression was one of disgust.

George struggled to keep his feelings under control. It didn't pay to show his anger around Madeline. She just got angry back and he couldn't face that, the days of not speaking to him. He always felt abandoned. "Well I don't think so," he answered.

"You're playing with fire, George."

He was caught off guard by her use of the same phrase that Lucas Bonaventure had used in talking about both his wife and his secretary. "Are you warning me?" He looked up at her, trying to read her expression.

She scowled at him. "Damn right I am. You can't afford to have your reputation compromised. Analytic patients don't grow on trees, and you haven't kept up with new developments in biological psychiatry enough to be able to do anything else. Other doctors can always fall back on something like moonlighting as emergency room physicians if their practices begin to fail. But what could you do in an emergency room, dear? I wouldn't allow you to give me a shot and I certainly wouldn't want you to be wielding a scalpel in my presence. You've become a one-trick pony, and that trick has a very limited audience."

He had a momentary vision of standing in front of his wife with a scalpel in his hand. He felt his palms beginning to sweat. He refocused his mind on their conversation. "You never complain about the money my one trick brings in."

"You earn well, I admit that dear. But your income is fragile. It's built upon a fading cultural phenomenon. Look at your colleagues. They're mostly in their seventies, some even older. You're always dreaming of publishing your cases in one of your hallowed journals, but half of those journals have gone out of publication. Nobody's coming into the profession but a few impressionable social workers. How many of *them* are going to want to claim that they received their training from the man who treated a psychopathic murderer and didn't even know it?"

He'd finished his third gin and tonic. He remembered his recent fugue episodes. He needed to rein in his anger... and his drinking. "I'll think about what you've said," he answered her, trying to sound sincere, perhaps even contrite. "Why don't we have dinner and then we can watch some TV?"

"Dinner is in the oven. I'll get it out. But after dinner I have some writing to do. The UC Irvine MFA program wants me to give a talk to their students next week and I have to come up with something."

"Really? That's great. You'll probably enjoy talking to some aspiring writers, you always enjoy teaching, and students love you." He knew he was trying to ingratiate himself, to change the tone of their conversation.

"Perhaps I should talk about knowing the difference between fiction and real life. How novelists are sometimes more perspicacious in this regard than others are. But then I'd have to censor my temptation to mention psychoanalysts as the prime example of those who fail to make this distinction. That would be difficult."

He knew she was joking, but he still felt a twinge of panic that she might talk about him and some of his cases in order to make a point. But then, she really was only interested in making her point to *him*, he reminded himself.

"I'm sure you'll come up with something," he said, standing. "I'll set the table for dinner."

# Chapter 5

"The police are on their way," Mrs. Schrempf greeted him. Her round face was fixed in a polite smile, but the look in her eyes suggested that she knew things she wasn't saying. Her voice was as cheery as if she were announcing a visit from the Girl Scouts.

George was standing in the waiting room, having not yet entered his office. He froze, thoughts of turning around and going back home flooding his mind. His stomach was churning. He willed himself to remain calm. "Did they say why they want to talk to me?" He knew it was about Lucas Bonaventure.

"A Detective Reynolds said that your new patient, the one you scheduled while I was away," she said pointedly, "told them that he was seeing you and they want to talk to you about him."

Was even Mrs. Schrempf distancing herself from him? Suddenly he was overwhelmed by the same sense of foreboding and guilt that he felt when he returned from one of his fugue episodes. He reminded himself that the police were interested in Lucas Bonaventure, not in him. He picked up his battered briefcase, which contained only unread journals and unused notebooks, items he ferried back and forth to the office each day because carrying the leather briefcase made him feel more like a doctor, or perhaps a scholar. Most of the time he felt like neither.

George greeted the two plain-clothes officers, a man and a woman, and offered them seats in front of his desk.

"You are aware that I can't divulge anything that Mr. Bonaventure has told me," George began. "If he hadn't told you that he was my patient, I wouldn't even be able to acknowledge that much to you." He had on his glasses, and he leaned back and looked down his nose, trying to convey an aura of authority, although the presence of the two detectives aroused his anxiety; as if he were about to be caught doing something wrong.

The woman, an early-thirties, dark-haired, slim Asian, dressed in a flowered dress with a high-neck oriental cut, who reminded George of a woman he'd once seen in a movie, although he couldn't remember which one, spoke first. "Lieutenant Reynolds is a detective, doctor," she said, looking over at her male partner. "I am Doctor Susan Lin, a forensic psychologist working with the Newport Beach Police Department."

George was impressed by the woman's delicate beauty. She was tall and willowy, with short black hair brushed back on the sides. He was surprised that the police would send a psychologist to talk to him. "If you're a psychologist, then you know that my professional ethics, as well as the confidentiality laws of this state, severely restrict any information that I'm allowed to provide you. Unless my client signs a release of information, I'm virtually prohibited from telling you anything he's said to me."

The psychologist looked over at her partner, as if she were seeking his permission before continuing. The detective gave a slight nod. "I'm quite aware of the rules about confidentiality, doctor," she said. "I'm here because we thought it might be easier for a psychologist, such as myself, to talk to you."

Detective Reynolds cleared his throat. He was a heavyset man, in his early fifties, with a swarthy complexion and a balding head of dark hair, glasses, and a habitual scowl on his face. "We're both aware of confidentiality, doctor, but Bonaventure is talking to you, which is more than he's done to us. He hasn't said diddly-squat to us about his relationship with his wife, except to say that his marriage was 'normal,' whatever that means."

"I'm assuming that he didn't sign a release of information or you would have shown it to me," George answered, looking from one to the other for confirmation.

Neither answered.

George nodded. "As I've said then, I can't discuss what he has said to me, or what he will say to me in the future or about his relationship with his wife or anything else without such a release." He turned to the young psychologist. "You, of all people, should be aware of this, Dr. Lin," he said, leaning back again to look down his nose at her. He hoped he was conveying the impression of a seasoned professional admonishing a neophyte, although he felt more fear than anything else at the moment.

"You said 'in the future,'" Doctor Lin answered, ignoring his remark.

"Then he is embarking on a course of treatment with you? Since you've already admitted you will be seeing him in the future, you can answer that." She gazed at him, smiling pleasantly.

She had caught him. He had a habit of divulging things he hadn't intended to share. It was an impulsive trait, which he was constantly trying to control with his rules and routines. He tried to quell his anxiety. "We've only met once, but it's possible."

"And this treatment would be psychoanalysis?" Doctor Lin asked, arching her eyebrows to indicate that she was not only interested but also skeptical. "I saw on your door that you were an analyst as well as a psychiatrist."

"Psychoanalysis requires an extraordinary commitment. I'm not sure it's indicated in the case of Mr. Bonaventure, nor that is what he is seeking."

"So you practice other therapies besides psychoanalysis?"

"Few people meet the requirements, either in time or money, intelligence, or ego strength, for full analysis. Most of my analytic clients are analysts in training. But I also see patients for shorter-term, analytically-oriented psychotherapy."

Detective Reynolds looked as if he were becoming impatient with the shop-talk between the two professionals. "So you've only seen Bonaventure one time, is that what you're saying?" he asked, casting an irritated glance at his partner.

George allowed his gaze to linger on Susan Lin before turning to the detective. "That's correct, detective. I saw him yesterday for fifty minutes. That was our first interview."

"And he's coming back when?" the detective asked, still scowling.

"Tomorrow," George answered, feeling as if it was futile to keep denying what he'd already implied.

"And after that?"

"I don't know. It will depend on his need."

"Psychoanalytically-oriented psychotherapy?" Susan Lin asked.

"I can't really discuss that."

"Have you given him a diagnosis?" she asked.

"If I had, I couldn't tell you what it is."

"I'm aware of that. I just wondered if you'd given him a diagnosis yet."

George replied with a noncommittal shrug. She might be attractive, but Doctor Lin was prying too much, and he had the feeling that she might trap him into saying more than he intended. Was that because of her skill or his lack of self-control? He just wanted the interview to be over. "I'm afraid I've told you all that I can tell you."

Detective Reynolds turned toward Doctor Lin and raised his eyebrows, as if to inquire if she had any more questions. "Are we done?" he asked.

She looked at George. "No more questions, Doctor Farquhar, except a general one. I had thought that psychoanalysis was a thing of the past. Do you still regard it as a valid theory for understanding human behavior?" A trace of a smile played about her lips.

He had the fleeting thought that Doctor Lin had been talking to his wife, but he knew that was his imagination conjuring such an idea. The majority of the psychological establishment shared the psychologist's opinion about his profession. She seemed friendly, but he felt as if she were baiting him. Despite his anxiety, he couldn't stop himself from answering. "Everyone has hidden reasons for his or her behavior. Psychoanalysis is one way of explaining those reasons and for the person being analyzed to understand those parts of his or her psyche that had previously seemed a mystery."

"I see." She still had a smile on her face, and he wondered if she was mocking him.

"I take it you subscribe to a different theory." He wasn't sure if he felt irritated or engaged by her manner.

"I'm less concerned with theory than with facts," she answered. Her smile was smug. Detective Reynolds shifted in his chair and glanced impatiently at the door.

"What kind of facts?" The psychologist's attitude definitely irritated George, but he also found himself becoming intrigued by the conversation, or perhaps it was with her.

"Those supported by research findings: personality traits, for instance, which are largely based upon genetics, although some, of course, are due to extreme trauma. Some too are based upon brain factors such as deficits in prefrontal cortices in psychopathic individuals, for instance."

"That's all well and good for large-scale studies of groups of people," George answered, her argument being a familiar one to him, "but they can't really be used to understand an individual." He was feeling more confident.

"If that were true I wouldn't have a job," she answered, laughing. She seemed to be enjoying their verbal joust.

Detective Reynolds stood up. "I think we've taken enough of your time, doctor. We're going to ask for a release from Bonaventure and then maybe we'll be back to ask you more questions." He glared at his partner.

She shrugged her shoulders, then gave George a warm smile. "I hope we can talk again, Doctor Farquhar."

George was relieved that their conversation was over, but he also hoped they could talk again.

# Chapter 6

"I hope you and the doctor had fun with your little debate about whatever you were talking about." Detective Abe Reynolds' broad face was covered by a frown. He and Doctor Susan Lin were sitting in his office, he behind his wooden desk and she in one of the hard plastic chairs in front of it. Behind him was a window looking out on a golf course across the street. They had just returned to the station from their interview with Dr. Farquhar.

"Sorry about that," Susan answered, although she really wasn't sorry. She had enjoyed the back and forth conversation with the psychoanalyst, but she knew that she had to maintain a good relationship with the investigating officer on the case. Abe Reynolds was a lieutenant, near the top of the hierarchy in the Newport Beach Police Department. He was twenty years her senior and he had a good reputation for solving crimes. She'd only worked with the Newport Beach Police Department for two years and her position was part-time, an experiment on the part of several Orange County police departments, which shared her services. She knew that she was regarded with suspicion and even distaste by some members of the force who distrusted her methods and disliked the fact that she was allowed on important cases despite only being a consultant. It might also be because she was a woman—an Asian woman. This was only her second case with Newport Beach, which had few murders or abductions, the kind of cases that required her services.

Reynolds shuffled through some papers on his desk. "Bonaventure doesn't have an alibi for the night his wife went missing, but there is nothing to suggest that he did anything peculiar or unusual that night, either. He says he was at home, had a few drinks, watched TV, and then went to bed. He wasn't aware that his wife didn't come home until he woke up on Saturday morning, and he reported it right after that."

"Isn't that unusual, to file a missing person report as soon as a spouse stays away for one night? Wouldn't most people assume that she stayed at a friend's or relative's place, try to make a few phone calls or wait for a while?"

"You tell me. You're the psychologist."

She wasn't sure if he was being sarcastic. She didn't want to alienate the lieutenant, but she needed to stand up for her opinion. "Right, but you're the one with the experience. Anyway, it seems unusual to me."

"I'm still putting my money on the man in the bar. He left right before Mrs. Bonaventure, and he could have waited for her in the parking lot."

"The odds are on the side of our perpetrator being her husband. Bonaventure is awfully blasé about his wife being missing, don't you think?"

The detective shrugged. He was still scowling. "Any other insights? You spent some time looking through a lot of papers yesterday."

"I had to get a court order to unseal Bonaventure's juvenile police record in Riverside. It took more than a week. We can't use any of the sealed information in court, but it gives me a better basis for building a profile of him. That's what I told the judge and he bought it."

"So Bonaventure was arrested as a juvenile?"

"For assault and robbery. The victim was another high school student. Bonaventure was a junior, just seventeen. He claimed the student owed him money and wouldn't pay him back. The other student claimed he was being extorted. Bonaventure beat him pretty badly and the other boy's parents called in the police. Bonaventure was convicted but his record was sealed when he turned eighteen."

Reynolds sighed. "So he was a badass in high school. But there must have just been that one incident or they wouldn't have sealed his record."

"Just that one when he was a minor. But I also checked his college record. He started at UC Riverside, but was caught cheating on an exam and kicked out of school. He went to community college, then was admitted to Cal State San Bernardino for his last two years."

Reynolds shrugged. "Not good, but I've seen worse. Anything else you turned up?" He leaned forward. He had gotten more interested in what she had to say.

"He worked for a firm that sold advertising when he got out of college. After three years he left and started his own company, which did the same thing. His former employer sued him for taking clients with him, but they lost the case because they couldn't prove that the clients didn't switch on their own. After five years with his own company, his partner took him to court for falsifying the company's books and reporting a smaller profit than they actually made so that his partner's share was less. Again, the partner lost. They dissolved the partnership after that."

"He doesn't make many friends in business, does he? But he won both of the cases."

"There's more. He got into an altercation with one of his neighbors here in Newport Beach. You showed me that record, remember? The neighbor dropped the charges. I tried to track down the neighbor, but he and his family moved away right after the incident. Another neighbor said that the family that moved was afraid of Bonaventure doing something to them."

"That's it?"

"That's it."

"Doesn't prove much. Except maybe Bonaventure is a jerk."

"Or a psychopath. That's what it suggests to me. I'd like to get his grade school records. I'll bet he had behavior problems even when he was young. Most psychopaths have very rocky childhoods: running away, fighting, bullying, animal cruelty. I'm willing to bet that's what I'll find."

"He grew up in Riverside?"

"Was born there. I've already contacted the judge. It's the same judge who gave me access to his sealed record. I'm pretty sure I'll get permission to look at his school records."

"And if he is a psychopath? What good will knowing that do us?" Reynolds' scowl had returned.

"In court, nothing. It's not the kind of thing you can use in court. But most psychopaths make mistakes. The same impulsiveness that leads them to commit their crimes leads them to leave clues, to do things that tip other people off. We already know that Bonaventure doesn't cover up his mistakes very well. He may not get convicted often, but his college, his business partner and his neighbor all were witnesses to his inability to control his impulses. He'll do something stupid. All we have to do is watch him closely enough to see it."

"Something stupid like going to see the psychiatrist?" Reynolds scowl had disappeared. He hated to admit it, but he was impressed with Doctor Lin's work. He'd assumed that a forensic psychologist limited herself to interviews and tests but Susan Lin did real investigating. She'd told him that a suspect's history was a better source of information about his personality than most of the psychological tests at her disposal.

"I can't figure that one out yet," Susan answered. "It could be that he's trying to lay the foundation for a defense of insanity or impaired judgment if he gets caught. But there's nothing in his record that suggests that he's clever enough to think of that, or even if he is, that he could fool someone like Doctor Farquhar. That's one reason that I wanted to find out more about the doctor. I'd like to talk to him again."

"Leave me out of it next time," Reynolds quipped. But this time he didn't seem angry. He pursed his lips. "Farquhar said he can't tell you anything."

"That's true. But maybe I can tell him some things. Like how to spot a psychopath, for instance. Maybe I can convince him to order some personality tests or a brain scan to help him in establishing a diagnosis. I had the feeling that he hadn't made a diagnosis on Bonaventure yet."

"That's all your area," Reynolds said. "Meanwhile, I'm going to keep looking for the mysterious man in the bar. But I'll step-up surveillance on Bonaventure too, and keep looking for his wife, or his wife's body, which is what I'm pretty sure we're going to find."

"Then you don't mind me poking around, meeting with Doctor Farquhar by myself?"

"The psychology part is your bailiwick. I'm just a fifth wheel when you start talking about that stuff. You've found some good stuff already without my help, so go ahead, I trust your judgment." His hostility appeared to have gone as he smiled at her across the desk.

Doctor Lin was pleased. She felt better working on her own, but she hadn't wanted to provoke Detective Reynolds. Besides his years of experience and his rank, he was the Chief Homicide Investigator in the department. If he opposed her, she'd be off the case. "I'll let you know what I find out. This sharing information is good for both of us, don't you think?"

He nodded. "I think it might be."

# Chapter 7

The large Golden Collie stood without moving. George let his Lexus idle as he stared at the dog in the arc of his headlights. Why was he waiting? What did the presence of the dog make him think about? Around him the fog blew in diaphanous clouds across the dark road, bringing the dog in and out of his field of vision. He watched as the animal stumbled forward, its legs unsteady, its noble head hung low, swinging from side to side, as if it were drugged. Slowly, it made it to the edge of the road and then disappeared into the fog. George's gaze trailed the dog into the darkness.

A half hour later he pulled into the shopping center and stopped in front of a restaurant that still had its lights on. George tried to clear his head. He had a vague recollection of a dog, a large one, sick, he thought. Why was he thinking of a dog? What was he doing in this shopping center at the bottom of Pelican Hill on PCH? Why were his hands covered in dirt? He wiped them on a rag next to him on the seat of the car.

George got out of his car and headed for the restaurant. He needed a drink. Maybe that would clear his head. He stepped inside the restaurant. It was Asian. Because of the hour, there were only a dozen or so customers in the restaurant and no one sitting at the bar. George headed straight for the bar.

"Gin and tonic, double" George said.

The handsome Eurasian waiter smiled at him. "It's good to see you again, sir."

His words caught George off guard. He had no recollection of visiting the restaurant before. He stared at the waiter, probing his mind for some shred of memory, but nothing surfaced.

"When was I here before?" George asked when the waiter brought him his drink.

The man shrugged. "A few weeks or so, I guess. I remember the double gin... and the beard."

Maybe the man was mistaken. George couldn't believe that his mind played such tricks on him. The last memory he had, other than the vague dreamlike visions of the Collie dog, was of sitting home, staring at his wife's empty chair and drinking his fourth gin and tonic. He looked down at his drink in front of him on the satiny wooden bar. He'd only taken a sip so far. How could he have forgotten that he'd already had four drinks that night? And this one was a double.

The barman was at the other end of the bar, fiddling with the glasses. George took a twenty from his wallet and left it on the counter. Leaving the rest of his drink unfinished, he walked quickly to the door and out into the night. Behind the wheel of his Lexus, he thought for a moment. He must have driven PCH to get to where he was now, despite his inebriated condition. His house was only ten minutes away with almost no traffic, but there was no other route than the highway. He put the car in gear and headed out of the parking lot onto the Pacific Coast Highway.

# Chapter 8

"You needn't lie down on the couch if you're more comfortable in a chair," George said as Lucas Bonaventure straightened the creases on the legs of his pants. He was lying on the analyst's couch in his shirt and tie, gazing at the ceiling. His coat was neatly folded on the seat of one of the chairs.

"I thought this was how it was done."

"It's up to you. I don't require you to lie down, but if it doesn't bother you, I find that it helps to free up a person's mind if he's not staring his doctor in the face." In fact, George felt that his position above and behind his client gave his clinical observations an additional air of authority they might not have had if he'd had to look the client directly in the face. Given Lucas Bonaventure's tendency to challenge him, George was relieved that Lucas had accepted the couch.

"I have no problem looking you in the face, doctor. But I want to do whatever is most helpful. This is fine, here." Despite his protestations, he continued to squirm to find a comfortable position, each time re-straightening the creases in his trousers.

"What kind of thoughts have you had about our first visit?" George asked.

"I don't think my wife has anything to do with this."

"With what?"

"With why I'm here."

"Your wife is missing."

"Of course. But that's not something I can do anything about by talking to you, is it? I can help Sherry if I know what's wrong with her."

"Does it bother you to talk about your wife?"

He started to sit up again, then lay back down. "Why should it bother me? I have nothing to hide."

"Why indeed?" George said. "So tell me about her."

"What do you want to know?"

"Whatever is important. What she was like." He noticed that he referred to the man's wife in the past tense. Why was he already thinking of her as dead?

Bonaventure heaved a loud sigh, as if it were a burden to acquiesce to George's request. "Regina comes across as gracious, even shy, wouldn't hurt a fly or step out of line even a bit. But that's not really her. She's used to being spoiled. Her father is a rich oilman with offshore rigs near Santa Barbara. He raised her like a princess. Once we got married, she expected me to give her everything her father gave her when she was growing up. When she didn't get what she wanted, she complained, always comparing me to her father. I'm successful, but I'm not filthy rich like he is. She was never really satisfied with me."

"You're feeling a lot of anger toward her."

"No. I'm just telling you what she's like. You asked."

"What made you want to marry her?"

He heaved another loud sigh. "Like I said, she seemed shy, not too assertive, always wanted to please me. That's what I was looking for."

"So you were looking for a docile woman?"

George could see from his vantage point that Lucas was frowning as he stared up at the ceiling. "I was looking for someone who wasn't like my mother. I had a very domineering mother. She turned my father into a wimp. I wasn't going to let any woman do that to me. Regina kept that side of herself hidden until after we were married."

George was surprised by Lucas' insight. It was at odds with his usual opacity with regard to his motivation. "But she ended up reminding you of your mother?"

"I heard this would happen, that you shrinks would want to blame everything on the mother." His hands, at his sides, were clenched.

"I thought I was asking about your wife."

"Wife, mother, it's the same thing. Neither of them was ever happy with me."

"They both treated you the same way?"

"Sure they did. The same way my mother treated my dad. Even playing around on him."

"Your mother played around on your father?"

"He thought so. I heard them arguing about it all the time. And she had men over when I was a kid. I remember that. She made me stay in my room whenever some guy came to visit." He was opening and closing his fists.

"You must have been angry at her."

"I hated her for that. She drove my father out of the house."

"Your father left?"

"When I was ten. She kept everything. He just took off. Never heard from him again."

"So your mother raised you after that?"

"If you can call it raising me. She was out all the time. The only thing she ever did with me was tell me that I was a failure. No matter what I did, it wasn't good enough for her." The hatred in his tone was palpable. His fists remained clenched at his sides.

"Is your mother still alive?"

"No. She died about ten years ago, drank herself to death. Well, not really. She drove off the road one night while she was drunk. She drank a lot as she got older."

"Do you still think about her?"

"Not really. Not unless my wife does something that reminds me of her." He turned his head to look over his shoulder at George. "Can we stop this about my wife and mother? I'm more worried about Sherry."

"You can talk about whatever is on your mind."

Lucas sat up for a moment, as if it took some effort to refocus his thoughts. He turned to face George, his legs hanging over the edge of the couch. "I tried to talk to Sherry's mother." The anger was gone from his voice.

"Her mother?"

"I wanted to find out if there was something in her history that would lead her to be the way she is, something her mother could tell me about."

"What did her mother say?"

"Said there was nothing wrong with her daughter. She was nice about it. She was worried when I told her that her daughter might be in danger."

"You told her that Sherry was in danger?"

"Sure. I needed to impress on her how serious this was. Her mother finally admitted that her daughter was naïve. She was glad that I was looking out for her. She offered to meet with me."

"The mother offered to meet with you?"

"Um hum. We didn't set anything up. I'm afraid of making Sherry mad if she finds out."

"So you're still looking for an explanation of Sherry's behavior."

"That's why I'm here. I need to find out how to help her so nothing bad happens."

"But I told you that I can't help you understand her. I've never met her."

"I could set something up." Lucas was still sitting on the edge of the couch. He stared at George, waiting for his response.

George was bothered that Lucas' suggestion aroused his interest. "That isn't how I work. She's not my client." It reassured him to cite the rules of therapy.

"What if I tell her that I'm getting help so I'll stop bothering her and my doctor wanted to meet her to find out who I was talking about. That would be true wouldn't it?"

Such a meeting violated all the tenets of therapy. George felt guilty and stimulated by the prospect at the same time. "Let me think about it. In the meantime, we'd better stop for today. Can you come back in another couple of days?"

Lucas smiled, as if he were satisfied with his therapist's answer. "Sure, depending on the time."

"I'll let you work that out with Mrs. Schrempf, my secretary. She will arrange the appointment."

Lucas got up and put his coat on. "This is interesting doc. I'm not sure whether it is going to help, but it is interesting."

He walked his client to the door. "Mrs. Schrempf will set up your next appointment."

# Chapter 9

"I can't believe you talked to him. I told you that the man was harassing me at work. Why didn't you just hang up on him?" Sherry Bennett was frustrated. Why did her mother do things like this? She scanned the parking garage as she exited the elevator. She didn't want anyone overhearing her conversation. She would have texted, but her mother refused to use her phone for anything but talking.

"He's your boss, honey, I couldn't hang up on him."

"He's not my boss for long. The man is acting weird and if I had another job to go to, I'd be out of here. He's creepy, mom. He keeps telling me that he's worried about me, but then he tells me that I'm acting like a whore. He wants me to wear long skirts and stop talking to any of the men in the office. He scares me."

"Maybe he's concerned. I've told you that your skirts are too short, remember? You have to be careful or men will think you're advertising that you're easy." Her mother's voice had taken on the lecture quality that usually made Sherry stop listening.

"C'mon mom. I don't dress like a whore and it's none of his business how I dress anyway. Nobody's ever tried to bother me except Mr. Bonaventure. You're just siding with him because you don't want me to lose my job."

"Of course I don't. I think you're overreacting to a boss who cares very much for you."

"I don't want him to care for me. Besides, his wife is missing. That's really creepy. He should be out looking for her, not stalking me." She had been so absorbed in the conversation that she'd forgotten where she was going. She stopped and looked around for her car, feeling disoriented. "I have to hang up mom. I'm paying so much attention to talking to you that I can't even find my car."

She closed her phone and tried to jog her memory. She didn't warrant her own parking space, as the executives in Bonaventure Enterprises did, so she had to take whatever space she could find in the parking structure that served the employees of the more than thirty firms occupying the building. She'd been upset when she'd arrived for work and she hadn't paid attention to where she had parked.

At least there weren't many cars left in the garage. She had stayed late talking to Gary Olson, one of the computer techs whom she knew was interested in her and who was always nice to her, even if she didn't reciprocate his amorous feelings. Then her mother had called and she'd talked to her until she was almost the last one in the office other than Mr. Bonaventure himself. She'd begun to worry that she'd have to talk to him if she didn't leave, so she continued talking to her mother but left the building.

She saw a van she thought she'd parked next to in the morning. Probably her car was behind it. Behind her she heard footsteps, hurrying across the floor. She froze, then stole a glance over her shoulder. She thought she saw someone moving behind a car off to her left, but no one emerged from the other side of the car. She quickened her pace, her anxiety beginning to turn to panic. Then the sound was there again, this time as if someone were running. She stopped and stared, but could see nothing. She thought about screaming, hoping someone would hear her.

"Sherry!"

She whirled around. Gary Olson was trotting across the parking garage floor. "Want me to walk you to your car?"

She felt a surge of relief. "Sure, I was feeling a little nervous with the garage being almost empty. I didn't realize you were still in the office when I left."

"Trying to impress the boss, I guess. But when I knocked on his door to tell him goodnight, it turned out he'd already left. I didn't even see him go."

She immediately tensed. "He'd already left?"

He had reached her side. He shrugged. "I guess so. Can't have been too long ago, though. I saw his car is still in its space, so he must still be in the building."

"Really?" She glanced over at the van behind which she thought her car was parked. She thought she saw someone move behind the van. "I'm glad you're here, Gary. I think my car's behind that van over there, but I'm not absolutely sure. Walk with me over there will you?"

"No problem. You know I like to walk with you, Sherry... and talk to you." He looked at her with an adoring expression.

He reminded her of a boy in junior high who'd followed her around like a faithful dog. "Me too, Gary." At least she wasn't alone, she thought.

She'd been right. The back of her car was coming into view. "That's it!" she cried, surprised at how relieved she felt. She reached the car and unlocked the door, checking in the back seat, just to make sure that no one was there. "You're a sweetie, Gary. I'll bring you coffee in the morning to repay you."

"How about a drink tonight instead?"

She looked at him and smiled. "Maybe some other time. I'm too tired right now. Thanks again for being my protector."

"Hey look," Gary said, gazing over her shoulder. A long black Mercedes was slowly exiting the parking garage. "There goes Bonaventure now. I guess he was still in the building."

*Or lurking in the parking garage*, she thought. Now she was sure that she was going to find another job.

# Chapter 10

George wasn't surprised at how pleased he was when Susan Lin called to ask if they could meet, but he *was* surprised that she had called him. She promised not to probe for information about Lucas Bonaventure. She said she wanted to talk about professional matters.

"Then if it's not about one of my clients, let's make it more social. How about if I meet you for lunch? My treat." What was he doing, inviting a young woman for lunch? He quickly pushed the thought out of his mind.

"We'll go Dutch, but lunch sounds good. I mostly want to learn about your approach to therapy anyway. And share some ideas. How about the Yard House?"

The Yard House was a gastropub, part of a chain, which advertised the largest selection of draft beer in the United States. He'd only been there once. His wife refused to enter the establishment. She never drank beer herself and frowned on those who did, labeling them "trailer park refugees who wear baseball caps indoors." "Perfect," he answered. "The ideal woman; one who likes beer." He was aware that he was making it sound like a first date. He immediately felt foolish for having said it, although the thought of a date with the attractive young woman excited him.

"See you at one," she said.

———   ———   ———

He walked to the restaurant and arrived fifteen minutes early, which gave him time to secure a table amidst the heavy lunch crowd, a table from which he could see the entrance and spot the young doctor when she came in. She arrived ten minutes after he did. He garnered her attention with a wave of his hand.

"Beer?" he asked. "It's their specialty."

"A Heineken," she said, smiling and sliding into the booth across the table from him.

He'd already ordered himself a strong Belgian beer, which the restaurant served in a goblet. He hoped she'd ask him about it. He'd looked up the beer's provenance on his iPhone, and he had an urge to show off, which made him self-conscious when he realized what he was doing. "Do you eat here often?" he asked, pushing his insecurities out of his mind.

"A few times. A lot of the police like the place."

"Then I had better watch myself," he joked.

"This is really a social visit, or a professional one, but not really police business." She had settled into her seat, and her smile remained, but her eyes looked serious. "I'm very interested in someone who practices psychoanalysis in this day and age. I'm not trying to be disrespectful, but I'd thought that almost no one was an analyst anymore, especially not someone young, like yourself."

Hearing her describe him as young pleased him, even though he knew that he was probably twenty years older than she. He was sure she was just being polite. He took off his glasses, realizing that he was hoping that not wearing them would make him seem younger. "You mean you thought it was only very old men, probably trained in Europe, who still had practices on the Upper East Side in New York?"

"Or Beverly Hills."

"Newport Beach is not that different from Beverly Hills," he reminded her.

She nodded. "That's true. This is only my second case here and I'm still getting used to the level of wealth in this community. Is that who most of your clients are?"

He'd had his share of film stars over the years and even a professional athlete or two, all of them local residents, but he didn't want to sound as if he were bragging. "Most of my analytic clients are trainees from either the local Analytic Institute or from the larger one in LA."

"You said you didn't get many criminals in your practice, but it sounds as if you don't get many real patients, that is people suffering from genuine disorders."

"It's about 50/50," he hastened to correct her. "Half of my practice is analysis with trainees, the other half is short term therapy with, as you call them, 'real patients.' "

"Like Lucas Bonaventure."

He wagged a finger at her. "Ah ah. That's forbidden territory."

Their beer had come. She looked with interest at his goblet of dark beer, but, to his disappointment, didn't ask about it. They both ordered their meals, his a club sandwich and French-fries, hers a salad.

"Why are you interested in psychoanalysis?" he asked.

"I guess I'm more interested in someone who practices it than in analysis itself. I learned all about it in grad school, but I've never met an analyst before."

"You mean it's like stumbling across a dinosaur in the middle of the modern world?" He was joking, using a phrase that had angered him when his wife had said it.

"I wouldn't put it that crassly. In fact, from what I learned about psychoanalysis, it's a very complex theory, one that is probably misunderstood by most people and one that takes years to learn."

Was she deliberately stroking his ego? She was correct, but it was hard to believe that she meant what she was saying. "I hate to say it because it doesn't sound scientific, but the power of psychoanalysis to explain behavior is not something you can fully understand until you've been analyzed yourself. I know that's what born-again Christians say about having a relationship with Jesus and what Zen Buddhists say about achieving enlightenment, but I still think it's true."

She smiled and nodded. "I'm willing to give you that. Do you feel that you understand your own behavior, why you do what you do, better than most people understand theirs?"

Did he? He wasn't about to tell her about the blank periods that had once again begun appearing in his life, the times he found himself someplace but didn't remember how he got there, or the impulsiveness he was constantly trying to subdue with his strict routines. "I think I can understand the reasons for what I do, see the patterns that fit my personality better than most people can."

"And does being able to understand the reasons for one's behavior help a person to change?"

"Sometimes. It's not enough by itself, but it's a necessary component."

She nodded slowly, as if thinking deeply about his answer. He was struck by her pensive beauty.

"Most psychopaths have a pretty clear understanding of why they do what they do," she said. "Unfortunately, very few of them want to change their behavior."

"Really? You don't think they're acting out some unconscious conflict and just rationalizing what they do without really knowing why they do it?" Other than a few classic papers from early in the last century, he had never really studied the psychology of psychopaths.

She shook her head. "In most cases, they just want things and don't want to postpone getting them and don't want to pay for them. They take what they want, whether it's money, property, sex or power. They're not conflicted about it. They're just unable to say no to their desires."

"But sometimes what they want is bizarre or sadistic, isn't it? What about their understanding of why they have such desires?"

"You mean like Ted Bundy or Jeffrey Dahmer, the Hannibal Lecter types? Those aren't your typical psychopaths. I admit that those people are deeply disturbed in some way and probably don't understand why they have such perverse appetites."

"And do *you* understand why they have such appetites?"

She shook her head, slowly. "I've studied such people. They all have very unusual childhoods, but do I understand why they are as sadistic as they are? No, I don't. Do you think psychoanalysis provides a way to understand them?"

"Only in theory. No such person would subject himself to analysis, I'm sure. From what I've read in the popular literature, Ted Bundy studied psychology, but apparently gained little self-insight from it."

She looked thoughtful "Then do you think the fact that Lucas Bonaventure is seeking analytic understanding means he's not a psychopath?"

"I think labeling his disorder is less important than helping him understand himself. That's what I'm interested in." He hoped his confident tone concealed his anxiety.

"You're very good at not answering questions directly," Susan said, smiling and holding up her glass as if she were toasting his skill. "I suppose that's something you've learned through years of being a therapist."

"You're not a therapist yourself?"

She shook her head. "I only do diagnostic work. I'm afraid I'm a skeptic when it comes to the power of psychotherapy to change people." She smiled uncertainly, as if she knew she was being critical of his profession.

"Change isn't always what therapy is about, except to lessen anxiety, perhaps. But there are more direct ways to do that with medication. Therapy primarily provides the client with understanding."

"Then I must learn more," she answered, brightly. "Now I'd better eat so I can get back to work on time. It's been a very interesting conversation, Doctor Farquhar. I've really enjoyed it."

"So have I," he answered.

# Chapter 11

Danny Rosberg sat in his motel room. His stomach ached with hunger, and he was sweating as though he had a fever. His description had been on the TV news again, a reminder that it was still dangerous for him to be seen in public. What a come down, he thought. He'd been staying at the Hyatt in Newport Beach, and now he was in a Motel 6 in Santa Ana, eating his meals at fast food drive-thrus. He still attended his business meetings, but, since they were mostly with the visiting Japanese executives from the company with which his employer was negotiating, he wasn't afraid that anyone at the meetings would identify him as the man who'd tried to buy the missing woman a drink in the bar in Newport Coast. He doubted any of his Asian business associates, who used a translator for all of their English conversations, watched the local news or read the local newspapers.

The police had put out a call for him to come forward, but there was no way that he was going to turn himself in. As soon as his business was over he was headed back to Boston. Then the nightmare would be over. Unless they found the woman's body. Then they would mount a national manhunt and he'd have no place to hide.

Guilty or not, his record would convict him—an assault on his girlfriend when he was in high school, two years in the Florida State Prison for assaulting another woman he hardly knew but had picked up as a one-night stand, then beat her when she tried to take his wallet. He was lucky he hadn't had to register as a sex offender. That he hadn't was only because the two other women he'd raped after picking them up in hotel bars were married and were afraid to report the incident to the authorities, lest their husbands find out. At least that was his theory. He'd never seen either woman after the nights when he'd forced himself on them. That's what he'd planned to do with Regina Bonaventure: a shared drink and then sex back at his hotel, but no rough stuff unless she didn't cooperate. She should have accepted his offer of a drink. If she had, she'd probably be OK right now. She might have been the recipient of some hard sex, even an unwilling recipient, but not "missing and presumed dead" as she had been described in the newspaper. Too bad for her that she had been such a stuck-up bitch. The more he thought about her, the more he thought that she deserved what she'd gotten, even though he was now in danger.

He was hungry. He'd gotten a hamburger after his meeting, but that was around two in the afternoon. Now it was ten at night and he hadn't eaten anything since the afternoon, nothing except whiskey, coke, and chips, which he'd bought at a grocery store near the place where his meetings were held. Without even a microwave in his room, there was no point in buying food, except potato chips and peanuts and candy bars, which he'd almost finished. He was only about a half-mile from three different fast food restaurants and a Denny's. He'd visited the drive-thrus at each of the fast food places several times over the last week and a half. Was it finally safe for him to enter the Denny's? There'd never been a picture of him in the paper or on TV. The papers had only published the written description of him that the bartender at the Asian restaurant had given to the police. The same description could fit a lot of people.

He finished the plastic cup of whiskey, his fifth since leaving work. The whiskey made him feel more confident. What could it hurt to go to Denny's? He changed into his most casual clothes. Although it was chilly at night, he decided not to wear a coat, since he'd been described on the news as wearing a sport coat.

When he entered the Denny's he found that the air conditioning brought the temperature even lower than it had been outside. He could take it. It was worthwhile in order to have a regular meal, maybe a steak and even a beer with his dinner, although he felt a little unsteady from the five cups of whiskey.

The steak was thin and overcooked—he'd ordered it rare—but it was delicious compared to the tacos and burgers he'd been eating. He devoured it eagerly and ordered a second beer. He felt better than he'd felt for the last week and a half, ever since his description had appeared on the news. He decided he'd order some pie. He hadn't had a piece of restaurant pie in years.

"Good thing you ordered the blueberry pie now," the waitress told him. "It's a favorite of both of those cops over there, and we only have one piece left."

Danny hadn't noticed the two policemen enter the restaurant. They were sitting in a booth three booths away from him, between him and the door. "Never mind," he said. "I'm not as hungry as I thought I was."

"I was just kidding," the waitress said. "We have plenty of pie, you don't need to worry."

"That's OK, I'm really not hungry."

"You sure? We've got plenty of pie for all of our customers."

He was getting irritated. He just wanted the waitress to bring him his bill so he could leave. "No pie," he said, raising his voice. "Just bring me the bill."

"How about some coffee? We have a whole dessert menu. Can I bring it to you?"

*Jeez*, he thought, *what's wrong with this bitch?* "Just bring me the goddammed bill!" he said, his voice nearly a shout.

The two policemen looked up. They stared at him.

Shit! He thought to himself. He lowered his head and put his hand on his forehead so they couldn't see his whole face. He shouldn't have shouted, but the beer and the whiskey had made him lose his temper. He kept his head down until the waitress returned. He gave her cash and told her to keep the change, even though he didn't think the stupid bimbo deserved a tip. He was ready to leave, which meant walking past the two cops.

He got up and walked as fast as he could past the policemen's booth, keeping his head turned away from them. Only too late, he discovered that he'd walked right past the entrance. Shit! He was drunk, and the cops were staring at him. He kept walking, pretending he had been headed for the restroom, which he entered. He looked at his face in the mirror. His face was red from the alcohol. He felt hot. He ran the cold water and splashed it on his face. He felt cooler. Grabbing a handful of paper towels, he dried his face and left the restroom, looking straight ahead as he passed the two cops, who both gave him a suspicious stare. When he got past the front door and into the night air, he breathed a sigh of relief. He resisted running toward his car. When he finally reached it and got inside, he ventured a look back at the restaurant. The two policemen were coming out the front door. They were looking his way. He started his car and pulled out of his parking space.

It was less than a mile back to the Motel 6. He held his breath. It seemed impossible that the two cops had identified him. He was sure they hadn't gotten a clear look at his face. They were only interested in him because of that stupid bitch of a waitress. If she'd just brought him his bill he wouldn't have yelled at her. He drove slowly and carefully, forcing himself to stay within the speed limit. Damn! Now he was going too slow. Behind him, blue and red lights began flashing.

He floored the gas pedal. He couldn't let the police pull him over. They'd pull him in for driving while intoxicated, and once they had him in custody, they'd figure out that he was the man who'd been at the bar with the missing woman. The police hit their siren. He kept his foot on the gas pedal. He was already up to seventy and it was a city street. He kept accelerating. On the right, he spotted a freeway entrance. He barely slowed as he spun the wheel to take the turn into the entrance. Only at the last second did he realize that it was an exit, not an entrance—just before he hit the truck coming off the freeway, his own car going sixty-five miles an hour, the two vehicles meeting head-on.

# Chapter 12

"Last night I had a dream. It was the second time I've had the same dream, or at least a similar one. You're supposed to be able to tell me what it means, right?" There was a note of dread in Lucas Bonaventure's voice as he lay on his back, staring at the ceiling, his head on the leather pillow.

"You sound worried," George said, mildly surprised that Lucas was already telling him a dream without any prompting.

"Both times it woke me up. The dream did. My heart was racing. I thought I might have a heart attack. Is that normal?"

"Dreams can often cause the same emotions we feel in our waking lives."

"There was nothing frightening going on in the dream, nothing that would have frightened me in real life."

"Tell me about it."

"I remembered it vividly when I woke up, but it's kind of vague now."

Lucas was retreating from the dream already, an indication to George of the level of anxiety the dream had provoked. George knew he had to push his client. "Tell me what you *think* you dreamt."

Bonaventure sighed and shifted his weight. He had turned away from the doctor, and lay on his side, facing the wall, as if to signal that he was complying against his will. "I was in a forest, it was dark. I was on a narrow pathway among tall trees, following a young woman, but for some reason, I thought it was my mother. Every time I tried to catch up with her, I moved more slowly, as if my legs were half-paralyzed. I couldn't get close to her." He rolled onto his back and his eyes searched the room, as if he were looking for an escape.

"Your legs felt paralyzed, or half-paralyzed, you said." George hoped his words would bring his client back to the rest of the dream. Whatever came next provoked enough fear to cause Lucas to try to avoid continuing.

"I know what being paralyzed is like," Lucas said, his voice quieting, so it was hard for George to hear. "Six years ago I lost function in my right leg.

It lasted more than six months. They never found a cause."

George wasn't sure he had heard his client correctly. "So the feeling in your legs in the dream reminded you of a time six years ago when your right leg was paralyzed?" Hysterical paralyses were rare. It took a massive effort of repression to cause such a symptom. In Freud's Victorian culture such symptoms had been common, but they were unusual in modern times.

"Yes," Lucas answered. "But in my dream, it was both of my legs and they were only partially paralyzed. I was able to move, but it was difficult."

"So you kept following the woman?"

"She went away at some point. After that, I came into a clearing in the forest. There was a man in the middle of the clearing. He looked like a workman. He was sawing something on a sawhorse. I couldn't tell what it was, but it terrified me. That was when I woke up."

Bonaventure's dream was a textbook Oedipal castration dream. George had recognized it immediately: the pursuit of the mother figure, the old man—a clear father figure—wielding a sharp instrument, one that could cut off a child's penis, the paralyzed legs, which represented the feeling of vulnerability of the male's sex organ. This was the kind of case George had dreamt of having, the symbolism of the symptoms so clear that he would have no difficulty writing it up for a clinical journal. His immediate task was to determine how deeply the psychological sources of the dream were buried in his client's unconscious. The closer they were to consciousness, the more anxiety Bonaventure would be feeling.

"And just now, did remembering the dream make you nervous?"

"A little, but not like when I woke up from the dream last night."

"Did you then or do you now have any thoughts about the dream?"

"What do you mean?"

"Something that pops into your mind. Some thoughts that the dream provokes."

"My brother."

"Your brother?"

"My older brother died around the time my leg was paralyzed."

"How did you feel when he died?"

"We weren't close, but I felt lost when he died. I had a panic attack. A lot like the feeling I had in my dream. Then my leg stopped working and I had to cope with that, using crutches, then a cane. I forgot about my brother and my panic went away."

"Do you remember what you were panicked about?"

Lucas hesitated before answering. "I guess the fact that I might die. He was only forty-eight, barely older than I am now. My father died at fifty. I felt doomed."

"So six years ago you were worried about dying, but after your leg became paralyzed you stopped thinking about dying?"

"I had too much else to deal with."

"What did the doctors say about your paralysis? What did they say caused it?"

"I never went to the doctor."

"You couldn't move one of your legs and you didn't go to the doctor?" George tried to keep the incredulity out of his voice. He didn't want to make his client defensive.

"No." Bonaventure's tone was blasé. As if what he was saying were perfectly natural.

George recognized Lucas' reaction as the classic *la belle indifference,* which often accompanied hysterical symptoms. Freud had written about it many times. "Why didn't you go to the doctor?" he asked, although he knew that his client would not have an answer.

"I guess I figured it was temporary. My problem was how to get around on one leg."

"And the paralysis just went away on its own?"

"After about six months I woke up one day and it was gone."

"How about your fear of dying?"

"I stopped thinking about it."

It was time to end the session. George regretted that he wouldn't be able to follow up on Bonaventure's dream further, or on his mysterious paralysis. Lucas Bonaventure had no insight into the unconscious sources of his behavior. Such cases were almost unheard of among educated Americans in the twenty-first century. But the rules of psychoanalytic sessions were ironclad, and despite George's curiosity, it was time to stop. "I'll see you next week," George said.

"You haven't told me yet whether you'll meet with Sherry," Bonaventure said, as he sat up and put on his jacket.

"I'm still thinking about it."

# Chapter 13

"That was our guy, all right," Abe Reynolds said. "He fits the description and he's got a record of assault against women, even did some time for it in Florida. And after the Bonaventure woman was reported missing, he changed his hotel."

Susan Lin looked skeptical. She was sitting across from him in his office in the Newport Beach station. Through the window, she could see golfers on the spacious course, which ran all the way down to PCH. Beyond that was Balboa Island and the sea. "He knew we were looking for him and he had a record. That's why he was at the Motel 6. Even if he was innocent, it made sense for him to switch hotels. And we don't have any other evidence against him. What's worse is that, if it was him, how are we going to find Mrs. Bonaventure if her kidnapper is dead?"

"C'mon, admit it. You can't let go of Bonaventure." Reynolds looked as if he were laughing at her. "After all, you've put in all that work on proving he's a psychopath."

"He's a psychopath whether he killed his wife or not," she answered, trying not to sound defensive.

"Our job's to find a killer, or at least a kidnapper, not to diagnose the victim's husband."

She raised her eyebrows. "You were convinced that Bonaventure killed his wife, just as much as I was. You know you were."

"Sure I was, but that was before this guy Danny Rosberg came along. He was the man who met Regina Bonaventure in the bar, he has a history of beating up women, and he changed his hotel so no one would find him. Not to mention that he panicked and tried to get away when the Santa Ana cops tried to stop him."

Susan nodded her head, grudgingly. Reynolds was making a lot of good points, but she knew that Lucas Bonaventure was at least capable of killing his wife and she wasn't ready to give up on him yet. "I want to continue looking into Bonaventure, but I'm going to find out more about Rosberg too.

He's clearly a psychopath himself."

"Good," Reynolds said. "Keep an open mind. 1 have to admit that, even though Rosberg looks like he's our man, I'd prefer that it be Bonaventure. At least with him, we have some chance of finding out what happened to Mrs. Bonaventure. We can't question Rosberg now that he's dead."

They were interrupted by the sergeant from the front desk. "Lieutenant, we've got a new development in the Bonaventure case. They've found the wife's car."

"Where?"

"Parking garage at John Wayne Airport."

Reynolds looked over at Susan. "The perfect hiding place. People leave cars there for long stretches of time without attracting attention." He turned his attention back to the sergeant. "Get the crime lab people over there and don't move the car until they've collected all their evidence."

"Maybe this will be the break we need," Reynolds said to Susan. "If Rosberg's prints are on the car, then he's our guy. If not, then Bonaventure is back in the picture."

"Or Regina Bonaventure parked her car at the airport and took a flight," Susan answered. "Remember we haven't got a body. She could have just left Orange County. Hadn't we better check that out too?"

"For a psychologist, you're a pretty good cop," Reynolds said, smiling. "I'll get someone to check the flights on the night she disappeared."

"And the next morning," Susan added.

"Right again."

———  ———  ———

"The only prints on the inside of the car were those of Mr. and Mrs. Bonaventure." Jerry Sloan, the crime lab detective had an apologetic expression on his face, as though he was at fault for bearing bad news.

"Any evidence that anything had been wiped?" Reynolds asked.

Sloan shook his head. "Nobody wiped anything, but the last driver wore gloves."

"So we don't know if it was Rosberg or not," Reynolds said, his discouragement evident in his voice.

"Not really. But there's no solid evidence that Rosberg was ever in the car. Unless you guys find a pair of gloves with Mrs. Bonaventure's blood on them in his hotel room."

Detective Reynolds shook his head. "Nada. There was nothing in his room with blood on it, none of the woman's possessions, nothing to tie him to Mrs. Bonaventure at all."

"We're still checking the back seat and the trunk—hairs, blood, you name it. If there's anything there we'll find it."

"Great. Keep me posted."

Danny Rosberg seemed a likely suspect, but with no direct evidence, other than his probably having been the man seen in the bar with Regina Bonaventure, Abe Reynolds knew it would be hard to prove anything. And, as Susan Lin had pointed out, if Rosberg had been responsible for Regina Bonaventure's disappearance, it would be next to impossible to find her, or her body. That would bother Abe. Newport Beach was a small town and murders were rare, less than one a year, most years without any at all. There hadn't been any unsolved cases since he'd been put in charge of homicides ten years ago. It was a record Abe was proud of, and he didn't want it spoiled.

It sounded to Abe Reynolds as if Susan Lin was on the right track. Barring any hairs or threads that would tie the car to the late Danny Rosberg, Lucas Bonaventure was still a suspect. Rosberg wasn't ruled out by any stretch of the imagination, but so far, because he was dead, there wasn't much that could be done to prove that he'd done anything except drive drunk and try to elude the police. Maybe Susan Lin would find something to point a finger more strongly in the direction of the husband. Abe hoped so. His pride would suffer if they never found Regina Bonaventure's murderer, but he didn't have any qualms about giving Susan the credit if it was her digging into Lucas Bonaventure's past that solved the crime. His pride was based on achieving results, not personal distinction. He was too professional to allow his vanity to cast a shadow over his work.

# Chapter 14

"See?" George held up the front page of the paper for his wife to see. "The police found the man who Regina Bonaventure met in the bar the night she went missing and he has a record of assaulting women."

His wife came out of the kitchen and into the living room where her husband was sitting with a gin and tonic on the table next to him. She had a drink in her own hand. She didn't bother to look at the paper he was holding in the air. "Has the man admitted anything yet?" Her words came out like an accusation

"He can't. He died in a police chase. Ran head-on into a truck coming off the freeway. But they're following up on him. It says here that a source in the police department said the man was a prime suspect in Mrs. Bonaventure's disappearance."

She sat opposite him in one of the Queen Anne chairs. "It sounds to me as if they don't know anything. You're still seeing the husband, right?" Her tone was disapproving.

"He's my patient. He hasn't done anything."

"Hasn't he? Do you know that for sure?" She stared at her husband, waiting for his answer, as if she had caught him in a lie.

"He has a classic neurosis. Some of his dreams are right out of a textbook. He hasn't a clue what they mean. And even better, he experienced a six-month hysterical paralysis when his brother died six years ago. I haven't had a case this good in years. I might even write it up."

She put down her drink. She was shaking her head. "Write a paper? Nobody would read it but your group of deluded colleagues in the Analytic Institute. You're practicing in the dark ages, you and the rest of your Analytic Society. I still can't believe people pay you for doing this stuff."

"You're perfectly happy to spend the money they pay me." He knew he was treading on thin ice with such a comment, but she was beginning to irritate him, as she often did when they discussed his practice.

"I admit you make a good living. But I bring in my share. My writing may not produce blockbusters, but it's very well respected in literary circles. Each of my novels has been reviewed by the New York Times. I was on the shortlist for a National Book Award with *Winter Song*. I may not make as much money as you do, but what I'm doing is at the forefront of progressive culture, not some leftover set of ideas from the last century."

"A lot of writers utilize psychoanalytic theory in their novels. It's very popular among intellectuals."

"*Was*, George, *was* popular. You're thinking of Faulkner or Capote, people of that era. It's fallen well out of favor in the last few decades."

He gulped down the rest of his second gin and tonic. "I couldn't understand human beings without it." He had the fleeting thought that he might have just admitted his own failing rather than made a point in favor of psychoanalysis.

"You can't understand them with it or you wouldn't be fooled by this Bonaventure deviate, who's obviously working you into his defense, in case they ever find his wife's body."

"You have no evidence of that. It's your theory and it's probably no longer even the theory of the police, who are following up on this Rosberg guy, the one who died. You're just using Bonaventure to mount another attack on my work, probably because you're jealous that I make more money doing what I do than you do doing what you do."

"Now you're acting like a child, George. I thought your training analysis was supposed to cure you of that. If there was ever proof that your method doesn't work, you're it. You play all day at being a doctor, even though nothing you do resembles medicine, and then you come home and carry on juvenile, competitive conversations with me. And now you're risking your livelihood—our livelihood—by insisting on treating this psychopathic wife-murderer, just to spite me."

He felt himself withdrawing under her withering attack. He wished he could run away or make her disappear. His wife always personalized everything. He thought about Susan Lin, the police psychologist. Doctor Lin didn't believe in psychoanalysis any more than his wife did, but that didn't stop her from respecting him as a doctor, or at least it hadn't seemed to the two times they'd met. Madeline used every conversation about his work as an excuse to belittle him, probably because she didn't respect him as a man. They hadn't had sex for over a year. Neither of them was clear if the other wanted it, and both of them were content to ignore the topic.

"You're not even listening to me, George. You never do. You drink yourself into a stupor and pretend that I don't exist. You're married to one of the most celebrated writers in America, and you can't take the time to listen to her opinions. Thank God I've got my university seminars and my academic colleagues. If I had to be content with talking to you, my IQ would probably plummet."

"Are we going to have dinner tonight?" he asked.

She stared at him. "Sure, George. I'm your wife; I can cook. I'll serve you dinner so you don't starve to death and then I'm going out. I'm going to find someone with whom I can have a real conversation"

"Great. Just make dinner, then do whatever you want." He got up to fix himself another gin and tonic.

# Chapter 15

"You're feeling powerless?" George asked.

"About helping Sherry."

"Not about finding your wife?"

Lucas started to sit up, then lay back down "No, not about my wife. I told you, I know I can't do anything about finding her."

"And that doesn't make you feel powerless?"

"Not really. I know the investigation is being handled by the police. I've put out a reward. There's nothing else I can do. It's Sherry that I'm worried about. That's something I *can* do something about."

"What can you do?"

"Get her to listen to me. Get her to change." He lay on the couch silently for a few moments. "I've come up with a plan."

"A plan?" George felt his pulse quicken.

"For getting Sherry to talk to you."

"I've told you…" His tone was half-hearted, and he was aware of that.

"No, no," Lucas interrupted him. "I don't want you to do therapy with her, I just want you to meet her, to get to see her, give me some idea what you think. I've figured out how to get you to meet her."

George knew that Bonaventure was using Sherry as a diversion from his unconscious fears, but he couldn't curb his interest in the idea. "Go ahead, tell me your plan."

"She's quitting. She sent me a formal letter resigning her position. She'll be gone in less than two weeks."

"And…?"

"I told her that we offer our employees exit interviews to help them find another job. It's true but only if we are the ones letting them go and only for our executives. But she doesn't know that. So I thought that you could interview her."

"You mean I should pose as your exit interviewer?" George leaned forward in his chair.

"You could even tell her that you are my therapist and that it's not a typical exit interview, that you're doing it as a favor to me."

"And then I'm supposed to help her find a job?" He felt let down. Such a plan would never work.

"No. We don't really do that anyway. After the interview, we just hook them up with an employment agency. It's more of a PR thing, to be sure someone doesn't come back and sue us for letting them go."

"So it's worthless to the employee."

"Most employees seem to appreciate it."

"I can't see someone under false pretenses."

"So how about I go back to plan A. I tell her that I know she's quitting because of me, and I'm sorry, and I'm trying to get help for myself and my therapist wants to talk to her to find out what I've done to drive her away."

"That's more honest." George felt his resistance melting.

"It even makes sense. How do you know that I've told you the whole story? Maybe I've done even more than I've told you."

"Have you?"

"I don't think so, but I'm not sure. Maybe I'm too ashamed to think about it, or I don't even realize what I've done."

Bonaventure might be talking about his wife as well as Sherry. George thought about Madeline's accusations about him not being aware that Bonaventure might be a wife-killer. This might be George's chance to find out for himself.

"OK, I'll do it," George said, his anxiety spiking even as he gave his answer. "But you have to be honest telling her who I am and what I'm doing this for. It has no real benefit for her. She's liable to turn you down."

"At least I can try." Lucas seemed calmed by George's acquiescence. "Thanks, doc. I think this will help me a lot."

# Chapter 16

"This feels odd. I've never talked to a psychiatrist before." Sherry Bennett seated herself in the chair in front of George's desk. She was an average height woman, appearing to be about thirty, not beautiful, but with a round, pleasant face, full lips, and a small turned up nose. She had soft blonde hair, which fell in waves to just below her shoulders. Her skin was pale, and she had striking blue eyes, which she kept glued to the floor. Her demeanor was modest and tentative, as if she were unsure of herself, which was quite appropriate for the situation, George thought. She was dressed in a rather short skirt, but not one that George would have thought of as risqué by any means. She wore an unrevealing satin blouse.

"Of course your being here isn't your idea, so I understand that this seems quite strange to you," George replied. He was doing his best to be nonthreatening. "Mr. Bonaventure is my client, and I understand that he is the reason for your wanting to leave his employ."

Her face reddened. "I can't believe that he wanted me to tell you what he's been doing."

"He's quite disturbed by his own behavior, as am I. I wanted to find out the extent of it before going too far in his treatment." What he said was true, although the idea for the woman's visit was Bonaventure's not his.

Her face stiffened, as though his words had reminded her of Bonaventure's offenses. "What has he told you?"

"I'd rather that you told me in your own words. I don't want to bias you by telling you what he's said."

She looked as if she was about to cry. She hung her head. "I don't think I deserved the things he said to me. I never did the things he said I did."

He felt like reaching out to her. "I'm not here to judge you, Miss Bennett. It's Mr. Bonaventure who is seeing me, and it's because he acknowledges that he has behaved inappropriately." What he'd said wasn't exactly true, but Lucas had acknowledged behavior that George regarded as inappropriate.

"I'm glad of that. I really didn't deserve to be treated that way. And I really am quitting, even if he is sorry for how he's acted."

"I understand that. This is not an attempt to get you to change your mind. Not in the least."

"Does Mr. Bonaventure have something wrong with him? Is it because of his wife?"

"His wife?"

She looked up at him, her eyes wide. "Being missing and all that. Everyone says that she must be dead. A lot of people think he killed her; even people at the office have said that." She looked away, as if she were embarrassed.

"And how about you, do you think his behavior toward you is related to his wife? Do you think he killed her?"

She glanced up at him, squinting her eyes as if she might be suspicious of his motives for asking the question. "I'm sure he didn't kill his wife. That's just talk around the office. But he changed after his wife disappeared. I'd noticed him looking at me before that, but he only began saying things to me after his wife went missing."

"So he seemed interested in you even before his wife died?"

"He noticed me, I think, but lots of men do." Her cheeks colored. She looked up at George and held his gaze.

George felt his own cheeks warming. Was she being provocative? He must be projecting because of what Lucas had said about the woman. He cleared his throat. "What was it he said to you when his behavior began to bother you?"

She took her eyes off him and let her gaze wander around the room. "He kept telling me he was worried about me. He thought that something terrible was going to happen to me. When I asked him why, he said it was because of the way I dressed and the way I acted. I didn't know what he meant so I asked him. He said that I was acting like a whore, a prostitute, that my skirts were too short, my blouses were too low, that I was flirting with the men in the office. He kept insisting that I was asking for trouble." Her gaze rested on George. She looked as if she were about to cry.

George resisted his urge to reach across the desk and pat her hand. "And what did you make of all this concern on his part?" he asked.

"At first I thought it was sweet, when he told me he was worried about me. He'd only looked at me before—not really talked to me—and I've worked there for two years. But when he accused me of dressing like a prostitute, I felt insulted. And then his warnings sounded like threats."

"Threats?"

"The way he said it. He said I'd pay for acting the way I was acting. It sounded like he was threatening me. I was scared. That's why I quit. That and because he was stalking me."

"Stalking you?" Lucas had never mentioned stalking her.

"In the parking lot a couple of times I thought that I saw him walking around near my car. Then when I went to dinner with a girlfriend, I saw him sitting in his car outside the restaurant. He was still there when I came out. And one day when I visited my mother, I saw his car parked near her apartment. Did he tell you that he called my mother and bothered her, too?"

"He told me about that, but I wasn't aware of the stalking until now. Were there other times?"

"I'm not sure. I became so paranoid that I thought I saw him everywhere, but probably sometimes it was my imagination. But he gave me the creeps. I mean, his wife is missing. He's supposed to be looking for her, not following me around." She looked up at him again with wide eyes.

He tried to hold her gaze but he began to feel embarrassed. He glanced away then looked back. "You said that he hadn't paid you much attention, other than looking at you, prior to when he started giving you these warnings, is that right?"

"Yes..." She sounded hesitant.

"You never gave him any reason to think you might be interested in him?"

She looked shocked. "Of course not. I don't date a lot, but I don't have any trouble finding men who are interested in me and I've had boyfriends in the past. I wouldn't be interested in an older married man."

He felt let down. Did she view him in the same category as she viewed Bonaventure: an uninteresting older man? "When are you actually stopping work?" he asked, attempting to move the conversation toward safer ground.

"At the end of this week."

"What will you do then?"

She let out a sigh. "I don't know. I felt like I had to quit, but jobs are scarce out there. I'm afraid to ask Mr. Bonaventure for a letter of reference."

"Why is that?"

"I think he's mad that I'm quitting. He still seems as interested in me as he ever was. It's as if I've become his obsession."

"I can ask him to write you a good letter of recommendation. After all it's not your fault that you had to quit." Why had he said that? Was he becoming concerned about Sherry Bennett himself?

She looked at him eagerly. "Would you do that? I'd really appreciate it. You probably have a lot of influence over him, being his doctor and all that." She looked embarrassed.

"I think it's the least he can do. Now we're finished, unless you have any questions. Is there anything I can do to help you?" He realized he was sounding like Lucas Bonaventure. He felt his face reddening.

She didn't seem to notice his embarrassment. "I don't have any questions and it's nice of you to ask, but no, there's nothing you need to do for me. I'll get along. I'm just glad that Mr. Bonaventure has someone like you to work with him. It makes me feel safer."

"Don't worry, he'll stop harassing you," he said, smiling. He knew he had no business reassuring her. He had no idea what Lucas Bonaventure would do in the future.

He saw her to the door. Just before leaving his office she stopped and put out her hand. He had an impulse to put an arm around her. He shook her hand. "Best of luck," he said.

# Chapter 17

"We found both blood and hair on the backseat of Mrs. Bonaventure's car. The blood's fairly fresh. I'd say it's from a couple of weeks ago. Barring some other explanation, I'm guessing that Mrs. Bonaventure was in the back seat of that car." Jerry Sloan was standing in the doorway to Abe Reynolds's office. He was holding a report, which he slid across the top of the desk to the detective.

Reynolds rested his hand on the paper but didn't pick it up. "How about prints?"

"There were some smudges that might have been the gloves on the door handle and on the back of the front seat. It would be hard to prove, but I'm guessing that whoever wore the gloves was waiting in the back seat for the woman and then did something to disable her—probably struck her, given the small amount of blood—and then he laid her down on the seat. The same person drove the car afterward."

"The blood makes it more likely that she's dead, but we figured that anyway, because there's been no ransom demand, and there might have been, since both her husband and her old man are loaded. But this rules out her having parked the car at the airport and taken a flight out of here. Whatever happened to the lady, it wasn't of her own doing."

"Call me if you have any questions about the report," Sloan said. He turned and left the office.

Reynolds wondered what Susan Lin was up to. She'd met with the psychiatrist and she thought she might have convinced him to use some modern methods to diagnose if Lucas Bonaventure was a psychopath, but the detective was skeptical about the usefulness of any of that. You couldn't arrest someone because you had evidence that he was *capable* of committing a crime. They needed something to tie the husband to his wife's activities that night. Or they needed a body.

His telephone rang. It was the front desk. Regina Bonaventure's father was on the line. He wanted to talk to Detective Reynolds. The detective hesitated, wondering if he should have the receptionist say he wasn't in, then he picked up the telephone.

"It's been more than two weeks," Bertram Knowles said without even a "hello." His voice was icy over the telephone. This wasn't the first time Reynolds had talked to the retired billionaire. The detective had called Knowles earlier to ask him to let Abe know if he received any calls demanding a ransom for returning his daughter.

"We're making some progress, we just haven't got a prime suspect yet," Reynolds told him.

"Not a *prime* suspect? Does that mean you have *a* suspect?"

The detective had no authority to divulge any of the lab reports to a family member. "We're checking out the man who was in the bar with her the night she disappeared, but he's dead so it's hard to piece things together."

"Do you think he did it?'

"We have no evidence one way or the other. We're still looking at anything that might give us a better idea about what happened." He was careful not to mention the blood on the back seat of Regina Bonaventure's car.

"What about Lucas, her husband? He'll profit from her death. She had more money than he did—my money—but it's in her name. Now it'll be in his." Knowles' voice had risen to a demanding pitch. "Lucas is a hot head. Did you know he beat up one of his neighbors?"

"We're aware of that."

"And the cheapskate only put up twenty-five thousand for Regina's reward. That's chump-change for him. She would have left him if I hadn't, like a fool, told her to stick it out. I thought he would be able to take care of her when I was gone. What an idiot I was."

"We're still considering suspects, Mr. Knowles. Trust me, we're leaving no stone unturned."

"But you haven't unearthed anything yet. I'm gonna up the ante, detective. I'm putting up a bigger reward: a million dollars for any information that leads you to my daughter's whereabouts. I'm releasing an announcement to the newspapers and TV today." His tone was matter-of-fact.

Abe felt his spirits sink. "That's generous of you sir, but it's going to flood us with crackpots giving false leads just so they can get their hands on the money. It'll slow down the investigation. We're a small department, we haven't got the staff to handle that many phone calls."

"I'm hiring someone to screen the calls. A private agency. I've been talking to a private detective. He's gonna start doing some investigating on his own. I told him to call you and find out what you know."

Abe's shoulders slumped. This was just what he *didn't* need. "I wish you wouldn't do that Mr. Knowles. It's just going to interfere with our investigation."

"How can it? You said yourself that you're a small department. I'll tell Ben Murphy, that's the private detective, to turn over anything he finds to you. It's like an extra set of hands. I'd think you'd be happy to have someone working full time on the case."

"I'm working full-time on the case. It's my top priority."

"So now you have some help. Anyway, Murphy will contact you. Tell him whatever you're allowed to tell him. And don't tell my son-in-law about him. I want Murphy to investigate Lucas too."

"If your son-in-law is guilty, don't you think that someone else asking questions is just going to make him more close-mouthed, less likely to give us any useful information?"

"C'mon Reynolds, you've had more than two weeks to get whatever you're going to get from Lucas. If he's still keeping things from you, then you won't find them out. Maybe my man will. Anyway, it's a done deal. I've already hired Murphy. And his agency will screen the calls after I announce the reward. He'll forward anything promising to you."

Bertram Knowles was used to getting his way. "Do whatever you want, Mr. Knowles. I'll give Murphy whatever I legally can give him. It won't be much."

"Suit yourself," Knowles said and hung up.

# Chapter 18

"What did you think?" Lucas Bonaventure had been early, fidgeting in his chair in the waiting room until it was time for his appointment. Now he was sitting in the same chair where Sherry Bennett had sat, in front of George's desk, rather than on the analyst's couch.

"I see you're sitting today," George said.

"I'll go on the couch later. I wanted to hear what you thought of Sherry. Can you tell what's wrong with her?"

George felt a stab of guilt, talking to Lucas about Sherry, but that was the reason he'd seen the woman. "Nothing's wrong with her so far as I can see."

Lucas looked as if he'd been slapped in the face. "What do you mean? You saw how she was dressed. That short skirt, the blouse."

"Her skirt was moderately short, but not unusually so. Her blouse was buttoned high on the neck." Why did George feel he had to defend her?

"The shirt was almost obscene it was so short. I saw it."

"You did? How is that?"

Lucas looked embarrassed but only for a moment. "I watched her come into the building." He looked up and met the doctor's gaze. "I wanted to make sure she came to her appointment with you."

"I didn't even tell you when the appointment was. And I'm sure that she didn't either. You must have followed her when she left work. She told me that you'd been following her. Stalking her was the word she used."

He looked irritated. "I've followed her a few times. So what? I was trying to make sure she was all right. I was trying to protect her."

"You've frightened her. She says you threatened her, too"

He looked surprised. "I never threatened her. I warned her that she was asking for trouble, that's all. I was looking out for her, not threatening her."

"That's not how she sees it."

"I get it," Lucas said, narrowing his eyes. "You fell for her. She seduced you the same way she's been seducing the men in the office."

George felt his face reddening. His hands were sweating. "That's ridiculous. I talked to her as a favor to you. You're projecting your own emotions onto me, and I think we need to examine that."

Lucas looked sheepish. "OK, maybe that's a stupid thing for me to say. But I thought you'd find something wrong with her, something I could help her fix."

George felt relieved that the focus was back on Lucas. "And if I had, how would you fix it? She doesn't want anything to do with you. As I said, you've frightened her."

Lucas shook his head in consternation. "Maybe there's something wrong with me. Ever since my wife disappeared, I've been unable to concentrate on anything. I just think about Sherry and what she's doing. My business is going to hell. What's wrong with me?"

"Why don't you come over to the couch?"

# Chapter 19

George didn't want Sherry Bennett to see him. He felt foolish, like a pervert or a criminal, parked in the parking garage in the building where Lucas Bonaventure's company was located, waiting for her to leave the building, but his session with Lucas hadn't convinced him that the man had given up his obsession with his soon-to-be former employee. What made him feel embarrassed, even ashamed, was that he knew that his motivation was his desire that Sherry Bennett remain safe. He was acting no different than his patient, and that frightened him.

He wasn't sure what he would do once he saw her. Follow her home or wherever she went after work, he guessed, see if he could spot Lucas doing the same thing.

To his surprise, the first familiar person he saw leave the elevator was Lucas Bonaventure. He watched Lucas walk to his car, unlock it and get in, then pull from his reserved parking spot. But instead of leaving, Lucas moved the car to another spot, in the middle of the parking garage: an unmarked space that gave him a clear view of the elevator, just as George's parking spot did for him.

A few minutes later, Sherry stepped from the elevator. She walked quickly to her car, three rows away, got in, then headed out of the garage. Lucas' car followed. George followed slowly behind them.

For the first few blocks he could keep both cars in view, but then the volume of traffic obscured Sherry's car, so he resigned himself to following Lucas, assuming that the man was still following his secretary's car, wherever it was headed. Finally, he was on a residential side street on which he could see Sherry's car five or six blocks ahead, and Lucas' about two blocks behind it. He saw Lucas pull over to the curb. He did the same. Several blocks ahead, Sherry's car pulled into the parking structure of an apartment building.

After about ten minutes Lucas pulled away from the curb and drove past the building, turned a corner and was out of sight. George guessed that Lucas had been satisfied that Sherry had simply gone home and was not doing anything dangerous. George continued to watch the apartment house. What was he doing? Lucas Bonaventure was no longer following Sherry, but George felt no impulse to leave. Perhaps Lucas had been fooled. Perhaps Sherry had only come home to freshen herself up before a date. He couldn't believe the thoughts that were swirling through his head like ugly creatures that wouldn't be still. He was acting stranger than his client.

He waited for another half-hour, then his own mortification persuaded him to leave. Instead of going straight home, he did something he almost never did and drove to the Yard House at Fashion Island. It was happy hour, and the restaurant was crowded, but he managed to find a seat at the bar. He ordered the Belgian beer he'd had when he'd lunched with Susan Lin, then looked around the bar. Was he wondering if Susan Lin would show up? Did he really want to talk to the psychologist? About what? His obsession with Sherry Bennett? She wouldn't understand and would think he was seriously disturbed, not to mention being a creep. He was an analyst. He had undergone a training analysis. He was supposed to understand himself.

He downed the entire goblet of beer in three drinks and ordered another. "We don't serve a customer more than two of these if they're driving," the bartender said, looking embarrassed.

"One more will be enough," George answered.

He sipped his second beer. Maybe there was something especially appealing about Sherry Bennett, he mused, something that made her seem vulnerable. He had no real feelings for the man's secretary. She wasn't as attractive to him as Susan Lin, whom he'd had no impulse to follow home from work. He guessed that it was something about Sherry Bennett herself that brought out such behavior. George knew that Lucas had given him lots of suggestions that Miss Bennett might be in danger. Perhaps that was all it was, he told himself, sipping his beer. Perhaps he had just been influenced by the suggestions coming from his own client. And, of course, there was the factor of his unhappiness at home with Madeline.

His wife didn't respect him. She made no secret of the fact. He was pretty sure she wouldn't turn to other men, as Lucas Bonaventure had apparently suspected his wife of doing, but George knew that his wife had her own coterie of confidants—professors of English and classics, fellow writers and editors—with whom she shared her disparagement of her husband and his profession. The ironic thing was that psychoanalysts, such as he, used to be celebrated by the very same intellectuals who now looked down upon them.

But despite their skepticism, despite the world's skepticism, George thought that he knew himself better because of what had been revealed during his own analysis. He knew the extent to which he feared powerful women, such as Madeline, even as he was attracted to them. He sometimes fantasized about finding someone who would simply serve him, respect him, agree with him, but he couldn't help being attracted when he met such a person's opposite, a Susan Lin. And he was competitive with successful and powerful men, men who resembled his father, a renowned surgeon who specialized in women and their diseases, something that had always engendered George's, as well as his mother's, suspicion. What had they suspected? That his father had chosen his specialty out of prurience? He'd never dared say as much to his father, although his mother, who was subservient to no one, had done so on more than one occasion and even in front of her son. And now George had a profession that allowed him to see inside his patient's innermost fantasies, especially their sexual ones. Was he just as prurient as his father may have been?

George was aware of how tortuous was the matrix of influences he'd acquired while growing up in his family. His own emotional growth had been twisted to fit within the volatile mold around him. Close to his mother, although secretive about his most precious feelings, distant from his father, seeking to outdo him without directly mounting a challenge. He'd learned all about it during his training analysis. But the emotional consequences and the behavioral patterns that his childhood had foisted upon him remained a part of his adult life, almost as powerful as they had been before his analysis, despite the understanding that he'd gained. It was the Achilles heel of his profession, the fact that was recognized but never mentioned by him and his colleagues: understanding is not mastery. Knowledge does not guarantee freedom from the chains of conflicts and motivations, which had previously been unconscious.

He finished his beer. Susan Lin was not coming in. If she had, he wouldn't have known what to say to her anyway, wasn't even sure that she'd be interested in talking to him if she were with her police colleagues. He paid for his drinks and left. It was time to go home and have cocktails with his wife.

# Chapter 20

Ben Murphy was older than Abe Reynolds expected him to be. He was at least in his early seventies. He sat slouched in the plastic chair in front of Abe's desk, one leg slung over the other, wearing a pair of jeans, sneakers and a checked flannel shirt. The shirt was open in front and under it was a tee shirt that had, "Peewee League Flag Football" written across the chest. Murphy wore a faded blue baseball cap with a Dodgers logo on it. A thin braid of white hair trailed from beneath the back of the baseball cap.

"Mostly I'm just gonna be fielding all these calls that come in for Knowles' ransom money," Murphy said. He had a friendly smile on his wrinkled face. "It'll make your job a lot easier."

"You're gonna do that all by yourself?"

"I've got some help. A couple of my grandkids are home from college for the break, and they need part-time jobs. They're both pretty bright—brighter than me—so they'll do a good job."

Abe looked skeptical. "You sure you can handle that? A million bucks is going to bring a lot of calls."

"I told you, my grandkids are bright. Lots of energy. They'll turn anything that sounds legit over to me."

"And you'll turn it over to us."

"Of course... after I check it out."

"How about you just turn it over right away?"

"You wouldn't want that. No telling how many calls are going to need follow-up but most of them, heck, maybe all of them, will be red herrings. You don't want to spend your time on wild goose chases."

"You've done this kind of thing before?"

"Yup."

"You work out of Santa Barbara?"

"I'll be down here for this. The grandkids will still be in Santa Barbara, but we're set up on a wireless phone exchange through the Internet. I can see all the numbers that call them, tap into a conversation anytime I need to. My grandson's a computer whiz. He set the whole thing up. No difference from being in the same room with them. No need to bring them down here."

"OK," Abe said, although he wasn't completely satisfied. "What do you want from me?"

"Where are you right now in your investigation?" Despite the affable expression on his face, Murphy's eyes showed his seriousness.

"I can only tell you what I've told the press. Bertram Knowles may be her father and he may be rich, but he doesn't have any right to special access to our information."

"Of course not, but you can share a lot more than you've given the press. You've got a lot of discretion in that."

Murphy wasn't the just friendly yokel that he appeared to be. "You've been a police officer?"

"Thirty-five years. Used to run the Santa Barbara department."

"You're *that* Ben Murphy?" Abe's eyes widened in surprise.

Murphy gave him an embarrassed smile. "I guess I am."

As the long-time Chief of the Santa Barbara Police Department, Murphy was legendary, not just for solving a number of high profile murder cases in Santa Barbara but also for cleaning up what was a corrupt police force. His reputation didn't match the laid-back old man slouching in Abe's plastic chair. "How long have you been a private detective?"

"Twelve years. I opened up shop right after I retired from the department. Now I'm retired as a private detective, except for some security work for Mr. Knowles. He wanted me personally on this. And I knew Regina, his daughter, when she was younger."

Abe relaxed a little. Murphy probably *did* know what he was doing. "Things aren't looking good for Regina Bonaventure. We found some blood in the back seat of her car. Can you keep that to yourself and not tell Mr. Knowles?"

Murphy's face showed his concern. "Blood?"

"I didn't tell her father."

Murphy nodded. "No sense getting him upset until we've got something real to go on. He's a hard-ass, but if he loses Regina, he's gonna take it real hard. What's the deal on this Rosberg fellow who got killed?"

"Still up in the air. None of his prints were in the car, but that may not mean anything because it looks as if the kidnapper wore gloves. You probably read about Rosberg's record in the newspaper. What a piece of work. He'd served time for assault on a woman. Been charged with the same thing another time. But that's all we've got. He changed his hotel when the papers ran his description, but that might just be because he knew that his record would make him a suspect. The bartender ID'd the corpse. Rosberg was definitely the guy in the bar that tried to buy Mrs. Bonaventure a drink the night she disappeared."

"You able to put together his movements later that night or the next day? He'd have had to get rid of the body or, if she was alive, stash her somewhere and put the car in the airport, then get back to his own car, which I assume was a rental."

Abe nodded. Murphy had analyzed the situation the same way he had. "The logistics are tough. The restaurant was down on PCH on the outskirts of Newport Beach. He'd have had to take a cab from the airport to get back there if he'd left his own car at the restaurant and drove hers. We've checked all the cab companies—Uber, Lyft—no one made that trip that night or the next morning. There were three passengers that went from the airport to the Hyatt where he was staying, but we've identified each of them, and it wasn't him."

"So nada on Rosberg so far. Sounds as if you're following up all the likely scenarios. What about Lucas? I met him once. At his and Regina's wedding. Didn't like him. Thought he married her for her father's money."

"I think Knowles thinks that too. He said Bonaventure will get a load of cash from his wife's estate."

"So there's motive. Except he probably had access to the money when she was alive, but maybe he didn't like having to share it with her."

"He's got no alibi. Said he was home sleeping. My partner thinks that it's strange that he reported her missing as soon as he woke up and she wasn't in the house. She's probably right, but that's not enough to hang someone. She also thinks he's a psychopath. She's a psychologist. Pretty bright."

Murphy rubbed his chin, smiling as if he were thinking of something pleasant. "My granddaughter is studying to be a psychologist. She's bright too. I hadn't thought about her going into police work. Maybe I'll talk to her about it."

"Bonaventure started seeing a shrink after his wife went missing. But the shrink won't tell us anything, and we don't have enough evidence to convince a judge to give us a subpoena. Anyway, he's just started with the shrink. Susan—Doctor Lin—that's my partner, is trying to get close to the shrink, hoping he'll tell her something more."

"Bonaventure's prints in the car?"

"All over it. He told us that he drives her car when they go on long trips together. Hers gets better gas mileage than his."

"Does it?'

"Does it what?"

"Get better gas mileage. I mean does she drive a Prius and he drives a Hummer, or what?'

"Couple of Mercedes. Looked identical to me."

"So maybe you caught him in a lie."

Abe nodded. The old man still had a good head on his shoulders.

"I imagine I'll be talking to him," Murphy said.

"Really? I thought you were just taking phone calls. Knowles told me not to let Bonaventure know that you were involved."

"Lucas is gonna know about the reward and that Bert Knowles is looking into things himself. I have to give him some explanation from his father-in-law about the reward, and that'll give me a chance to form an opinion myself. But of course opinions are just opinions and, like I said, I didn't like him the one time I did meet him. That doesn't make him a murderer, though."

It sounded to Abe as if Ben Murphy was planning to do a lot more investigating than he'd first implied. Abe wasn't sure how he felt about that. The old ex-police chief probably knew what he was doing and he was even more experienced than Abe. "I need you to keep me informed if you find anything."

"Of course. I can't arrest anyone. You can. I know about preserving evidence and not biasing a case. If I find anything, I don't want to nullify its use in a trial by screwing around with it myself. Trust me, you'll be the first to know if I find anything." He uncrossed his legs and looked as if he was getting ready to leave.

"So let me know if you get any leads from those phone calls," Abe said.

"Like I said, you'll be the first to know." Murphy stood up. He massaged his knee as if sitting too long had stiffened it. "Oh, and sometime I'd like to talk to that bright psychologist on your staff. I want to learn more so maybe I can steer my granddaughter into police work. That would be nice, at least for me." He stuck out his hand.

They shook hands and Murphy ambled out the door.

# Chapter 21

"Have the police made any progress in finding your wife?" George asked. It was three weeks since Regina Bonaventure had gone missing.

Lucas lay on the couch and talked to the ceiling. "They found the guy she met in the bar. You probably read about that. He died in a car crash trying to get away from the police. I'd think that should pretty much seal his guilt, but the detective who talked to me says that he's not sure that's the guy who took her."

George had read about it. He'd felt relieved. Was it because he no longer had to fear that Lucas was the killer, or was there something else he'd been afraid of? "How do you feel about that?" he asked.

"I'm not sure what you mean by how do I feel about it. I can tell you what I think. He sounds guilty to me. But it's what the police think that matters."

"You're not angry at the man? I know he's dead, but you must have some feelings about him. He might be your wife's killer."

"Why would I feel anything? Like I said, they don't know if he's the one who took her or not."

Lucas' comment brought back George's anxiety. "And they still don't have any theories about what happened to your wife?"

"This police psychologist told me to prepare for the worst. I guess she meant that they think my wife is dead." He said it without emotion.

"Doctor Lin said that?"

Lucas looked surprised. "You know her?"

"She and Detective Reynolds came to my office to talk to me, remember. You told them you were seeing me." George wasn't going to mention his lunch with Susan Lin.

"Right. But you can't tell them anything we say, right?"

"Everything you say is confidential. They could subpoena my records, but they would need a good reason to convince a judge to grant a subpoena. Doctor-patient privilege is sacred in California."

Lucas sighed, as if he were relieved. "My father-in-law has offered a reward. And he's hired a private detective. Some old guy who wants to talk to me."

"How do you feel about that? You've offered a reward yourself."

"Bert—that's Regina's father—is just trying to one-up me. I offered twenty-five thousand dollars and he's offered a million. He can afford that. I can't, and he knows it."

"Maybe he's just trying to help."

"And show that he's better than me. He and Regina always played that card. They both tried to make me feel inadequate."

"And that's how his reward makes you feel?"

"Not really, but I know that's what he's hoping for."

"Sounds as if you feel competitive with him."

"He's the competitive one. And Regina pushed it. She constantly told me that her father was more successful than I was. He let me know, too, without directly telling me, but in other ways."

"Did he ever remind you of your own father?"

"My father wasn't a success. I'm more of a success than my father ever was."

"Do you know what happened to your father after he left you?"

"No, except he died when he was fifty. But he never was a financial success, I know that much."

Lucas had a different issue with his father than George had with his.

"So there have been some developments in your wife's case since you last saw me. Is that what's been on your mind since our last visit?"

"Not really. Sherry has quit, but I'm still worried about her."

George felt his pulse quickening. Was it because they were now talking about Sherry Bennett? "She's gone, so what can you do?"

"I can't just give up. I can't let something happen to her."

"Are you still following her?" He knew that Lucas had followed her less than a week ago, because he'd seen it with his own eyes.

"I can't. I'm at work all day, and I have no idea where she is or who she's with."

"What about at night? You can still follow her at night."

Lucas started to sit up. Then he lay back down. When he spoke, he sounded irritated. "This isn't about me. It's about her. You were supposed to tell me how to help her."

"No, I'm supposed to help you understand yourself, which includes why you're so concerned with Sherry Bennett and whether you're spending your free time following her around. Her welfare is not something that concerns me." He knew that he was lying. He was concerned about the secretary; that's why he'd followed her earlier. But he was just being safe and trying to make sure his patient didn't get himself into trouble, wasn't he?

"I dreamed again," Lucas said abruptly, interrupting George's thoughts.

"The same dream as before?"

"A different one."

"Tell me about it."

"This time I was near the ocean. It might have been that stretch of beach along the Pacific Coast Highway near where I live: Crystal Cove. I was up on the cliff looking down at the beach below. It was daylight, and I could see this couple down on the beach, near some rocks that stuck out into the ocean. They were fighting with each other, really fighting, like wrestling. The man was on top of her. I wanted to go down and help her, but I couldn't find a way down the cliff. Every time I got close to the edge I got scared, I froze. My legs became wooden. I was afraid of falling. I just kept looking down, watching them, searching for a way to get to them, but I was completely paralyzed by fear. Then I woke up."

"And what did you think when you woke up?"

"I wondered if the woman was Sherry."

"In your dream, did it feel to you as if it *was* Sherry?"

"I can't remember. I think it must have been her because that's who I've been worrying about. But honestly, I can't say."

"You couldn't see her clearly?"

"She was under the man much of the time. I saw her bare legs sticking out, kicking. Maybe she had on a bathing suit, or a short skirt, or a dress that had been pulled up."

"And you're sure they were fighting?"

There was silence. After a few seconds, Lucas spoke. "At first I thought they were having sex. But the man was fully dressed."

"Were you frightened when you thought they were having sex?"

Lucas hesitated again. "I guess I was. I don't know why."

Another textbook dream, George thought. A child seeing his parents having sex often mistook what was going on as a fight, as violence in which his mother was being hurt. A child traumatized by such a memory often had dreams in which the original act was repeated. Such dreams sometimes persisted into adulthood. Lucas hated his domineering mother, but perhaps such feelings were a reaction formation to his own Oedipal desires for his mother, stirred by that first observation of his parents in bed.

Sometimes a boy's observation of his mother's genitals in such a situation, his first realization that his mother was devoid of a penis, was the beginning of his castration anxiety. Such anxiety was certainly present in Lucas' dream in the form of the paralysis of his legs, his feeling that they were "wooden," which was reminiscent of his earlier dream when the man was using a saw to cut something, and Lucas again felt his legs become paralyzed.

"I think we can explore this dream further, but we'll have to do it next session," George said. He was reluctant to end the session but it was time to stop.

Lucas sat up. "I'm not sure why, but I always feel better after our sessions. I do now."

"I'm glad to hear that," George said.

# Chapter 22

Madeline had gone out and not told George where she was going. He had celebrated his abandonment by finishing the dinner she'd left for him and then pouring himself a large, fourth, gin and tonic. He was interrupted by his cell phone ringing. He expected that it was Madeline, but the caller ID said it was his after-hours answering service. Most of his clients underwent only minor crises, and he rarely received after-hours calls. Occasionally a client became distressed, even suicidal, and he needed to respond to his or her need with immediacy.

It was Sherry Bennett. The service had her on hold; she was asking to talk to him. George took her call.

"I'm frightened. I didn't know who else to call." Her tone was apologetic, but she sounded as if she were holding back a sob. "I think Mr. Bonaventure is stalking me again. I got a call about a job interview and I was supposed to meet someone in Irvine at this office building, but everything is closed, and when I came back to my car the tire had been cut." Her voice was rising in anxiety. "I know that Mr. Bonaventure is behind this, and I'm afraid he's going to show up." She started to cry.

George needed her to regain control of herself. "Who called you about the interview?" he asked, his voice as calm as he could muster.

She inhaled deeply. "A woman. She said she was with the employment agency that Mr. Bonaventure's company provided to ex-employees and that a prospective employer wanted to interview me. I was supposed to come to the office at eight o'clock tonight. I questioned her to make sure it was eight at night and not eight in the morning because that didn't sound right, but she said she was sure that eight at night was what the employer had said. The building's locked but there's no such employer even listed on the sign in front." Her voice was rising again, the hysteria just below the surface.

He tried to clear his mind. The gin was making it difficult to think. The story about the interview sounded suspicious, although Bonaventure had told him that his company sometimes referred former employees to an employment agency. "Do you have Triple-A or some other emergency car service?" He wanted someone else involved.

"I've got Triple-A."

"Call them to come and change your tire." He took a long sip from his gin and tonic. "And give me the address. I'll come and wait with you, so you won't have to worry about Bonaventure." Why had he offered? She wasn't his patient, he hardly knew her.

"Would you? I know it's ridiculous of me. But if it's him, you'll be able to talk to him instead of me."

What would happen if Lucas showed up and found him with Sherry Bennett? Was he hoping that would happen? Was he now competing with his own client for a woman? The gin must be getting to him. He'd told the woman that he would come, and now he had to go there.

———  ———  ———

The building was about a fifteen minutes drive, on the edge of Irvine, near the Santa Ana border, in a cluster of office buildings, some of which were still lit, but most were dark. The parking garage where Sherry had said her car was stranded was dimly lit. He saw her car, with its rear tire flat, sitting near the entrance to the building's basement. He could see Sherry sitting in the driver's seat. He drove toward her car.

———  ———  ———

He was leaning over her, one of his knees on the seat next to her leg, the other foot on the floor of the garage. He had no recollection of how he had gotten there. The last thing he remembered was driving across the floor of the garage in the direction of Sherry's car. He stared at her face, only inches in front of him. Her eyes were wide open, bulging. Around her neck was a nylon rope, one end of it looped around the headrest. George began to feverishly undo the rope, tearing at it until his fingers were raw.

The parking garage was suddenly illuminated by flashing red and blue lights. An Irvine police cruiser pulled up next to the car. Two uniformed police officers stepped from the car with their hands resting on their holstered guns. "Step away from the car!" one of them shouted.

George was confused. "She's been murdered, help me get the rope off her neck!"

"Step away from the car!" the officer repeated, both of them advancing toward him.

He stepped back.

"Turn around and put your hands on the roof of the car."

He obeyed. "She's dead. I found her and I was trying to take the rope off her neck. I'm a doctor."

One of the officers was bending over Sherry's body. He was feeling her pulse. He put on a pair of rubber gloves and then began loosening the rope.

"She called me and said she was frightened. She wanted me to wait with her until Triple-A arrived," George said. "She was dead when I got here." He felt as if he had to explain himself.

The officer who had stood him against the car looked at him suspiciously. "You're her doctor?"

What was he going to say? "I'm not *her* doctor. I'm *a* doctor, a psychiatrist. I interviewed her recently because a patient of mine is stalking her. She called me tonight on my answering service to tell me that she was stranded here and she was afraid he was going to show up to harass her."

The policeman turned him back around. "What is this patient's name?"

Sherry Bennett wasn't his patient so nothing she'd told him was confidential. He could divulge Bonaventure's name as the person she was afraid of. "Lucas Bonaventure."

The police officer didn't recognize the name. He wrote it down using a stylus and an iPad he'd fetched from his car. "When did you get here?"

He had no idea how long he'd been there or how long his fugue state had lasted. "I got here about thirty seconds before you did. What brought you here, anyway?"

"She made a 911 call, saying that she was here with a flat tire. She thought it had been cut. She thought someone was going to harm her."

"She didn't say who it was?"

"She got cut off before she finished talking. We located her from her cell phone."

A tow truck with the Triple-A logo on the side pulled up. "Somebody need a tire changed?" the driver asked.

"Stay in your truck and don't leave. We want to talk to you," the officer told the man.

"I've called the paramedics," the other cop said, straightening up after having worked over Sherry's body for about five minutes. "There's nothing they can do except take her to the hospital and have her declared dead." He walked over to his partner. "Let's let the detectives question this one. They'll get pissed off if we do anything more than secure the crime scene. Put him in the cruiser."

The officer who'd questioned him led George to the police car and put him in the back seat. The two officers began stringing tape in a wide perimeter around the car.

After about five minutes, an unmarked police car pulled up. Behind them was a black and white SUV marked "Crime Scene Investigation" on the side. Two plain-clothed officers stepped out of the first car and walked over to the body, each sticking his head inside the car for at least a minute, then conferring with the two uniformed cops. George couldn't hear what they were saying. The uniformed cops and the detectives were joined by two more officers, a male and a female, who were in the process of donning head-to-toe protective outfits, each of them carrying a bag of some kind of equipment. The detectives and the CSI people talked briefly, then one of the detectives headed toward the two uniformed cops, who had moved off to the side. The other came over to the cruiser where George was sitting and opened the back door.

"Name, please," the detective said. He was in his thirties, clean-shaven with blonde, straight hair, and freckles on his face. He might have been a surfer dressed in a suit for work.

George gave him his name and address.

Unlike the uniformed officer who'd recorded his notes on an iPad, the detective wrote down George's name in a worn, leather-bound notebook, using a ballpoint pen. "So tell me what you were doing here."

George tried to control his panic. He reminded himself that he hadn't done anything, at least as far as he knew. He explained how Sherry Bennett had called him to say that she had come to what had turned out to be a bogus job interview, had her tire slashed and had grown fearful that his patient was stalking her. He had told her to call Triple-A and he would come and keep her company while she waited."

"You told the officer that she's not your patient. Is that right?"

"I only met her once."

"Yet you volunteered to come here and keep her company while she waited for a tow truck?"

He knew how strange his story sounded. "I felt bad. It was my client she was scared of."

The detective, who hadn't given his name, stared at him long and hard. "This patient, his name is Lucas Bonaventure?" The uniformed cop must have given the detective Lucas' name.

"Yes."

"You're a psychiatrist, right?"

"Correct."

"Lucas Bonaventure is the name of the man from Newport Beach whose wife is missing. Are you aware of that?"

"I am."

"It's the same guy?"

"Yes."

They were interrupted by the sound of a dying siren as an ambulance, its emergency lights flashing, pulled up and parked next to the detectives' car. Two paramedics were met by one of the uniformed cops who escorted them to Sherry Bennett's car.

The detective turned his attention back to George. "Officer Dramond said that you had your hands on the rope around her neck when he and Officer Wilshire drove up."

The roof of his mouth was dry. George ran his tongue over it. He cleared his throat. His anxiety was almost overwhelming. He was afraid of losing his voice. "I thought maybe I could revive her if I could get the rope off of her neck, but the two officers told me to step away from the car. I presumed that the police officer knew first aid. It wouldn't take a doctor to try to resuscitate her." He was aware that his voice sounded strained.

The detective stared at him for a few seconds. "He seemed to think she was beyond resuscitation."

George couldn't hold the man's gaze. "He was probably right," he said, looking over the detective's shoulder at the ambulance. "I was just panicked and wanting to try everything I could think of."

The detective looked over at the crime scene. The two uniformed officers were standing next to the open door of the car. After a quick examination of the body, the paramedics had stepped back and were waiting before doing anything more. The detective squinted his eyes as if he were thinking. "What's the number for your answering service?"

"It's on my cell phone. I can speed dial it for you."

"What's the number?"

George told him the number.

The detective dialed the service on his own cell phone and identified himself as a police officer, then asked if a call had come in for Doctor Farquhar that evening. The operator gave him the time that Sherry had called and told him the caller's name. The service had recorded her call up to the point when they'd transferred it to George. "Your story fits," the detective said, looking at George. "She called about thirty minutes before our guys arrived. How long did it take you to get here?"

"I live in Newport Beach." He knew that it had only taken him fifteen minutes to get from his house to the parking garage. But even granting five minutes to get himself out of his house, that left at least ten minutes unaccounted for before the police arrived. He had no idea what he had been doing for those ten minutes. "It took me a while to find the address."

"How do we know you weren't already here when she called you? Your answering service reached you on your cell, even though you say you were at home."

"They always call my cell. That's the first number they call because I always have it with me. Does it make sense that I was already here, lurking around somewhere, and she just happened to call me to tell me to come here? If you check her cell phone I'm sure you can verify that she called Triple-A after she got off the phone with me. I told her to call them."

The detective scowled. "You can get out of the car, but don't go anywhere. My partner and I will want to ask you some more questions." It appeared to irritate the detective that George's story made sense. George knew that it wasn't the whole truth, but he didn't know what the whole truth was. He had no memory for the first ten minutes after he'd driven up next to Sherry Bennett's car.

For the next hour, the detectives, whose names turned out to be Jensen and Morovitch, went back and forth between the tow truck driver, the crime scene detectives, and George. The crime scene people were still poring over the car, but the paramedics had taken the body away. The two detectives were mostly interested in Lucas Bonaventure and the phone call that George had received in which Sherry had told him about someone calling and telling her to come to the office building for an interview with a company that didn't have an office in that building.

"I suppose she could have been mistaken and gone to the wrong address," George volunteered.

"It's more like someone knew she'd be here," Detective Jensen, the young surfer type who'd talked to him earlier, said. "Probably that same someone slashed her tire so she couldn't leave. Is that the kind of thing your patient is capable of doing?"

George told him that he couldn't divulge anything about his client because of confidentiality.

Jensen shook his head in disgust. "I'm gonna talk to the DA about how far your confidentiality extends and I want to do that before we go any further. I want you to come in tomorrow so we can get a statement. I think you can tell us more than you're saying, doctor."

The detective was right. All of Lucas' statements to him were covered by client confidentiality, but nothing Sherry Bennett had told him was confidential. She hadn't been his client. Everything she'd told George about Bonaventure's stalking, his threats, his talking to her mother, were things George could tell the police, probably things he had an obligation to tell them. And he had the added incentive that it would point the finger of guilt away from him, although the two detectives seemed to be satisfied with his story and no longer regarded him with suspicion.

"So I can go now?"

"You're free as a bird," Jensen said without smiling.

George headed for his car. He was going to pour himself a tall gin and tonic as soon as he got home, maybe more than one.

# Chapter 23

"I can't talk to you very long," Lucas told Ben Murphy, whom he has just led into his den and offered a chair. "I have an appointment at noon." He didn't mention that the appointment was with Detective Jensen of the Irvine Police Department, who wanted to talk to him about Sherry Bennett's murder, which had been all over the morning news.

"This is mostly a courtesy call," the detective said. "Bert didn't want you thinking he was doing anything behind your back by hiring me and putting up his own reward."

"No problem. Bert can do whatever he wants to do. It has nothing to do with me."

"It's his daughter, but it's your wife who's missing. Whatever Bert does has a lot to do with you." The old detective's expression was bland.

"I mean he can use his money to do whatever he wants," Lucas answered, his irritation evident in his voice. "He doesn't have to ask my permission. He hasn't talked to me since Regina disappeared, except to call and say he's putting up his own reward and that he thought mine was too small to be useful. I could tell he thought I was being cheap, even though he didn't come right out and say it. He can use you, Mr. Murphy, but I'm working closely with the Newport Beach Police Department, which I think is perfectly capable of finding my wife."

"Even after three weeks and still no clues?"

He stared at the private detective. It seemed odd to him that his father-in-law with all his money and after offering a million dollar reward for information, would hire someone like this to try to find his daughter. The man was wearing a pair of faded jeans, an open flannel shirt over a tee shirt, a baseball cap, and sneakers. His hair in back hung in a short white braid that just touched his shoulders. He was tall and skinny and looked more like an aging hippie than a private detective.

"You've made your courtesy visit. Is there anything else I can do for you?"

Murphy stood and began walking around the den, his pace leisurely. He appeared to be examining the books on Lucas' shelves. "I know you've told the police, but once more for me, can you tell me what happened that led to Regina going out by herself that night?"

"Nothing happened. We ate dinner; she had a few glasses of wine, then she went up to her room. I heard her showering, and I thought she was going to bed. Then she came downstairs all dressed and told me she was going out. That was the last time I saw her."

Murphy was running a finger over the spines of the books on the shelf. "Did you argue? Was she angry when she left?"

"We'd been talking. We weren't arguing. She didn't seem angry to me."

"Talking about what?"

"She wanted to go on a vacation. She said she was bored. I told her I'd love to take a vacation, but this is the worst time of year for me, too much to do at work."

"So you argued."

"We didn't argue. She wanted to take a vacation right now and I wanted to postpone it until I could more easily take time off work."

"Where'd she want to go?"

"Europe, she said, France and Spain, I think. She'd attended school in France for a year during college, some kind of exchange thing, and she had never been back."

"She'd never been back to Europe since college?"

"No."

"Where do you usually take your vacations?"

"We have a cabin at Big Bear, we go skiing on the weekends during winter. She likes to ski. We don't leave Newport Beach very often; why would we? It's like Santa Barbara. It's got everything you could find anywhere else."

"Except your wife didn't think so."

"She wanted to get away. I can understand that. I didn't oppose the idea, just the timing. Don't try to make more of this than it was." Lucas' tight smile showed his growing irritation with the detective's questions.

"And what was it?'

"A typical after-dinner discussion between a husband and wife."

"And then you didn't notice that she didn't come home until when you woke up the next morning?"

"I went to bed early and I'm a sound sleeper."

"You had a lot to drink?"

"That's none of your business. Why are you questioning me? I don't know what happened to Regina." He was leaning forward in his chair, as if he were about to stand up.

"Just trying to be sure that I have all my facts straight." He bent down as if he was reading the title of one of the books. "You've got a lot of psychology books here. More than a dozen books by Freud."

"Those are Regina's." Lucas eased back in his chair.

"She didn't major in psychology, did she? My granddaughter is majoring in psychology at UCSB."

"Romance languages. Regina majored in Romance Languages."

"Like French?"

"French, Spanish, Italian, she could read and speak all of them."

"But you never took her to Europe?"

"I think we've been over this."

"Right." Murphy pulled a book from the shelf. "*The Interpretation of Dreams*. Interesting title. Somebody's spent a lot of time with this one. It's pretty well worn. You ever read it? It's by Sigmund Freud."

Lucas shook his head. "I told you the psychology stuff was Regina's interest. She read a lot of Freud."

"She in therapy?"

"No."

"How about you?"

"Why do you want to know that?"

"Just wondering. Have you gone to a therapist?"

"I'm seeing one now. It's been hard for me to handle Regina's disappearance. I've been anxious. I've seen a psychiatrist a few times."

"Somebody local?"

"He's in Newport Beach. But before you ask, he's not allowed to talk to you. What I tell him is confidential."

"Why would I want to talk to him?"

"You seem to want to know everything about me."

"Not really. It's Regina I'm worried about. Anyway, I guess I've asked enough questions."

"Good, because I've got an appointment. I have to go to."

Murphy stood waiting for Lucas to get up. When Lucas stood, Murphy held out his hand. "Good to see you again, Lucas. Last time we met it was at yours and Regina's wedding. You probably don't remember. So many people that day. Anyway, it's too bad to meet again under these circumstances."

"Right," Lucas answered, cautiously. "Good luck with following up the phone tips. I hope someone gives you something useful."

"Me too," Murphy said as he headed for the door.

Now Lucas had to talk to a real detective, one who worked for the police and not for his father-in-law. He could feel his anxiety starting to rise.

# Chapter 24

Detective Frank Jensen hung up the telephone. Abe Reynolds, the Newport Beach detective in charge of Lucas Bonaventure's missing wife's case hadn't been able to give him much information about the businessman that he was about to interview. Reynolds had voiced his suspicions about Bonaventure but had no real evidence against him. The most helpful thing Reynolds had been able to tell him was that Susan Lin, the psychologist who was working on the case, had pegged Bonaventure as a psychopath.

Jensen was young—in his early-thirties—but it wasn't his first homicide case. He had worked on a case with Susan Lin a year ago and he had a lot of respect for her opinion. He'd minored in psychology in college himself, and he knew what the term *psychopath* meant and that Doctor Lin wouldn't have used it loosely, especially about someone who wasn't even officially a suspect in their investigation.

"I'm devastated to hear about Sherry Bennett's death," Lucas said, as he sat down in the chair opposite Detective Jensen's desk in the Irvine Police Station. The room was tiny, and one side was floor-to-ceiling glass, although it was frosted so no one could see in. The detective's desk was Oak and marred by numerous chips and scratches. There were two hard-back wooden chairs covered in green plastic cushions in front of the detective's desk, and Lucas was seated on one of them. "She'd been a valuable employee for over two years," he continued. "She just quit my firm last week. I'm not sure why you called me in on this, though."

Bonaventure might not have appeared "devastated" to Jensen, but he certainly looked uncomfortable. He loosened his figured silk tie as soon as he sat down, as if he were finding it hard to get enough air. There was a thin film of perspiration on his forehead. His eyes kept darting toward the leather-bound notebook in which the detective was taking notes. Despite possessing the computer literacy of his fellow Millennials, Detective Jensen preferred a pen and notebook, the time-honored recording tools of all the detectives in his department.

"Miss Bennett told someone that she was afraid you were following her last night. I understand that she'd previously complained that you were stalking her, harassing her."

Lucas looked over at the door. "I was worried about her, that's all. She misinterpreted my worry. That's why I backed off. But that was all in the past. I certainly wasn't following her last night. Why would I?"

"Where were you last night?"

"Do you think I killed her?"

The young detective gave Lucas a flat stare. "I asked where you were."

"I was at home, working at home."

"By yourself?"

"I'm afraid so." He hung his head. "My wife is missing. You know that, right?"

Jensen nodded. "I know that. I'm sorry about your wife." He smiled perfunctorily. He preferred keeping his demeanor neutral when he interviewed someone who could become a suspect.

"Her disappearance has had me very upset. I'm afraid I've acted a little strangely. Some of my behavior toward Sherry Bennett was because of that. I'm trying to get some psychiatric help."

"From Doctor Farquhar?"

Lucas raised his head, a look of alarm on his face. "How did you know that?"

"Doctor Farquhar was the one who found Miss Bennett's body. He said she'd called him to tell him that she thought you were stalking her."

Bonaventure's eyes widened in surprise. "Doctor Farquhar found her? I don't understand."

"He said that she had called him because she was afraid that you had set up a phony job interview and that you were going to show up in the parking garage where we found her."

"Doctor Farquhar said she told him that? I don't understand. Why would she even be talking to him? She wasn't his patient."

"We verified that she called him. He told us what she said. Do you admit that you were harassing Miss Bennett, that you were stalking her?" The young detective's square face looked innocent enough, but his eyes had a steely quality when he looked at Lucas, waiting for his answer.

Lucas returned the detective's hard stare, but he finally had to look away. "That's how she perceived it. I was trying to help her. You can ask Doctor

Farquhar. He should have told you that already."

"He says he can't talk to us about you. Not unless you give him permission."

"It sounds as if he's already told you a lot, even without my permission." Lucas' anger was barely concealed behind his tight smile.

"He's told us what Sherry Bennett told him, not what you told him. He made that distinction clear to us. We have to get your permission to talk to him about anything you've told him. I presume you'll give that to us unless you're hiding something."

Lucas heaved a dramatic sigh. His face showed his irritation. "You have my permission. Do you want me to sign something?"

"We'll do that later." Jensen looked down at his notebook, turned a page, and then seemed to find something he'd been looking for. "Do you know anything about Eureka Industries?"

Lucas' expression was blank. He shook his head. "Never heard of them. What do they do?"

"Apparently nothing. That was who Miss Bennett had an interview with last night. Except they don't exist. Torelli Associates, an employment agency, was contacted by someone who said they were from this Eureka company and asked them to set up an interview with Miss Bennett for last night at their firm. Only they gave a fake address. Torelli said your company paid for their services."

"That's true. We use them to help our former employees find employment. But we don't have any knowledge about who Torelli matches them up with. We're out of the loop once we've referred them to Torelli."

"And who makes the referral to Torelli?"

"One of my employees. It's not something I have anything to do with."

Jensen flipped a page in his notebook. "What is that employee's name? I'd like to talk to him—or her."

"Certainly. It's Mrs. Schwartz, one of my secretaries."

Jensen wrote the name in his notebook. "It looks as if the interview was a set-up. She wasn't a random victim. Someone wanted to kill her."

"She went out with a lot of men; even some from my company, I think."

"Can you give me some names? Phone numbers?"

"Gary Olson was the one I knew about. I can give you his number after I get back to my office."

"Do that. It sounds a little odd for someone she dated to go to this length to get her to drive somewhere. Why wouldn't he just make a date with her?"

Lucas shrugged his shoulders. "Doesn't make sense to me either. Maybe she'd stopped seeing him. Maybe she refused to go out with him."

"We'll talk to him." Jensen sat back in his chair, and then glanced at the clock above the door. "Anything else you can tell us about Miss Bennett?"

"She was very flirtatious, very provocative. That's what I was warning her about. I thought she wasn't using good judgment around the men in the office."

"You thought what she was doing was dangerous for her?"

"I think I was proved correct."

"So you think it was an admirer who killed her?"

"I really have no idea. You're the detective."

"Right." He opened a file drawer in his desk and rustled around in it for a minute, then came out with a piece of paper. "Here's the release of information form. Put your doctor's name on it and then print your own and sign it."

"And you'll talk to him?"

"I'm not sure. But at least we'll have your permission to do so."

"I think he can convince you that I had no ill intentions toward Miss Bennett. I was distraught about my wife, and I was acting strangely at work, and it bothered her. I'm sorry for that. He'll tell you that, himself."

"Then you don't have anything to worry about," the detective said, giving Lucas a polite smile.

Lucas signed the paper and left. As soon as he was out of the room, Detective Jensen picked up his phone. "Captain, do we still have access to Doctor Lin, the psychologist we're sharing with some other departments? I think I'd like to pull her in on this Bennett case."

# Chapter 25

"I can't believe you did all that and didn't tell me until now," Madeline said. Her eyes were narrowed in anger as she looked at her husband as if she could literally kill him. It was the night after Sherry Bennett's murder, and George and his wife were sitting in their chairs in the living room having drinks.

George sipped his gin and tonic slowly, trying to maintain his composure in the face of his wife's withering attack. He was emotionally exhausted, hoping for the solace of an alcohol-befogged mind. But Madeline's reaction, which had been no real surprise to him, had robbed him of any hope of respite from the turmoil that had begun with the call from Sherry Bennett the night before. "You were asleep when I got home last night, and out of the house before I was even up this morning. You seemed to have a full agenda, and I really had no opportunity to tell you any of this. I wasn't avoiding telling you, you can trust me on that."

His wife's eyebrows were arched, as she stared at him accusingly. "Can I, George? Can I trust you? You've continued to see your murderer-client despite my objections. It turns out that you talked to his girlfriend or secretary or whatever she might have been, but neglected to tell me that, although it is entirely outside the bounds of any normal method of doing therapy, even I know that. And finally, you responded to the poor dumb woman's cry for help when she was being stalked by your client and drove to some unknown parking garage in Irvine, where you discovered her dead, moments before the police drove up to find you with your hands around her neck. You're lucky you weren't charged with murder or killed by the same person who killed her. And what would I have thought? I wasn't even aware you had left the house."

"How would you have been aware? You had already left, yourself, without telling me where you were going, I might add." He tried to make his own tone accusing, but he was too afraid of provoking another of her attacks to sound anything more than petulant. He had no intention of telling

Madeline about the ten-minute dissociative fugue he'd experienced before finding himself bending over Sherry Bennett's dead body. He couldn't even let himself think about it. It bothered him, not just because he didn't know what he had been doing for those ten minutes, but also because this was the fourth such fugue episode in less than two months. The symptoms he had thought had been resolved through his analysis had returned with a vengeance.

"I was attending a lecture at UCI," Madeline answered dismissively. "I'm sure that I told you about it, probably weeks ago. You just didn't pay any attention when I told you; you never do, which is why you never know what I'm doing. Sometimes it's like you're off in another world, completely unreachable."

Her words frightened him. Were there other times in which he'd been in a dissociative state? Times he hadn't even noticed? "Anyway, I'm still alive and I'm not a suspect. They let me go home last night and only called me in today to find out what I knew about Bonaventure harassing the woman."

"Are they going to arrest him? Bonaventure?"

"I have no idea. I had the impression that they had no other evidence against him other than what I told them that Sherry told me."

"Well, of course he did it. Just as he killed his wife. The man's not just a psychopath, now he's a serial killer. I hope that this has convinced you to drop him as a patient."

"I don't have any proof that he did anything." He looked into his glass; there were only ice and the remains of a lime. He knew that his answer would anger Madeline, and he wanted another drink before he listened to her tirade. He swirled the ice in his glass and started to stand.

Madeline was glaring at him. " Proof?" she asked shrilly. "You don't need proof. You're not a judge, you're a psychiatrist. You know for sure that he killed that woman and his wife. You can't keep treating him. That's absurd."

George sat back down. He stared wistfully at the bottom of his glass. "I'm not sure that he killed his wife, or if he did, that he's aware of it. He had no motive for killing Sherry. He was worried about her. He wanted to protect her."

"Sherry? You talk about her as if she were your girlfriend."

He felt his face getting hot. "Nonsense. That's her name. I was just using her name. I've gotten used to calling her Sherry in my sessions with Bonaventure since that's all he talks about."

"And you can't see that that makes him guilty? What's wrong with you,

George? Why can't you let this go? This man is going to take you down with him."

He sighed and gazed into his empty drink glass. He stood up again and gazed longingly toward the kitchen. "I haven't decided yet. If he's charged with anything I'll drop him for sure. But right now, I'm fascinated by him. I want to see how he reacts to Sherry's death; will he be as indifferent to it as he has been to his wife's disappearance?"

"Fix me another, too," she said, holding out her glass. "I think you've got a death wish, George. Either that or you're doing this to deliberately frustrate me. If that's the case, it's just another sign of your immaturity. What am I going to tell my friends if it turns out that you're embroiled in two murders?"

"Tell them that it's unfortunate for your husband but that it's giving you great material for your next novel. They'll be jealous of you." His voice sounded bitter, even to him.

"That shows how much you know about my friends and colleagues; or even my own literary work. I don't write lurid murder mysteries. And that's what this is, a cheap, low-class murder mystery. Only my husband is involved in it."

He continued into the kitchen, a glass in each hand. "I forgot that your literary crowd doesn't write popular fiction. In fact, they don't write anything anyone other than them actually reads. And neither do you. So forgive me for letting the real world intrude into your pristine intellectual domain. But I'm a psychiatrist, and the welfare of my client is my first concern."

"Hurry up with my drink, George. And if the welfare of your clients was your first concern, you'd refer them all to someone else, someone who practiced a therapy that worked. You don't fool me, you're in this to excite your own prurient interests with your client's peccadilloes. You're not curing anyone of anything. Only this time your voyeurism is going to cost you. It's going to cost us both, and I hope you remember that I told you so."

Her words frightened him. They reminded him of his own doubts about himself and whether, in his choice of a profession, he was engaging in the same vices that he had suspected were his father's. "How could I forget," he answered, standing in front of her with full glasses in each of his hands. His own was straight gin. He handed Madeline her drink then sat down in his chair. "Shall we watch the news on CNN?"

"Fine. Just let's not watch the local news. I have no interest in seeing my husband's face on television, listed as a witness to a murder."

———   ———   ———

George awoke with a start. Something was wrong. He looked over at his wife's place next to him in bed. She was gone. He swung his legs over the side of the bed. He was still wearing his pants and his shirt. Why had he gone to bed in his clothes? And where was Madeline?

He stumbled downstairs, feeling lightheaded. Madeline wasn't in the kitchen, but the gin bottle was still out on the countertop. It was empty. How much had he had to drink? The wooden knife block was in the center of the counter instead of against the tile splashguard where it belonged. The largest knife was missing. George felt a wave of panic. What had he done? He called his wife's name but no one answered. Had she left? He checked the garage. Her car was still next to his. What had happened last night? Why had he no memory? He called her cell phone. There was no answer.

# Chapter 26

Susan Lin had agreed to meet Ben Murphy in the coffee shop of the Marriott hotel where he was staying. She'd been briefed on the private detective by Abe Reynolds and she was looking forward to meeting him, given his legendary status among Southern California peace officers. She felt touched that Murphy's main interest in talking to her was to find out information about the field of forensic psychology so he could advise his granddaughter, who was studying psychology at UC Santa Barbara.

The seventy-two-year-old detective was dressed in a pair of faded jeans and an unbuttoned green and white checked flannel shirt with a tee shirt underneath, his sleeves rolled up to his elbows. He wore a faded Dodgers baseball cap behind which his hair was in a braid, and he wore a pair of worn white sneakers. As he walked into the coffee shop, Susan stood up to greet him.

"Doctor Lin, I presume," Murphy said, smiling a broad smile and sticking out his hand.

"Call me Susan. It's a real honor to meet you, Chief Murphy."

"I'm just Ben now—no more Chief. You're doing me a favor. We're working on the same case, but my reasons for wanting to meet with you are personal." He slid into the booth opposite her.

"I understand you have a granddaughter who is studying psychology," Susan said.

He nodded, his mouth crinkled in a smile. "She's a bright kid. I've even got her working with me during her vacation. She and her brother, who's a whiz with computers, are taking calls on a hotline I set up for tips on Bertram Knowles' daughter, Regina. My granddaughter's a junior at UCSB."

"Is she planning to go to graduate school?"

"She says so. She's really into psychology. Not so much mental health kind of stuff, more research. I think she wants to teach someday. But I'm not sure that she's aware that there are police psychologists. It might be something that interests her. She's always had a keen interest in my work. She's got the kind of mind that figures stuff out quickly. She's intuitive and observant."

"You know the value of those qualities for police work more than I do."

"So why don't you tell me what you do and how you got involved in doing it? And by the way, are you hungry? It's on me since you're doing me the favor by being here. I'm going to have a bagel with my coffee. Go ahead and order whatever you like."

"Just coffee is fine." Susan relaxed. It was rare that anyone asked her about herself, and, like many Asians, she usually avoided making herself the topic of conversation. But Ben Murphy's casual friendliness was inviting, and she felt as if she were helping him with his granddaughter. "I was like your granddaughter. I wanted to teach, still do someday. But teaching jobs are few and far between. They want you to have published several papers before even hiring you as an assistant professor. Also, like your daughter, I was enchanted with police work. My father was a policeman, a homicide detective in Chicago." She saw the surprised look on his face. "I know most people don't think of a Chinese-American when they envision a police detective. My family has been in the U.S. for generations. My great-great-grandfather came to America to work on the railroad at the beginning of the last century. My Parents are much more American than they are Chinese. Anyway, my father's retired now. When I was in graduate school at Northwestern, he got me a consulting job on a couple of cases with his department. When I got my Ph.D., I looked around for openings for forensic psychologists—that's what the field is called—and the first one I found was here in Orange County. I work with several different cities' departments, depending on the kind of cases they have."

"How do the guys on the force accept you... and the gals?"

She gave him a "so-so" gesture. "Most are pretty open, especially the higher ups. Abe Reynolds, whom you met, was a little slow to warm up to me, but we got through it, and now we work well together. An Irvine detective just called me to invite me in on one of their cases. Both Lucas Bonaventure and his psychiatrist are involved in some way with the case. I have to meet with him this afternoon and find out more, but Frank Jensen, that's the Irvine detective, got Bonaventure to sign a release so I can question his psychiatrist, which is something I've been wanting to do."

Murphy sipped his coffee. His bagel had arrived, but he ignored it. "So you do investigating as well as psychology?"

"I wouldn't call it investigating so much as establishing a suspect's history. Psychology has its own methods—personality tests, neuroimaging, specialized interviewing techniques—but the best clue to a suspect's behavior, even with regard to his psychological profile, is gained from analyzing background information. A person's past behavior is the best clue to his personality."

"And talking to his shrink—excuse me, I didn't mean that as a disrespectful term—is part of gaining background information?" Murphy was looking at her with a rapt expression, as if everything she was saying was important to him.

"Shrinks, as you call them, are experts at gathering information about people. I'm hoping that Lucas Bonaventure told his psychiatrist things he'd never tell an investigating officer or even a private detective like yourself."

Murphy nodded as if he understood. "I talked to Lucas Bonaventure yesterday. Kind of a courtesy visit, since I'm working for his father-in-law."

She was surprised. She knew that Ben Murphy was handling the phone tips that came in as a result of Bertram Knowles' million-dollar reward, but she didn't know that the former police chief would talk to Bonaventure himself. "How did that go?"

"I think Lucas is a little put out that his father-in-law has offered such a big reward. Thinks the old man is trying to one-up him since he only offered twenty-five thousand himself. Wouldn't own up to saying that he and Regina had a fight the night she left, even though I'm willing to bet that they did. She wasn't the type to go out to a bar by herself, or at least she didn't use to be."

"You knew her?" she asked.

"Bert Knowles and I have been friends for years. I was always fond of Regina, but I haven't seen her much since she got married."

"Bonaventure hasn't told us anything about his relationship with his wife. He just describes it as 'normal'."

"He's not your most forthcoming person. Always has been arrogant... and distant. Bert thought that Lucas was a business genius, that's why he wanted his daughter to marry him, to give her security, although, God knows, Bert's money is security enough for her. But Lucas hasn't really panned out as a businessman."

"I thought he was very successful." She was learning all sorts of things she hadn't known before.

"He acts the part, but the truth is that Bert has had to bail him out a couple of times. Too impulsive, Bert says. I wouldn't know since that's not my bailiwick."

"His wife has a lot of money in her name, but being California, that's half her husband's anyway."

"Could become all his." Murphy narrowed his eyes as if he were thinking of something, then took a bite of his unbuttered bagel.

"Learn anything else from talking to Bonaventure?" Susan wasn't sure that Murphy would be willing to share more of what he'd found out, but it didn't hurt to ask.

"One of them was really into psychology. The bookshelves in their den are full of the stuff. Lucas said all the books were Regina's. Said she was a big fan of Freud."

"Really? That's odd for a nonprofessional unless she's into the arts or literature. Freud is a lot more popular with the artsy crowd than with psychologists. Bonaventure's psychiatrist is a psychoanalyst, so maybe that's why he picked him, if his wife had told him about Freud."

"Or if Lucas reads the stuff himself. He looked uncomfortable when I asked him about it. His denial was too emphatic. One of the books, something about interpreting dreams, was a big hit with one of them. Its pages were pretty dog-eared."

"*The Interpretation of Dreams?*"

"That was it."

"It's a classic. Not that I'm an expert on Freud. I'm into research and neuroscience, like your granddaughter. But that would be interesting if Bonaventure was reading Freud. He'd know just what to tell his shrink."

"What do you mean?"

"I wonder if Bonaventure isn't seeing the psychiatrist in order to lay the groundwork for a diminished capacity defense, although I doubt that he knows how hard that kind of defense is to make."

"And now you've got permission to talk to the psychiatrist?"

She smiled, as if they shared a secret. "Yes I do, and I plan to make the most of it."

"Sounds as if being a police psychologist is as much police work as it is psychology."

"I'll take that as a compliment, especially coming from you."

"I'm impressed. A good policeman has to be an amateur psychologist, but that doesn't mean that a professional psychologist wouldn't make an even better policeman—or policewoman—especially if he or she had the respect you seem to have for real investigating. I think my granddaughter would like you and what you do. Maybe I can bring her down here to talk to you."

"I'd be happy to talk to her."

# Chapter 27

George was surprised at how happy he felt that Susan Lin, the young police psychologist had called to ask to meet with him again. He was also worried. How could he talk to someone from the police department when he had no idea what had happened to Madeline?

He was still at home. He had told Mrs. Schrempf to cancel his appointments for the day, claiming to feel too ill to come in. In fact, he was overcome with anxiety, paralyzed by the fear that, during one of his amnesic fugue episodes he had done the unthinkable: harmed his own wife. He was sitting in bed, still dressed, leaning against the headboard. He knew it was bad for him, but he was sipping on a gin and tonic from a newly opened bottle. He needed something to calm his nerves.

Think as he might, he could not recall anything from the night before. His last memory was of eating dinner with Madeline, both of them in silence, both of them drinking more than eating. He seemed to remember her leaving to go up to their bedroom, heaving a loud sigh but saying nothing, but perhaps she had said something after all. He had a vague recollection of her threatening him. With what? Leaving? Her car was still in the garage. He'd checked her closet and her drawers. Nothing seemed to be missing. All the suitcases were still in the auxiliary closet where they were kept. He'd called her cell phone twice. She hadn't answered either time.

When Susan Lin called him on his cell phone he had been relieved. Suddenly, his thoughts about Madeline's hostility toward him had been erased by his interest in the psychologist. For the length of the conversation, he hadn't thought about Madeline at all. Now, his terror had returned full bore, combined with his apprehension about focusing on Susan Lin instead of his missing wife, just as Lucas had focused on Sherry Bennett instead of his own wife.

He roused himself from the bed and went downstairs to the kitchen. The knife block was still in the middle of the counter. He stared at it, trying to jog his memory. They had eaten steaks for dinner, so two steak knives were missing, as they should be. He opened the dishwasher. The steak knives were there. There was no sign of the butcher knife.

The front door opened.

"George? "His wife stood in the entryway, looking at him standing in the doorway to the kitchen in his wrinkled clothing and a drink in his hand. "What are you doing? Why aren't you at work?"

He almost dropped his drink. He felt a wave of relief. "Where have you been?"

She walked into the living room and threw her purse on a chair. "Where have I been? I was at Cecily Engle's house. I told you that when I left last night."

"But your car...."

"She picked me up. I'd had too much to drink to drive. You'd had too much also, which is why I left. You followed me upstairs, trying to pick a fight with me." She looked at him with curiosity. "You don't remember, do you?"

He shook his head. "I can't remember what happened. I called you, but you didn't answer your phone."

" I didn't want to talk to you. Your drinking is getting out of control, George." She stood gazing at him. "Look at you. You're already drinking and it's 10:30 in the morning. You're not even at work. Are those the same clothes you were wearing last night?"

He looked down at his wrinkled shirt and pants. "The butcher knife was missing. I thought..."

"You thought what, that I had been attacked, kidnapped, murdered? You're losing it, George. That knife has been missing for at least three weeks.

"I was terrified." He didn't say that he'd been terrified that he had done something to harm her.

She shook her head. "Worry about yourself, George. This ridiculous case is making you ill." She glanced at the staircase. "I have to change my clothes. I have a lunch appointment." She picked up her purse and started up the stairs. "Stop drinking George, and go to work. Pull yourself together for God's sake."

He watched her climb the stairs, feeling as though he had been through this experience before.

———  ———  ———

"So we meet again, Doctor Farquhar, but this time I need to ask you specifically about what Lucas Bonaventure has told you." Susan Lin sat in the soft leather chair in front of George Farquhar's desk. She appeared surprised by the psychiatrist's cordiality after she had produced a copy of the release of information form, signed by his client. He seemed genuinely pleased to see her.

Although George had been pleased when Susan Lin had called and asked to meet with him, he now felt his suspicion growing. "I thought you were working with the Newport Beach Police Department. This release is from the Irvine Police."

"I work for several departments at the same time. I'm working on both Bonaventure's wife's disappearance and Sherry Bennett's murder, which I've heard you're also connected to in some way." Her statement sounded like a question.

George felt his anxiety rising. "I'm afraid I found the poor woman after she was already dead." After his experience with Madeline's absence, he was even more worried about the fugue state that surrounded his finding Sherry Bennett's body. He felt as if he might be capable of doing anything and not remembering it.

"And you already knew the victim?"

"I interviewed her at Bonaventure's request."

"And why did he ask you to interview her?"

"He was stalking her. He felt she needed protection. She felt harassed and had quit working for him, and he wanted me to find out what he'd done that had forced her to quit."

"That doesn't sound like analytic therapy. It doesn't sound like any kind of therapy. Why did you consent to do it?"

His face reddened. He remembered his wife asking the same question. "It's rather complicated."

She smiled politely. "I have time to listen."

He shifted uncomfortably in his chair. "Lucas Bonaventure is a very complex man. He has a neurosis." He noticed the young psychologist raise her eyebrows at his use of the old-fashioned term. "I know we don't talk about neuroses anymore. Instead, we classify people by symptom syndromes, clusters of symptoms that occur together and can be observed even by poorly trained therapists. Of course, Bonaventure fits one of those categories, too. He has what the DSM would classify as a dissociative disorder." Even as he said it, George felt self-conscious, realizing that his own fugue states fell into the same category.

"You mean he has amnesia or a dual personality?" Her frown conveyed her skepticism.

"Not a dual personality, but he utilizes repression much more than normal. That's one of the drawbacks of the new diagnostic system. It doesn't allow us to diagnose someone on the basis of how he copes with his unconscious conflicts, the extent to which he employs specific defense mechanisms."

"Those were the kinds of things no two clinicians could ever agree upon, which is why we changed to the new system."

George smiled at her. Engaging with the young psychologist in theoretical repartee was more comfortable than talking about why he had interviewed someone who was not his client. "I'm afraid you're right. Such things require knowledge not just of a client's symptoms, but also of the inner workings of his mind, both on a conscious and unconscious level. Most modern clinicians are not trained nor capable of gaining such knowledge about their clients."

"Only psychoanalysts?"

He wondered if she was teasing him. "Only clinicians with an appreciation of unconscious processes and defense mechanisms," he answered, aware that he was speaking somewhat stiffly.

"We could argue about this for a long time," she replied. "But what about Lucas Bonaventure? You were going to tell me how he convinced you to interview Sherry Bennett."

George felt his face getting hot. Doctor Lin wasn't letting him off the hook. If he were talking to Madeline, he'd pour himself a drink about now. "Mr. Bonaventure was living under the delusion that Sherry Bennett was in danger. I believe it was a displacement of his anxiety caused by the loss of his wife, by his failure to protect her."

"So some harm befell his wife and since he didn't do anything to prevent that, he made up a danger for this other woman and was determined to protect her as a substitute for not protecting his wife?"

"In a nutshell." He was impressed by how easily she comprehended the psychological situation.

"But she obviously *was* in danger. And she felt that he was the one who posed that danger to her. Did he ask you to reassure her that he wasn't a threat to her?"

"Not at all. He wanted my opinion on whether I felt she was in danger or if he was deluded about it."

"How could you determine if she was in danger?"

"It was Mr. Bonaventure's idea that Miss Bennett was courting danger by behaving sexually provocatively and he wanted my opinion about that. He also wanted my advice on what he could do to persuade her to be more careful."

"And you agreed to that?"

"I knew that he was delusional on the topic. But I felt that I needed my own first-hand observation in order to change Mr. Bonaventure's mind." George was trying his best to make his behavior sound logical. It was hard to keep his thoughts straight.

"And did you change his mind?"

"Not really. He continued to believe that she was, in his words, 'courting danger.' He also continued to stalk her."

"Stalk her? I don't know if the Irvine Police are aware of that."

"I told them, at least I thought I did. But I know that he followed her after work on more than one occasion. He admitted as much to me." He couldn't tell her that he had also followed Sherry in order to confirm that Lucas was stalking her. Such a confession would reveal too much about him.

"And when she called you on the night she died, she said he was following her?"

"That was her assumption. I don't believe she had any direct evidence that that was the case."

"What's your opinion?"

"I don't have one. I know she was terrified, and I believe that someone deliberately sent her to that address, and then disabled her car so they could kill her. I have no idea who it was."

"And why did you go there that night?'

George felt a wave of anxiety. He rubbed his hands together. His palms were slick with sweat, and he could feel the moisture from his armpits sliding down his side. He worried that Susan Lin might smell his fear. "Miss Bennet sounded terrified. She called me because she thought that my client was after her and that if he appeared, I could stop him. I had no idea if that was correct, but I knew that she was paralyzed with fear and I felt an obligation to try to help her." He knew that his behavior made no sense from the point of view of his being Lucas' therapist.

"I'm not an analyst, nor even a therapist, but I thought that meeting with other people in a client's life carries the danger of biasing your relationship with your client, that it harms the transference relationship or something. Am I wrong?"

She was not wrong and George felt trapped by having to admit that, by meeting with Sherry Bennett and then by responding to her distress call, he had violated the very theory that underlay his therapy. He shook his head to try to clear it. "What was your question?"

"It doesn't matter. It was only theoretical. Tell me more about Lucas Bonaventure's mental state."

His shoulders relaxed. Talking about his client was easier than talking about himself. "As I said, he's severely repressed, quite unaware of the reasons he does some of the things he does."

"What do you mean?"

"Exactly what I told you before. His reaction to his wife's disappearance has been one of complete emotional denial. He knows she's missing, but he feels no emotion about it. Instead, he transferred all of his fear about his wife to a woman he picked virtually at random from his office staff. And he has no idea that he's displaced his anxiety from one person to the other. None at all." He was struck by the recollection that he had reacted similarly by focusing on Susan Lin when she had called, despite thinking his own wife was missing. He tried to refocus his thoughts. He felt as if his mind were swirling in circles.

"You said that Bonaventure felt that Sherry Bennett was behaving provocatively, that he said she was asking to have something bad happen to her. Do you think those feelings were also displaced from his wife?"

For someone without analytic training, Susan Lin was amazingly quick to grasp psychological phenomena. "I have to assume so. I met Miss Bennett and I got no impression that she was behaving provocatively. That was all projection on Bonaventure's part."

"Your client certainly seems to have little knowledge of himself, doctor."

"I told you, Bonaventure is neurotic. He had conversion symptoms long before his wife went missing."

"What kind of conversion symptoms?"

"One of his legs became paralyzed, apparently as a reaction to his brother's death."

Doctor Lin's face showed her surprise. "Really? Conversion symptoms are rare in our current culture, especially among educated people, such as your client. In many cases, they actually have a neurological basis. Are you sure there was no physical reason for the paralysis?"

He shook his head. "None. Paralyses don't come and go, not unless they're psychosomatic."

"Did his come and go? Did it happen again?"

"Not in real life, but he dreams about it."

"Dreams that he's paralyzed?"

"It's not an uncommon thing. But his dreams are what we call anxiety dreams. They wake him up and he continues to feel terrified when he wakes up. The first thing he does when he awakens from such a dream is to check if his legs are able to move."

"Do you have an explanation for his dreams? I know that's what psychoanalysts do, explain dreams."

He wasn't sure if she was making fun of him or was sincere in wanting to hear his explanation. "I'm sure you don't want to hear my Freudian interpretations. Anyway, dream analysis isn't the immediate, shoot-from-the-hip process that most people think it is. I will need to hear much more about his dreams before I can understand their significance." George wasn't about to go into the Oedipal and castration fears that motivated Lucas' dreams, not when his own dissociative episodes might be related to the same unconscious conflicts.

She looked as if she was considering asking more but then changed the subject. "Bonaventure has a copy of *The Interpretation of Dreams* on his shelf in his den. In fact, he has an extensive psychological library, mostly Freud. He says that it's his wife's."

George tried to conceal his shock. "That's news to me. He's given no indication that his wife was interested in psychology and certainly not that he was." Bonaventure's naiveté about psychology was one of the assumptions that underlay George's treatment of the man, and was part of the analyst's explanation for Lucas' lack of insight into his own mind.

"But he did choose to see a psychoanalyst. Even if he picked a therapist randomly, what's the chance that he would pick one of the few analysts in Newport Beach? Did he say why he picked you?"

"He said he picked me out of the phone book." In fact, George had no idea why Lucas had picked him, since he had no recollection of the phone call that had secured Lucas his first appointment.

"I've never read much of Freud. I'm afraid they don't teach it much in research psychology programs these days. Would you recognize if he was feeding you material from some of Freud's books to make it seem as if he was neurotic?"

This time he couldn't conceal his shock. She was voicing the same opinion as his wife's. He felt let down that she believed he could so easily be fooled. "I'm hardly capable of failing to recognize if someone is feigning a neurosis by copying his symptoms from one of Freud's texts."

"Of course not. I just wondered if it made a difference knowing that he might have some knowledge of Freudian theory."

He gave her a quick smile. "I've told you all I know at this point."

She sensed that he'd said all that he was going to say. "I'd like to talk to you again, kind of touch base every once in a while. Your client's release allows us to talk as much as we'd like." Her request sounded as much social as professional.

George felt relieved. Perhaps she didn't question his clinical acumen. He guessed that Madeline's comments had made him overly sensitive. "I'd like to talk again, too. Anytime you want to. I also enjoy our talks."

She stood to leave. George came around his deck and took her arm as he walked her to his door.

# Chapter 28

Susan Lin poured hot water from the electric pot on her kitchen counter into a cup in which she'd place a bag with green tea. She carried the steaming cup of tea and its saucer to her small living room and placed it on the coffee table in front of her flowered couch. Then she picked up the copy of *The Interpretation of Dreams* she'd checked out from the Irvine Public Library that afternoon. She plumped a throw pillow behind her back and put her feet up on the coffee table, careful to not disturb the cup of steeping tea. She enjoyed her nights of solitude in her condominium, one of nearly one hundred similar residences in the three-year-old Irvine complex. The apartment had been her first big purchase after graduating with her Ph.D. and getting her first job as a forensic psychologist. She didn't think of it as her life-long home. It was a one-bedroom and too small for the husband and two children that she hoped to have someday. But it was comfortable, and it was home, and it was hers.

She'd read *about* Freud's theories in graduate school, but she'd never read Freud in the translated original. Her doctoral program had been based upon a combination of neuroscience and advanced psychometric theory. She had delved deeply into how the brain worked and learned how to use the most recent and sophisticated neuroimaging techniques to study what was happening and where it was happening in the brain when individuals engaged in cognitive tasks. And she had learned how to use the most advanced personality and attitudinal measures to compare an individual to his peers in every area from political sentiments to control of his aggressive impulses. Classical Freudian theory had only been mentioned as an example of unscientific, subjectively validated psychology, something from the ancient past.

She set down the book and reached over and removed the tea bag from her cup and laid it on the edge of the saucer. Then she took a sip of the tea— still too hot to drink—and picked up the book. She skipped the long introduction and the several prefaces to earlier editions and instead turned to the book's beginning. It was a history of the work on dreams up to the point of the publication of the book, which was in 1900. She read just enough to be amazed by the author's confidence and lack of ambiguity in claiming the validity of his method. Phrases claiming "proof" or that "there can be no doubt as to the truth of this assertion," proliferated. Sigmund Freud was persuasive, although his exhortative language would be shunned by any modern-day scientific journal or publisher.

It would take forever to wade through the book, the writing of which was dense and arcane, filled with concepts and constructions from a previous era, more like reading a Dickens novel, or, given its subject matter, a story by the Marquis de Sade, than a scientific treatise. She flipped to the index and found several mentions of anxiety dreams in chapter seven, which she knew was the most famous and oft-quoted chapter of the book.

She turned to the section, which was labeled "The Function of Dreams." Taking a sip of her now sufficiently cooled tea, she began reading.

Freud claimed that one of the functions of dreams was to allow the dreamer to continue sleeping, despite the presence of disturbing thoughts from his unconscious mind, such thoughts having been provoked by experiences during the recent waking hours. These thoughts became disguised and acted out in the imagination in such forms that, while they might contain some anxiety, would not wake the sleeper. As such, they allowed for some "discharge" of excitation from the unconscious, which, although the original unconscious thought was pleasurable because it represented the fulfillment of a sexual wish, had turned into anxiety because of the need for repression of the wish.

She had to admit that she found the theory fascinating, even compelling, had she not known that modern theorists seriously questioned Freud's findings. Not that there was universal agreement as to "the function of dreams," or even that they had a function. Current theories ranged from the idea that dreaming is an evolutionary adaptation that allows us to practice "flight or fight" reactions in our sleep to Sir Francis Crick's idea that "we dream in order to forget." Crick, the discoverer of DNA, thought that dreaming allowed us to form new connections between experiences to replace older, outmoded ones—a nightly updating that rids us of useless mental connections and thoughts, much as a computer overwrites old information on its disk and replaces it with new.

Susan couldn't help but reflect on some of her own dreams. She still had nearly monthly somnolent, anxiety-filled reveries related to graduate school, particularly the examinations she'd had to pass in order to obtain her doctorate. That had been the period of her life most filled with anxiety and, despite Sir Francis Crick's claims, not something she seemed able to forget. She suspected that those situations in her present life that re-aroused her own questions regarding her competence were what provoked the reminiscences of the examinations taken several years ago.

But Freud had a different idea. He claimed that anxiety dreams represented subconscious sexual thoughts. And, as if to cement his legacy as one who chose his own path toward scientific validation, he picked one of his own dreams to prove his point. His explanation of the sources of his dream, which had occurred when he was seven or eight years old and which he interpreted thirty years later, ranged from a play upon a childhood friend's name, to Biblical illustrations, to a memory of his grandfather's face when he was in a coma, which was then transferred to the face of his mother in the dream. Most of Freud's analysis seemed to Susan to be of not only questionable scientific status, if not veracity, but extremely forced.

The second dream offered in proof of Freud's conjectures caught her attention. It was from a twenty-seven-year-old man who recalled a recurrent nightmare from his childhood. The dreamer had been physically abusive to a younger brother whom his mother had predicted would be killed by him one day. Susan immediately thought of Bonaventure's bizarre reaction to the death of his own brother, with Bonaventure having become paralyzed in one leg. The dream described by Freud was one in which the dreamer was pursued by a man with an axe, but the dreamer's legs became paralyzed and he was unable to run away. He awoke in a state of anxiety. Here again was the paralysis, which Doctor Farquhar had described as a component of Lucas Bonaventure's dream. Freud's interpretation was that the axe and the paralysis represented castration anxiety, this time provoked by Oedipal wishes toward the dreamer's mother, but related also to his anxiety about the death of his brother.

Had Lucas Bonaventure read this dream and Freud's interpretation and provided it to his psychiatrist in order to prove that he was neurotic? She knew that she was grasping at straws. The evidence for her theory was even more insubstantial than Freud's supposed confirmation of his anxiety dream theory on the basis of the two childhood dreams he had cited. What would Doctor Farquhar say to her conjectures? No doubt that she understood neither psychoanalytic theory nor how the unconscious mind works, both points to which she was forced to agree. But she did understand the cleverness of psychopaths, despite their almost always fatal impulsivity and poor judgment. After all, it didn't take the intelligence of a Ted Bundy, who had in fact studied psychology, to copy a dream from the most famous work ever written on the subject and to try to pass it off as his own.

She did not know, for a fact, how closely Lucas Bonaventure's dream resembled the one discussed by Freud. She knew that it involved a feeling of paralysis in his legs and that his symptoms, and perhaps the dream also, were related in some way to his brother's death. She would have to find out more. She took a long sip of her tea and reflected on the fact that it was fortunate that Doctor Farquhar seemed eager to talk to her. She would take advantage of his eagerness.

# Chapter 29

Ben Murphy got off the telephone with his granddaughter. She had told her grandfather that the caller was sincere, she was certain of it. However, when she had put her on hold to put her grandfather on the line, the caller had hung up. Luckily, Terri, his granddaughter, had typed the message even as the caller was speaking it, and it had appeared almost instantly on her grandfather's computer. After she had hung up, Terri could only tell Murphy that the caller had been a female.

The caller's message was that she had seen a car fitting the description of Regina Bonaventure's Mercedes the night of the woman's disappearance. It had been parked near the edge of the parking lot overlooking Crystal Cove beach. Someone, a man or woman, had gotten out of the car and was pulling something large out of the back seat, then carried it into the grass and underbrush between the parking lot and the cliff overlooking the beach. The caller hadn't called the police because she herself wasn't supposed to have been in the parking lot that night. Following that statement, Ben's granddaughter had tried to transfer the call to her grandfather, but the caller had hung up. Her phone had left no caller ID.

Perhaps it was an underage girl who had been parked with a boyfriend in the parking lot, Ben thought to himself. Someone who didn't want her parents to find out she'd been there or whom she was with. He debated whether to call Abe Reynolds. It was already eight o'clock at night and Reynolds probably wouldn't be in his office. The information could wait until morning. It was the third week since Regina's disappearance anyway. Another twelve hours wouldn't matter. But Ben's curiosity wouldn't let *him* wait.

The sign on the gate to the parking lot, which was on the Pacific Coast Highway, about a half mile from the shopping center from which Regina Bonaventure had disappeared, said that it closed at ten p.m. Ben didn't know if that meant that the gate would be locked or just that anyone still there would be told to leave. Anyway, it was only eight-thirty so he drove through the gate and parked at the other side of the lot, nearest the cliffs. There were still about twenty other cars in the lot, presumably their occupants still on the beach below, even though it was already dark.

Ben got out and walked to the edge of the parking lot. The lot itself was several hundred yards long. In the quiet of the evening, he could hear the waves rolling in on the sandy beach below. The car that had been seen—perhaps Regina's car—could have been parked anywhere along the cliff's edge. Ben walked to the end of the pavement. There were several trails, perhaps six of them, leading toward the beach. He assumed that if a killer were attempting to hide a body, he either would have carried it down to the beach and thrown it into the sea or buried it among the underbrush, but not near one of the well- worn trails. No bodies had washed ashore since Regina went missing, so the odds were that if a body had been disposed of, it was still somewhere on top of the cliffs.

The body, if there was a body, could be anywhere. He wished that he had the been able to talk to the person who'd made the phone call so that he would have a better idea as to the exact spot, but that was not the case. Unless the person called back, there was no way Ben could figure out where the car had been parked or where to search among the underbrush. If he just began tramping around at random, it was highly unlikely that he would be able to find the body and very likely that he would destroy any evidence that might be present near the crime scene. He got back in his car. Better call Abe Reynolds in the morning.

———  ———  ———

Thirty uniformed cops and two cadaver-sniffing dogs, both German Shepherds, combed the brushy area around the Crystal Cove parking lot and the beach below. Abe Reynolds had asked the park rangers to close the parking lot at Crystal Cove, since the beach area was designated as a state park. The men and dogs fanned out along the cliff-top between the parking lot and the cliff's edge and combed every inch of the underbrush. The dogs found no scent along any of the six trails leading to the beach. Abe's men made a thorough search among the rocks and sand spits leading into the water but found nothing.

As the search crew made its way slowly through the underbrush between the edge of the parking lot and the cliff, the two dogs suddenly became alert, their bodies stiffening and their ears pointing forward as they sniffed the air. Both of them ran directly to a spot between two three-foot high coastal shrubs. Both dogs pawed and sniffed at the recently disturbed ground. Their handlers pulled the straining dogs back.

"Bring shovels," Abe Reynolds shouted. He and Ben Murphy stood back while crime scene photographers took pictures of the area before any digging began. Murphy was dressed casually in jeans and sneakers and his usual Dodgers baseball cap, but this time he wore a blue nylon windbreaker and dark sunglasses. The temperature was in the high sixties with a strong wind blowing in from the ocean, and the sky was pristinely blue.

As soon as the officers with shovels began digging, one of them shouted, "There's something buried here." The crime scene team took over, carefully lifting shovelfuls of dirt and putting them in bags. A dark plastic bag began to be revealed. The diggers carefully dug around the bag, their hands in gloves so as not to destroy any fingerprints. Soon two plastic bags, taped together, emerged from the shallow grave. When it was completely visible, one of the crime scene men cut one end of the bag open with a scalpel-like instrument. He peeled back the plastic to reveal the contents "It's a dog!" the officer cried.

"Shit!" Abe Reynolds said.

As the crime scene officer peeled back more of the plastic, the head and torso of a large Collie dog, in the early stages of decomposition, emerged.

"That's a young dog," Ben Murphy told the detective. "Odd for him to die. Odd place to bury him."

Abe looked at him. "I don't know. My daughter's cat got hit by a car and I buried the body in a field away from the house. Told my daughter the cat had run away. People do that kind of thing." He bent down and looked more closely at the dog "This isn't what we're looking for."

Ben wasn't sure if he was frustrated or relieved. Finding the dog's body left him no closer to finding Regina, but it did keep open the possibility that she was still alive. It was becoming an increasingly slim possibility, he thought. "Why don't you have your lab find out what killed it?" he said.

Reynolds gave him a skeptical look. "That's a lot of wasted effort. It's just a dog. This has nothing to do with Regina Bonaventure's disappearance."

"It happened the same night, according to my anonymous caller and we're only a half mile from the restaurant where she was last seen."

"That dog hasn't been in the ground more than a week, I can almost guarantee that," Reynolds answered.

Ben agreed. "So keep your men and dogs looking. This might not be the only grave around here. But I'd still be curious how a dog this young died."

Reynolds's instructed his men to continue the search. "We'll see. Depends on how backed up the coroner is. I don't even know if the coroner will autopsy a dog, come to think of it."

"If he will, it could give us some more information. You never know," Ben replied.

An hour later, the head of the search crew declared the area clean.

"A wild-goose chase, I guess," Ben Murphy told Detective Reynolds. Ben was leaning against Reynolds's car.

"Thanks for calling us anyway," Reynolds said. He held a paper cup from Starbucks in one hand and now and then took a sip of coffee. "Too bad the caller didn't identify herself."

"Probably wasn't supposed to be here herself. Afraid her parents would find out if she made an official report. But there are lots of white Mercedes and lots of reasons someone might park here and dispose of something at night. I'd say it was the dog, except I agree with you that it would be more decomposed if it had been here for nearly three weeks, even wrapped in plastic bags."

"How many calls you getting a day?'

"Thirty to forty. More at first, but now it's settled down. Probably go down to just a few a day in a week or so."

"And this is the first one that looked like it might be something worth following up?"

"First one. Mostly they're inquiries about the size of the reward rather than real tips. Since it's known that Bert Knowles is putting up the money, and it's his daughter that is missing, a lot of them are from the Santa Barbara area. A lot of people up there have seen a lot of suspicious things. They don't seem to realize Regina went missing down here."

Reynolds shook his head. "That's the downside of offering a reward for tips on a crime. People will report almost anything. Don't know why they think they'll get paid when they know their tip is bogus."

Ben nodded. "This one seemed real, though. This beach is less than a mile from where Regina was last seen. It made sense that maybe someone dumped her body here; except they didn't I guess."

"I'll talk to the coroner about autopsying the dog, but I think you're right, this one was a red herring. But don't let that stop you from calling me if you get another one that sounds promising. We've got almost nada ourselves."

"Nothing more on the guy who smashed his car into the truck?"

"None of his prints, no evidence that he did anything that night other than go to the bar and have a few drinks. We're not giving up on him, but frankly, I hope it's not him or we won't be able to get any clues as to what happened to the Bonaventure woman."

"How about Lucas, the husband? I talked to him and he doesn't seem very broken up about his wife being missing."

"He's a person of interest, verging on becoming a suspect in another case over in Irvine. This time it was definitely murder. But all the evidence is circumstantial. Our psychologist thinks he's responsible for that one too."

"I met with her—your psychologist—she's bright. We talked about my granddaughter's interest in psychology. Dr. Lin mentioned that Irvine had called her in on another case that involved Lucas and his shrink, but she didn't tell me that Lucas was actually a suspect."

"His shrink could be too, for that matter. He found the body and he knew the victim."

"That case got anything to do with this one?"

"Other than Bonaventure being involved, you mean? Not that I know of, but Doctor Lin is talking to the shrink. Bonaventure signed a release, so she may dig up connections we don't know about."

"Always distrust a coincidence, is one of my mottos," Ben said. "I hope Doctor Lin finds some connections, because I'm willing to bet they're there."

"We'll see," Abe said, throwing his empty coffee cup into a trashcan next to his car. "But I think you're right."

# Chapter 30

When Lucas arrived he headed straight for the couch and lay down, putting one arm across his eyes. "I can't stop thinking about Regina. I know that something bad has happened to her. The police seem to think so too."

George was surprised that Lucas' defenses had collapsed so easily. He had become more concerned about his wife since Sherry died, probably because he had lost the person upon whom he'd displaced his anxiety since his wife's disappearance. "You're worried more about your wife than you were before?"

"I'm terrified. I know something terrible has happened to her. I've even started dreaming about her."

Even though he couldn't see his face, George noticed that there were beads of sweat on Lucas' forehead. Whatever he'd dreamed bothered him even more than usual. "Tell me about your dream."

"I saw her dead. Her dead body laid out in the ground. But my dreams have become weird."

"What do you mean, weird?"

"Last night I dreamed I was walking through this field, only it was at the edge of a cliff. And then there was a hole in front of me. I was going to go around it, but it kept getting wider. Then I decided to jump across it. I backed up and took a run at it, but then my legs wouldn't move. No matter how hard I tried, my legs were stiff, paralyzed, I couldn't run at all."

"What happened?"

"I kind of dragged myself up to the edge of the hole, like a paraplegic in a movie I saw once. When I got to the edge, I looked down and there was Regina's body, naked."

"Naked?"

"But that wasn't the weird thing. She was naked and I could see she had a penis. It had a card attached to it with a string." He raised up enough to turn and look at George. His face was red.

George decided to ignore Lucas' embarrassment. He was too interested in the dream. "A card?" he asked.

Lucas lay back down. "Like when they attach a card—a tag—with a number on it to the toe of a body in the morgue, only this was attached to her penis, Regina's penis."

"What happened in the dream after you saw her body with the card attached to her penis?"

"I woke up. I was sweating, shaking almost. I moved both my legs to be sure they weren't paralyzed, then I tried to get the picture of Regina's body out of my mind."

"And were you able to get it out of your mind?"

"I had to get up and have a drink of Scotch... two in fact. I was afraid I was going to have a heart attack."

"What frightened you so much about the dream?"

"The card tied to the penis, Regina's penis, I guess, even though that doesn't make sense. Like I said, it was weird."

"Why do you think the card attached to the penis frightened you? Did it make you think of anything?"

Lucas heaved a sigh, as if explaining any further was difficult. "My brother. When he died, I had to go to the morgue and identify his body. He died suddenly, in his car while driving. He had a heart attack but he crashed his car and the paramedics took him to the hospital. The doctors at the hospital declared him dead, but they needed someone to confirm that it was my brother. He had my name and number in his wallet so they called me."

"And the card attached to the penis reminded you of when you identified your brother's body?"

"There was a card just like that tied to his toe in the morgue."

"To his toe, not to his penis?"

"His toe. I guess they do that."

"And were you frightened then, when you saw your brother's body with the card tied to his toe?"

"First I was angry. They hadn't cleaned him up at all from the traffic accident. His face still had streaks of blood on it, and his arm was bent at this impossible angle. I was mad that they had just left him like that. I mean, he was dead, couldn't they have cleaned him up and made him presentable before they showed him to me?"

"So you were angry, but not frightened."

"At first. I mean I was anxious going into the hospital morgue, hoping that it wouldn't be Jerry, that they'd made a mistake. But when I saw him, I got mad. Then after I cooled off, I looked around and I saw these other bodies, all with similar tags attached to their toes. Suddenly I panicked. I remember I got dizzy. They made me sit down, brought me some water. When I tried to stand up, my right leg wouldn't move."

"It was paralyzed?"

"Completely. They had to get me a wheelchair. They took me upstairs, and one of the hospital doctors examined me. I had an MRI, then the doctor told me that there was nothing wrong with me."

"But why was your leg paralyzed?"

"I don't know. The doctors there didn't know what was wrong with my leg so they said it was all in my head. I didn't believe them. I could tell that my leg wouldn't move. It was paralyzed and I had no feeling in it. That couldn't have been in my head."

"And you never saw another doctor to diagnose what the problem was? I seem to remember you telling me that."

"Like I said, I was busy, then it went away on its own. Maybe they were right, it was some kind of stress reaction."

The symbolism of castration anxiety was almost too blatant to be real. George reminded himself of Susan Lin's warning about Lucas having read *The Interpretation of Dreams*. "Paralysis shows up in your dreams a lot. It was in the dream when you were following your mother through the forest and came upon the man with the saw; it was in your dream you had last night about seeing your wife's body. It seems as if when you become anxious, you think of losing power in your legs."

"I don't know why I think that way."

"Boys often think of their penis' as a 'third leg'."

"Really? Yeah, I guess, maybe. A third leg that boys have but girls don't. I remember thinking that when I was a kid."

"It can be frightening to a boy when he first sees his sister or his mother, that she doesn't have a penis. It's like something happened to her penis and she lost it." George watched Lucas' body, to see how he reacted to such a direct suggestion of castration fear.

Lucas showed no visible reaction. "I didn't have a sister. I don't remember seeing my mother without clothes on."

"We don't always remember something that frightened us."

Lucas shifted his weight on the couch. "I don't remember anything like that."

"But you've somehow connected the thought of death with losing power in your legs, as you did when your brother died. When you dreamt of your wife being dead, you gave her a penis but tied the tag that signaled she was dead to her penis. And in your dream, you were paralyzed again."

Bonaventure was silent. George could see that his eyes were closed. Lucas' breathing had quickened. "You're getting pretty complicated, doc. I can't say that it makes a lot of sense to me," he finally said.

George knew that Lucas' defenses were fighting against his realization of the truth. "It's a lot for you to absorb," he said. "I think we should talk more about this next session."

"Can you stop me from having these dreams?"

"I don't want you to stop. Your dreams are messages from your unconscious telling us what you're really thinking about. I'm sorry that they make you uncomfortable, but that's because you're fighting against realizing what they mean. Once we decipher them completely, they won't bother you anymore."

"I hope you're right," Lucas said, sitting up.

"Oh I am," George said, but he was less sure than he sounded.

# Chapter 31

The "tip line" set up by Ben Murphy with the aid of his grandchildren was yielding diminishing returns. Nothing substantive had come in since the anonymous call sending him on the wild goose chase to Crystal Cove State Park. The volume of calls had been reduced to a trickle. It was time for Ben to take more aggressive action. He decided to follow Lucas Bonaventure.

Lucas spent his days at his office, with occasional forays into the nearby community: to Doctor Farquhar's, to the bank, or to lunch, often by himself, usually at a high-priced restaurant. After a few days, Ben dismissed Lucas' daytime activities and waited until he left work, at the end of the day, to begin his vigil as the man's shadow.

Lucas' evenings were even less adventuresome than his days. Typically, he went straight home from work, or stopped at a restaurant, often a fast-food drive-thru to grab something quickly, then went home and stayed there. Ben was almost ready to give up his nighttime monitoring, as he had his daytime surveillance, when, at ten o'clock on a Wednesday evening, he observed Lucas backing his car out of his driveway and heading down the winding hill from his house toward PCH.

Ben could tell that Lucas had been drinking. He took the curves on the narrow street leading down the hill too fast, almost hitting the curb on one occasion. Luckily, no one was coming up the street in the opposite direction. When he reached the Pacific Coast Highway, the road was crowded with cars, mostly traveling above the fifty-five miles per hour speed limit. A least, with this much traffic, Ben was less likely to be noticed following Lucas.

Once on PCH, Bonaventure turned up the coast, heading toward central Newport Beach. Ben followed him past Newport Center, then past the bridge leading onto Balboa Peninsula. After passing Hoag Hospital, Bonaventure signaled his intention to turn right and head up into the hills, inland toward Costa Mesa, rather than continue toward Huntington Beach. Ben followed a quarter mile behind.

Before crossing the border into Costa Mesa, Lucas took a left down one of the small side streets. The street led to a vacant office building on the edge of a wide field of grass on a tall cliff overlooking PCH and the beach beyond. Ben recognized the field, which lay behind a wire fence, as part of Banning Ranch, the controversial new housing development that was perched on a cliff overlooking the beaches and had been favored as a nature preserve by environmentalists. Ben had read about the losing battle by the environmentalists in the newspaper. Although there were no homes on the property yet, there were the beginnings of a network of roads and several leveled homesites.

Lucas parked his car at the rear of the parking lot of the vacant building. Ben parked on the street. He watched as Lucas slipped through a break in the fence, and then began walking down the hill toward one of the homesites. Ben followed.

The site had been recently leveled and there were open ditches on the street side of it where power lines would eventually be laid. Ben watched as Lucas walked around the perimeter of the site, then stood for a minute, looking past the edge of the bluff at the end of the property and out to sea. When he turned and headed back toward his car, Ben crouched down in the brush and waited until he had passed him. After Lucas drove away, Ben walked toward the homesite.

The site was enormous. Whatever kind of homes were going to be built there would be mansions, at least in size. Ben took a turn around the edge of the site, just as Lucas had done, but he didn't see anything unusual. What had he been hoping for, he asked himself, an open grave? Perhaps Lucas was thinking of moving here. It would garner him a better view of the ocean, he would be within walking distance to the beach, and, because of the size of the lots, he would have considerably more privacy than in his Pelican Hill home. Ben would check it out.

He trudged back up the hill, slipped through the fence and returned to his car. Had his evening been productive? He wasn't sure. Lucas had led him somewhere, but the significance of his destination was still a mystery.

# Chapter 32

"The coroner says the dog was poisoned," Abe Reynolds told Ben Murphy over the telephone. "Been dead about a week."

"Six days ago," Ben answered.

"How do you know?'

"A family reported their two-year-old Collie missing six days ago. I called Animal Control."

Reynolds was impressed. Murphy was still a sharp investigator. "So someone killed someone else's dog and then buried it? I guess we've got a crime on our hands. But that's for someone else to follow up. I'm busy with the Bonaventure case and this looks like this has nothing to do with that."

"Except the family that lost their dog lived two houses away from Lucas Bonaventure."

"Jesus Christ. Just a coincidence, you think?"

"I told you, I distrust coincidences. Can you keep the dog's body so the family can identify it?"

"I'd better tell the coroner soon, or they'll dispose of it. Have you talked to the family?"

"I did. They haven't a clue what happened to their dog. I didn't tell them. I lied to them on the phone and said I was with Animal Control. I can give you their number if you want to call them."

"I'll do that. I still don't know what it all means, though. Any hunches?"

"Just a suspicious coincidence as far as I can tell right now," Ben answered. "But the more pieces you have in a puzzle, the more the whole picture begins to emerge. This may be a piece."

"I'm not ruling anything out right now, not with the little we have to go on."

"Any progress on that other case that Bonaventure is involved with? The murder in Irvine?"

"Zip. I think the Irvine people are as suspicious of the shrink as they are of Bonaventure on that one. Could be neither of them, though. They haven't got much to go on except a body and a murder weapon."

"What was the weapon?"

"A rope."

"Should have prints on it then. Unless the perpetrator used gloves."

"The shrink's prints are all over it," Abe answered. "But he was trying to untie it when the uniforms arrived. His are the only prints."

"Doctor Lin still talking to him?"

"Every once in a while. She actually likes the guy. Says he's a bit out of touch with recent developments in his field, but she doesn't see him as a murderer."

"She seemed pretty savvy to me," Ben said.

"Savvy and smart, but she's also new at this. A psychiatrist might be pretty good at acting innocent."

"I'm willing to bet she figures him out if he's acting."

"I hope so. Keep me informed if you get any more hot tips," Reynolds said, sounding as if he was ready to hang up.

"I'll let you know whatever I find out. The well has gone pretty dry though. We're down to a few calls a day."

"Sometimes the ones who know something wait a long time to tell anyone," Reynolds said.

"We can always hope."

———    ———    ———

The family that had lost its Collie identified the dog that had been found at Crystal Cove as theirs. Ben Murphy thought it was time to pay another visit to Lucas Bonaventure.

"Just thought I'd drop by and see how you were holding up, maybe update you on our reward call-ins," Ben told Lucas. He had been shown into the den where he had visited with Lucas the previous time. Bonaventure looked less confident than before. He looked as if he were tired.

"Drink?" Lucas asked. He still wore his work slacks but on his feet were a pair of leather slippers. He had taken off his dress shirt and wore only a white T-shirt. He was starting to get a belly, probably from drinking, Ben thought, but his arms and his shoulders were still large and muscled. He already had a Scotch in his hand. It was seven in the evening.

"I'll have whatever you're having," Ben answered.

Lucas fixed Ben a drink, then sank heavily into a big leather armchair. "I'd hoped something would have turned up by now. The police act as if they've already concluded that Regina is dead." His face looked strained. He finished the remnants of his drink in one long sip, then got up and poured himself another. "I'm having trouble sleeping," he said, holding up his drink as if to acknowledge that he was using it to deaden his senses.

"What's changed?" Ben asked.

"Time I guess. At first, I thought it would just be a few days, maybe a couple of weeks before I had some news; now it's been more than three weeks and still nothing. I've read enough about disappearances to know that the longer they go on the less the likelihood of finding the victim alive. And that guy who got killed isn't going to tell anyone anything. If he did it, we may never know what happened to Regina." He took another long drink, a morose expression on his face.

"I understand the police talked to you about another case... a murder over in Irvine?"

"My secretary, or former secretary. They just talked to me is all. She'd quit a few days before. I didn't have anything to do with her at the time she died." He looked disinterested in talking about the topic.

"How many times did the police talk to you about her?"

"A couple. Two or three times, I guess. My psychiatrist found the body. I think they may suspect him."

"They think your psychiatrist killed your secretary?"

"Former secretary. They haven't come out and said it, but it looks suspicious even to me. What was he doing with her in some lonely parking lot? He'd only met her once before."

"How did your psychiatrist know your secretary at all? That sounds odd."

"I asked him to talk to her once. She was complaining about me and I wanted him to evaluate her complaints, tell me if I was doing anything inappropriate."

"She said you had?

"She was acting that way. Anyway, it turned out to be nothing. But maybe my doctor saw her again after that."

"Did he?"

"Who knows? Anyway, it might just all be one big coincidence."

"Speaking of coincidences, we got a tip on our hotline that someone had seen a car just like Regina's parked down at Crystal Cove on the night she disappeared. I told the police and they searched the area. Found a grave with a dog in it... a Collie dog. Turns out that your neighbors just down the street lost their Collie about a week ago and that was it. He'd been poisoned and buried."

Lucas shook his head. "Bizarre. But what's the coincidence?"

"Can I have another drink?" Ben asked.

"Sure," Lucas said, draining his own glass for the second time. He got up and fixed them each another drink.

"The coincidence is that we got a tip about someone taking a large object out of the back seat of a car on the night Regina went missing, then we found a grave at that very spot, and it turned out to have your neighbor's dog in it." Ben studied the man's face to see if he showed any reaction.

"But you said the dog was only missing for a week. Regina's been gone for three weeks now." Lucas looked confused.

"I can't explain that. Probably just a coincidence is all."

"Sounds as if you and the police are grasping at straws." There was no hostility in Lucas' voice.

"I'm as disappointed as you are that there are no leads yet, but even coincidences have to be followed up."

"So the police are following up on my neighbor's dog?" Lucas looked puzzled.

"They already did. That's why they did the autopsy and found the poison. It's not clear where they go from there. Probably nowhere."

Lucas looked glum. "I'm glad it was a dog and not Regina. I want her to be alive."

"Me too, Lucas, me too."

# Chapter 33

"Have you figured out whether Bonaventure's dreams are real?" Susan Lin asked.

George felt a pang of regret that Susan had called him on the telephone, rather than requested another lunch meeting. "Some of them are real. Maybe all of them." He was thinking about Lucas' most recent dream of finding his wife buried with a tag tied to her mysterious penis. The dream fit psychoanalytic theory perfectly, but George was unaware of any report of such a dream in the literature, especially in any of Freud's writings. It certainly wasn't included in *The Interpretation of Dreams*. George had gotten out one of his copies of the text to make sure. "I haven't asked him directly about his knowledge of psychoanalytic theory."

"It sounds as if he's had more dreams."

"Everybody has dreams."

"Don't become evasive, doctor. I thought we were working together on this." Her voice sounded more playful than irritated.

"We're discussing my case because my client has signed a release. But you're trying to catch a killer and I'm trying to cure my client's neurosis."

"And you still believe that Bonaventure has a neurosis?"

"Absolutely. I'm more convinced than ever." Was he? Or was he just susceptible to Bonaventure's suggestions because they mirrored his own neurotic tendencies? Every time he thought about it George became more confused.

"You're more convinced because...?

"Because the material he's brought up in therapy since our talk has convinced me of that. It fits with his particular neurosis and it's not copied out of any book, at least not any that I've ever read. His dreams are too bizarre to have been made up."

"Really?"

He had to control his defensiveness. He knew it was as related to him as it was to Lucas Bonaventure. "Listen, I'm keeping my mind open because I respect your opinion. I can be as wrong as anyone else, even when it comes to my professional judgment. That's part of the beauty of psychoanalysis, it makes all of us aware that we can be subject to blunders, sometimes deliberate blunders because of our unconscious motivations."

"Your own unconscious motivation might be leading you astray in Bonaventure's case?"

Why had he suggested that to her? He felt a sense of panic. "I was talking generically, not specifically about myself."

"Of course," the psychologist replied. "Anyway, I just wanted to check in with you and see if you'd learned anything new. It sounds as if you haven't. Or at least nothing new that would heighten our suspicion about Bonaventure. How about we do lunch again, maybe next week? Would Wednesday work? This one will be on me."

He felt elated. He was amazed at how the thought of seeing the psychologist again wiped the fears from his mind. "Sounds great. You pick the place this time."

"I'll have to think about that. I'll give you a call before Wednesday, OK?"

"Perfect."

———  ———  ———

Lucas was still agitated. He went straight to the couch and lay down and began talking. "I'm still having dreams, disturbing dreams."

"Tell me about them," George said.

"Last night's dream really bothered me. It woke me up, just like the last one I told you about."

"What did you dream?'

"I was driving my car—I think it was along PCH, I'm not sure—anyway, I drove up this long hill, then down a small street until I came to this big field overlooking the ocean."

George could sense his own anxiety rising. "Crystal Cove?"

"No, definitely not Crystal Cove. This was different. The ocean was off in the distance, but I could see it in the dark. There were lights below me. I could see a highway and then lots of houses and streets before the ocean. I walked into the field and there was this big flat surface of dirt with nothing growing on it, like it had recently been plowed, or the soil had been dumped on it. There was a ditch all around it, and I began walking along the ditch.

At some point, the ditch widened out into a big hole. As soon as I saw the hole I began to have a feeling of dread. I was afraid to look inside of it." He paused and rubbed both of his eyes with his hands, as if he were trying to stay awake. Then he lay silently.

"Are you alright?"

He nodded his head. "I still get nervous thinking about it."

"Thinking about the dream makes you nervous. Can you continue telling me about it?"

He nodded again. "I wanted to look inside the hole, but, just like before, my legs became paralyzed. I don't remember actually moving toward the hole, but suddenly I was standing over it. Regina was inside, naked again."

"She was naked? With a penis again?"

"No, thank God. She was just staring up at me. I couldn't tell if she was alive or dead. I looked around for help, but there was no one else there. There was some sort of construction equipment parked nearby, but it was almost black outside and there was no one there but me. Then I looked down again and Regina was gone. I became dizzy. I tried to back away from the hole, but my legs still wouldn't move. I felt myself tipping forward like I was going to fall into the hole. Then I woke up."

George felt a wave of relief that the dream had not gone any further. Something about the dream had made him intensely anxious. "And how did you feel when you woke up?"

"Still panicked. I felt my legs and they were OK, so I got out of bed and poured myself a drink. Just like before, I had to have a couple of Scotch's before I was calm enough to go back to sleep."

Lucas' dream departed a little from his earlier ones, George thought. The paralysis was still there, suggesting the castration fear behind the dream, but there was no direct symbol of castration such as the workman's saw in the first dream or the tag on the penis in the second. In this case, it seemed as if the fear of seeing his wife's corpse was enough to trigger Lucas' fear—and his paralysis—in the dream. "Do you think about your own death very often?" George asked.

"Almost never," Lucas said, although his tone was tentative.

"You don't sound completely sure."

"When I wake up from one of these dreams and feel my heart pounding, then I'm afraid I'm going to die. My brother died of a heart attack. He was the same age I am now."

"That's interesting."

"Why is it interesting?"

"Freud thought that the fear of death was a displaced fear of castration. He believed that castration anxiety was the more primary fear. But there have been others, Ernest Becker being one, who thought it was just the opposite: that castration anxiety was a displacement of the fear of dying, and that the fear of dying was at the bottom of much of neurotic behavior."

"So what does that mean?"

"It means we have a lot more work to do to figure out why these dreams frighten you so much and why you're having them in the first place."

"You can't stop them?"

"As I said before, they are our roadmap as to what is bothering you. We don't want to destroy our roadmap or we will become completely lost."

"So next time I'm supposed to tell you about more of my dreams?" Lucas' had apparently noticed that their time was up. He was sitting up on the couch.

"Or we continue to plumb the ones you've already told me about. We haven't gotten to the bottom of them yet, have we?"

"I guess not."

———   ———   ———

When Lucas had left, George sat back in his chair to think. There was something else about Lucas' dream that George hadn't divulged to his client. That something else was the source of George's anxiety. The description of the field off of PCH and the newly excavated ground, with the ocean in the distance, fit one place that George was aware of: Banning Ranch. The land was in West Newport Beach, at the beginning of Balboa Peninsula, high on a bluff overlooking PCH, the peninsula and the ocean. George knew it very well.

He and Madeline had bought a homesite there.

# Chapter 34

It was eating away at George that Lucas had envisioned his wife's body in an open grave on what sounded as if it was where George and Madeline had bought land. The anxiety he had felt when Lucas had told him the dream had returned. He finished his gin and tonic and looked over at his wife. "Have you been by Banning Ranch lately to see how the homesite is coming along?"

"What do you mean, 'coming along?'" Madeline had been sitting on the couch reading. Her face showed her irritation at George's question.

"Progress. Have they made any new progress, like finished laying the sewer, or put up street lights, that sort of thing?"

She put her book face down on the couch next to her and looked over at him with her eyebrows raised. "Is that the kind of thing that interests me? You know me about as well as you know any of my literary friends, which is not much. When they're done turning that hillside into streets and sidewalks and places where it might actually be possible to build a house, instead of the no man's land that it is now, then I'll take another look at it and decide if we really want to build there or sell it."

"I thought you liked that location." His wife's negativity about the lot they'd purchased, surprised him.

"I love the view, I like the location, although it's a bit farther from the university than we are now. But I want to see what it looks like when it's not raw land. It's hard to visualize how close the houses will be to each other, especially since the homes are going to be so big that their acreage will seem to have shrunk. And I'd like to know who else is going to live there."

"They'll be rich, whoever they are."

"Everyone who lives around us now is rich. In Newport Beach being rich doesn't mean being sophisticated. We're surrounded by a bunch of millionaire Neanderthals. They're nothing but land developers, dot-com entrepreneurs, get-rich-quick hedge fund managers or cooks who now own restaurant chains."

"I've never heard you this negative about Newport Beach before. I always thought you enjoyed living here."

"When did you ever ask? Irvine is a much more vibrant community. It's not all White, for one thing. Do you know that Irvine has the highest proportion of Asians of any city in Orange County? Higher than Garden Grove or Westminster where all the Vietnamese live, even."

"Yes, I knew that. So what?"

"So don't you ever get tired of living in an all-White community, where everyone who went to college majored in business administration, if he or she went to college at all, and a place where everyone thinks that USC is a superior academic school to UCLA or Berkeley because it beats them in football."

George peered inside his empty glass. "I hadn't thought about it," he said. "So I guess you haven't been by the Banning Ranch property."

She picked up her book. "No, George, I haven't. And thank you for being so interested in my point of view."

He got up and went to the kitchen and fixed himself another drink. His hand was shaking when he poured the gin.

After dinner, George had another drink. He couldn't quell his agitation, wondering why Lucas Bonaventure had dreamt of a place where George and his wife had recently bought property. Could Bonaventure have buried his wife there? And if he had, was that just a coincidence, or did Bonaventure have another reason? But then perhaps Bonaventure's dream hadn't been about Banning Ranch at all. Perhaps that was just a projection on George's part. But why? "I'm going out," George announced.

"Out? Where?"

"I want to go look at our property. I want to see if they've made any improvements yet."

"At this time of night? You won't be able to see a thing."

"Maybe they've put the street lights in."

"They don't even have paved streets yet, George. Why would they have street lights?"

"Anyway, I'm going. I'll be back in about an hour."

"I may go out myself."

"Where are you going?"

"There's a group of writers meeting at the Newport Beach Yacht Club tonight to discuss what they're working on. I wasn't going to go, but since you're going out anyway, maybe I'll drop in and see what everyone is doing."

"Yacht club? And you were the one who said that you were tired of rich White people."

"It's just where they're meeting. It doesn't mean they subscribe to that lifestyle. One of the authors, Jack Kingsley, who happens to write thrillers—the kind I never read—likes to hang around with types who are more literary than he is, and he owns a boat and is a member of the yacht club. Besides, I've never been there. It might be interesting. Maybe I'll learn something I can use in a future book."

"Don't drink too much and then drive. They stop people along PCH."

"How many have you had tonight, George? I'd worry about myself if I were you."

"Whatever," he said. "I'll see you later."

———  ———  ———

Madeline had been right. George could see no streetlights ahead as he passed through the gate leading into Banning Ranch. As a property owner, he had a key to the otherwise inaccessible property. The road was graveled at least as far as the real estate office just to the left inside the gate, but leading up the hill to his homesite, which sat on the edge of the bluff, there was only a dirt road, heavily rutted from the construction equipment, which traversed it during the day. Nevertheless, his Lexus had no difficulty climbing the hill. He passed two leveled homesites before arriving at the one he and Madeline had purchased. It had been just grass and brush when they'd first seen it, but the view was spectacular. He pulled onto the lot and parked his car, then sat for a moment, gazing out at the panorama of lights below. Off in the distance, in the great void of the night ocean, were the sparkling pinpoints of the lights of Catalina Island. Up the coast, he could see two of the several offshore oil platforms, which dotted the coastline in front of Huntington Beach. He remembered that they had once belonged to Regina Bonaventure's father. How had he known that? He began to feel anxious.

He got out of his car and looked around. There were no obvious holes in the ground. Of course, there wouldn't be, he thought to himself. He was being ridiculous. If Regina Bonaventure had lain in an open grave for three weeks, one of the workmen on the site would have found her. There was a ditch running along the side of the road and George assumed that either sewage pipes or electrical conduits would occupy the ditch at some time in the future. There was a short offshoot of the ditch leading into his property from the main road. He followed it until it ended abruptly in a mound of loose earth. He stared at the mound, his heart beginning to race. Why was he feeling such panic? There was nothing special about the bump in the ground to distinguish it from several other areas of uneven surface, which he could see in the shadows surrounding him, yet he couldn't take his eyes off of this particular pile of dirt. His head began to spin. He tried to walk toward the mound of earth, but his legs wouldn't move.

———   ———   ———

He was on his knees, digging in the dirt with his hands. He had no idea how he had gotten there. The last thing that he remembered thinking was that he needed to move toward the mysterious mound of dirt, and now here he was, digging frantically, having removed almost a foot of soil already. He must have been digging for several minutes without even knowing it. His hand felt something soft and sticky. He drew it back as if he'd been stung. He could smell the putrid odor of rotting flesh. He stood up in horror.

Behind him, there were flashing red and blue lights coming up the hill. He knew he should move—return to his car—but his legs were frozen. Besides, if this was Bonaventure's wife, and he was sure that it was, the police needed to know. He began waving his arms in the air.

# Chapter 35

Susan Lin stood outside the door to the autopsy laboratory in the basement of the county hospital. Her partner, Abe Reynolds was inside, talking to the pathologist in charge of the lab. They couldn't begin the autopsy of Regina Bonaventure, assuming it really was her who had been buried, naked, in the shallow grave at Banning Ranch, until Lucas Bonaventure arrived to provide positive identification. Susan had never been in the morgue before, but she wanted to be here today. She wanted to watch Bonaventure's reaction to seeing his wife's body.

Lucas Bonaventure had a strained expression on his face as he rounded the corner. He seemed relieved to see Doctor Lin. "This is where Regina is?" he asked her.

She nodded, noting the tremor in his voice. He seemed terrified. She had an impulse to reach out and take his hand, but she reminded herself that, in her mind, Lucas was his wife's killer, and possibly Sherry Bennett's also. He looked pathetic. His clothes were well-pressed and expensive-looking: a camel-hair sport coat over a light blue Oxford Cloth shirt, open at the collar, a pair of light khaki pants and boat shoes rounding out his typical Newport Beach casual look. But his dark hair was uncombed and he had not shaved, his eyes had dark circles under them. Even from a distance, she could smell the alcohol on his breath.

"Shall we go in? Are you ready for this?" she asked, unable to keep the concern from her voice.

He shook his head. "I'm not ready, but I guess I have to go in there." He straightened himself and took a deep breath, then pushed through the swinging doors.

There were several long and narrow tables in the room, two of them occupied by bodies draped with white sheets. Along one wall were rows of steel doors, the repository for other bodies being kept in the morgue for identification or autopsy. Detective Reynolds and a doctor in blue surgical scrubs were standing next to one of the tables on which a clean white sheet revealed the outlines of a body beneath it. Behind them was a wheeled cart carrying an impressive array of surgical instruments.

Abe Reynolds came forward and held out his hand. "Thank you for coming this morning. I know this is difficult for you." Although his words were meant to be comforting, there was a hard edge to his voice. Susan knew that Reynolds regarded Bonaventure as a prime suspect, along with Doctor Farquhar, in Regina Bonaventure's murder.

"Is that her?" Lucas asked, ignoring the detective's greeting. He stood stock still, staring at the table. He seemed unable to move.

"I'm going to remove the sheet just enough to show you her face," the pathologist said, looking at Lucas. "I just want you to tell us if this is your wife." His concern for Lucas' condition showed on his face. "I know this is stressful, Mr. Bonaventure, but you'll have to come closer to make the identification."

Lucas moved woodenly toward the table. Abe Reynolds moved aside to let him stand next to the pathologist, whose hand was holding the edge of the sheet. Lucas was staring down at the form on the table. The pathologist pulled back the sheet. The woman's face had traces of mud and her hair was filthy with remnants of the soil in which she'd been buried.

Lucas looked down at his wife's face. He swallowed hard, as if he was trying not to retch. Then he turned toward the pathologist, his face livid. "How dare you show me her with mud on her face? Look at her hair, it's filled with dirt!" His fists were balled, as if he were ready to attack the pathologist.

The pathologist lowered the sheet and backed away, a look of fear in his eyes. "We couldn't clean her up until you made your identification. We have to examine all of the fragments of dirt on her face and in her hair. I'm sorry to show her to you this way, but it was necessary."

"I don't feel well," Lucas said. His anger had disappeared. He looked as if he might pass out.

Abe Reynolds took him by the arm and led him to a chair at one side of the room. "Why don't you sit down for a moment? You're in shock."

"Can I bring you anything? Water?" Susan asked.

Lucas' face was ashen. "Give me a minute. I just wasn't prepared to see my brother like this."

"Your brother?" Susan said.

He looked up at her, as if he were confused by her question. Then he looked over at the table where his wife's body lay. "I mean my wife, of course."

"You seem a little disoriented," Susan said. She looked over at Detective Reynolds, who was still next to the table but was staring at Lucas. His face showed his skepticism.

"I'll be all right. It was just a shock, seeing her like that, especially so dirty. Why was she so dirty?" He still looked confused.

"She'd been buried. They can't remove all the dirt right away. It needs to be analyzed. They were waiting for you to identify her before proceeding."

"Analyzed? The dirt? I don't understand. What does the dirt have to do with anything?"

"In case your wife's body had been moved. They need to see if all the dirt came from the site where they found her or from somewhere else."

"You mean someone could have moved her after she was dead?"

"They just have to rule that out. It's routine." She worried that she might have told him too much, but he seemed to need an explanation and she was worried about his mental health.

"Can I go?" he suddenly asked.

"Do you feel well enough to walk?"

He nodded and began to stand up. His right leg seemed not to move and he teetered for a moment on one leg then crumpled to the floor. Detective Reynolds and the pathologist both rushed over and assisted Susan with picking him up and putting him back on the chair.

"Are you all right?" The pathologist asked.

Lucas appeared calm. He looked up at the three worried faces peering down at him. "I'm fine. It's just that my right leg doesn't seem to move."

"Did you injure it when you fell?" the pathologist asked. He bent to examine Lucas' leg.

"Never mind, it's OK. Perhaps if you could get me a wheelchair or a cane or something?" There was no panic in Lucas' voice. He spoke as if becoming paralyzed in one leg was a perfectly ordinary occurrence.

Susan remembered her conversation with Doctor Farquhar. Bonaventure had a history of hysterical paralysis. It had happened before when his brother died. "He'll be OK," she told the pathologist, who was feeling Lucas' knee and calf for evidence of an injury. "I believe this has happened before, hasn't it Mr. Bonaventure?"

Lucas' head snapped up. He narrowed his eyes as he looked at her. "How did you know that?"

"Doctor Farquhar told me. Remember you signed a release for us to speak to him about you."

"And he told you about that?"

"I'm a psychologist. I needed to know what his assessment of you was."

"I don't want you talking to him anymore. I had no idea that he'd tell you things like that."

"It was important to know your history," Susan answered, surprised by Lucas' alarm.

"I'm rescinding your permission to talk to him. Is that understood?"

"The release you signed was with the Irvine Police Department, with regard to the Sherry Bennett case. You'll need to contact them to rescind your release on paper, although, of course, I'll honor it now that you've told me in person."

"Why are you talking to Doctor Farquhar about Sherry Bennett anyway?" Bonaventure seemed both angry and confused. "You work for Newport Beach."

"I'm working for Irvine, too. I'm involved in both your wife's case and Sherry Bennett's case."

He looked up at her with fury in his eyes. "Well, no more access to my doctor. Is that understood? Now bring me a cane or something so I can leave here."

She looked over at Abe Reynolds, who nodded, then turned to the pathologist. "Have you got some crutches or a wheelchair we can loan Mr. Bonaventure so he can leave?"

# Chapter 36

"Lucas Bonaventure has rescinded his permission for you to release information to us," Susan Lin said. She and Abe Reynolds were sitting in the detective's office, the detective behind his desk and she in a chair next to it. George Farquhar sat facing the two of them. He was neatly dressed in a Hunter Green sport coat and brown slacks with a light blue Oxford Cloth shirt and a green tie that matched the color of his jacket. His face looked tired, but his eyes moved back and forth between Abe and Susan, as if he were frightened of what they would ask him.

"You didn't have to tell me that," George said, looking back at her. "You might have gotten me to tell you something important before you told me that he had taken back his release."

"It would have been disingenuous for me to not tell you," Susan said, looking over at Detective Reynolds, who was scowling at her, as if he agreed with the doctor. "Anything you told us about what he said to you could not be used in court."

"We're not interested in Bonaventure right now," Reynolds said. "We want to know what you were doing at Banning Ranch last night."

George sighed. He felt an immense weight pressing down on his whole body. "My wife and I had a discussion about our new house site there. I wondered if they had started any of the improvements yet and she told me she no longer wanted to live there. We argued. I'd had a few drinks after dinner and I decided to drive over there and see if anything had been done, and, to tell you the truth, whether I still felt attached to the property."

"So that was why you were there?" Susan Lin asked. Her voice was friendly and reassuring.

"Yes."

"So why were you digging in a mound of soil? Were you wondering how attached you were to the dirt?" Reynolds asked, making no attempt to conceal the sarcasm in his voice.

George could feel his panic rising. The truth was, he didn't know how he had come to dig up Regina Bonaventure's burial place. The last thing he remembered was staring at the pile of dirt and then suddenly he'd found himself digging up her body. "I guess it looked odd, as if it didn't belong there." His gaze darted from Reynolds to Susan Lin. His panic was growing. "I really don't know what made me start digging."

"Maybe you knew that there was something buried under the dirt," Reynolds said, as he bored into George with his gaze.

"How would I have known that?"

"You tell us. You were the one who was digging in the dirt," Reynolds said, making no effort to hide his hostility.

"I told you, it just looked odd, that pile of dirt right there." George was still feeling panicky. He wished that Susan hadn't told him that Lucas had taken back his waiver of confidentiality. Without telling them about Lucas' dream, there was no way to explain why he was there or what he was doing digging in the dirt. Even if he had been able to tell them, he wasn't sure that the story would have made sense. Why *did* he go there? If he thought that Lucas' dream had suggested that his wife might be buried there, why hadn't he called the police?

"So you see a mysterious pile of dirt and you decide to start digging underneath it, and voila, you dig up Regina Bonaventure, a woman who has been missing for over three weeks and was stabbed to death and buried on your property." It was obvious to George that Reynolds wasn't buying his story

"She was stabbed to death? What with?" George felt an acute sense of panic.

"A knife," Reynolds said. "What else would she be stabbed with?"

"What kind of knife?"

"Why do you care what kind of knife she was killed with?" Reynolds looked at him suspiciously.

George shook his head, trying to clear his thoughts. "I don't know. I don't really. It just sounded shocking."

"You must have felt shocked when you dug up her body," Reynolds said.

"I didn't dig up her body, the cops did. I just felt something under the dirt and I stopped digging."

"Why did you stop digging?" Susan asked. Her voice was still supportive.

"I felt something and then I smelled something... a dead smell. I was frightened. Then the police drove up."

"They caught you digging up her body," Reynolds said.

"They didn't 'catch me,' " George answered. "I waved to the police, called them over to where I was. Anyway, would I have driven there at night to dig up a body and not brought anything to dig with but my own hands? No shovel, not even gloves?" He returned Detective Reynolds's angry stare.

Reynolds heaved a sigh. What the doctor said was true. Digging in the ground with his bare hands was bizarre. "We're gonna want to talk to you again about this. Don't think I buy your story, doc. It just doesn't hold water."

"Not everything makes sense," George said, looking over at Susan.

"Lucas Bonaventure identified his wife's body," Susan said, examining George's face for a reaction. "Then he experienced a hysterical paralysis, just like the one you told me he'd experienced before."

"My God," George said. He'd almost forgotten that Lucas would need to view his wife's body for identification.

"He also referred to his wife as his brother. Then his leg became paralyzed. Didn't you tell me that a similar thing happened before when his brother died?"

"I can't tell you anything, I'm afraid, now that he has taken back his permission for me to speak to you about him." The news about Lucas astounded him. It made him almost forget about himself and that he seemed to be a suspect, at least in Detective Reynolds's eyes.

"I'm just verifying what you already told me when you did have permission," Susan said.

"It seems to me there's something weird going on between you and your patient, doctor," Abe Reynolds interjected. He was sitting forward in his chair, his eyes again narrowed as he looked at George. "This is two murders that both of you have something to do with. Don't you find that strange?"

"I certainly find it strange that Bonaventure's wife's body was on my property. In fact, it makes absolutely no sense to me. But he was my connection to Sherry Bennett. I knew her because I had interviewed her at his request, which was something I already told Doctor Lin. That connection isn't mysterious at all."

"But the fact that you found both bodies is, don't you think?" Reynolds answered.

George didn't say anything. He had no idea what to say. "I think we've gone over that," he finally answered. "Am I done here?"

"For now," Reynolds answered. "We're probably going to want to talk to you some more."

"About what? I can't tell you anything more about Lucas Bonaventure."

"About you, doctor, about you." Reynolds sat back and smiled, not warmly.

"Well, I'd like to talk to you more," Susan said. Her smile was an inviting one.

George nodded. Despite his apprehension, he found himself buoyed by her friendliness.

"Let's have that lunch we talked about," he said, smiling back at her. She nodded.

As he left, George saw that Detective Reynolds was scowling at both the young psychologist and him.

———   ———   ———

"What was that all about?" Reynolds said to Susan after Doctor Farquhar had left the station.

"I still want to get information from him. I can't have him hating me the way he hates you."

"He's not telling us the truth," Reynolds answered.

"I agree. But you catch more flies with honey than vinegar. Besides, do you really think he murdered Regina Bonaventure?"

"He found her body, but he didn't even know the woman. And he's right, he wouldn't have gone to dig up her body bare handed."

"Right. So Doctor Farquhar is more important to us as a witness than as a suspect."

"A witness to what?"

"To whatever Lucas Bonaventure told him that made him go to that site last evening."

"You think that's what happened?"

"Definitely. There's no reason that the doctor would have gone to the site at night just to check on the property."

"But Farquhar can't tell us what Bonaventure is telling him. Bonaventure rescinded his release."

"Farquhar couldn't tell the Irvine police that Bonaventure had asked him to talk to Sherry Bennett or that Bonaventure was stalking her, but he managed to get around that by telling them what Miss Bennett was afraid of. He'll find a way to tell us if we don't frighten him too much."

"So how do you plan to get that information from him?"

"Charm..." she smiled coyly at her partner. "Charm and a lunch invitation."

"The psychological approach?" He grinned back at her.

"Something like that," she laughed.

# Chapter 37

George wasn't surprised to see Lucas Bonaventure supporting himself with a cane and dragging his right leg, but he was shocked at the man's frail appearance. Lucas sat down heavily on the edge of the couch. "I don't understand how you were the one who found my wife." It wasn't clear if he was confused or angry.

"She was buried on my property. I don't understand that either. I found her because that was where you dreamt that she was buried and I decided to look." George gazed steadily at his patient, closely watching his reaction.

"I didn't dream that she was buried on your property." Lucas' tone was flat, as if he were stating a fact.

"Not my property specifically, but on one of the lots at Banning Ranch. You described it to a tee."

"It could have been anyplace. I've passed Banning Ranch many times, driving along PCH. It never occurred to me that that was the place in my dream."

George could feel his anxiety rising. The assumption that the location in Lucas' dream was Banning Ranch was his. Was his conclusion just a projection based upon his owning property there? But Lucas' wife's body *had* been buried there. "It seemed clear to me. Which raises the question of why you dreamed accurately of the location of your wife's body."

"What question does it raise?" The suspicion was evident in Lucas' voice.

"Whether you are really reporting your dreams to me or making them up. Whether you're telling me things you want me to hear."

"Why would I do that?"

"I don't know. I understand you own a copy of Freud's *Interpretation of Dreams.*"

"Do I? It must be my wife's then. I don't recall it."

"Some of your dreams are remarkably similar to those described in Freud's book."

"A coincidence I guess. How did you know that I owned a copy of that book?" He stared at George.

"The police told me."

"Really? The police haven't been to my house since the day I reported Regina missing."

"So perhaps they noticed it then."

"I don't recall them entering my den."

"So you *do* know where the book is located."

"All the books are in the den."

"Well, we're getting nowhere with this. I don't know how the police knew about the book but they told me and I was familiar with the dreams that Freud mentioned in his book."

"You talked to that psychologist, Doctor Lin. Wasn't she the one you talked to after Sherry was killed?"

George felt himself getting uncomfortable again. He didn't want to implicate Susan Lin. "I talked to Detective Reynolds, too."

"Which one told you about the book?"

"I don't recall."

"Really?" Lucas smiled at him. "By the way, doctor, you haven't commented on my leg. You didn't even act surprised when I walked in your office with a cane."

"The police told me that you'd suffered another paralysis after viewing your wife's body in the morgue."

"You seem to be pretty cozy with the police. I would have thought that they'd be treating you as a suspect since you found my wife's body... and Sherry Bennett's, too." George could have sworn that Lucas was gloating.

"I *am* a suspect or, as they say to the press, a person of interest. Being present when two dead bodies are found by the police makes them wonder about me. I understand their point of view."

"So we're both suspects. That's an interesting development." Lucas reached down and took his right leg in both hands and hoisted it onto the couch, leaning back and putting his other leg up next to his right leg. "Shall we start our session doctor? I had another dream."

George didn't know what to think. He felt as if he were being manipulated, but perhaps he was being paranoid. He was not used to being this confused with a patient. "I'd like to hear about your leg, first," he said.

"What about my leg?"

"As you pointed out, your paralysis is back. Tell me how that happened."

Even as he asked, he felt a sharp twinge of anxiety. He remembered his own feeling of being paralyzed when he saw the mound of earth under which Regina Bonaventure was buried. Then he'd blanked out. One of his fugue states had disrupted his consciousness, just as it had when he had found Sherry Bennett's body. George knew that it meant something, but he could feel his resistance to finding out what it was. Was he more involved in the women's deaths than he was aware?

"I had a flashback to my brother's death, to the time when I had to identify his body in the morgue," Lucas said. "Everything seemed similar. After I saw Regina's face, I got mad because they hadn't cleaned her up. It was just like my brother after his heart attack when he had the traffic accident. I started to yell at the pathologist, then this white light exploded in my face. I couldn't see anything. I was dizzy. It was just like when I identified my brother's body. As soon as they sat me down, I knew that I wouldn't be able to move my leg. It was just like before."

"Just like when you viewed your brother's body?'

"Exactly like it. Or it felt that way to me."

George was sure the man's paralysis was real. Everything he'd said fit psychologically. "What were you thinking when you were sitting there?"

"I imagined myself on one of the tables. My body with a tag on my toe."

"On your toe?"

"I thought about being dead."

"And how did that feel?"

"I don't know. It was just a momentary thought. Then I tried to get up and I couldn't. My leg wouldn't work."

Was Lucas suffering from castration anxiety or was he afraid of dying? Ernest Becker had said that Freud manufactured his theory of sexuality, and particularly the castration complex, in order to divert his own thinking away from the topic of death. Freud himself was terrified of dying, according to Becker. George had regarded Becker's suggestions as brilliant speculation, but they had never shaken his belief in the sexual basis of neurosis as put forward by Freud. But Lucas Bonaventure presented exactly the kind of case that put the two theories in competition.

"What did you think when you found yourself paralyzed?"

There was a long pause before Lucas answered. "I'm embarrassed to say this doctor, it sounds so cold, but I was angry at Regina for reminding me of my brother. I knew it wasn't her fault. My God, she'd been stabbed to death. But that was my reaction."

"How did you know she'd been stabbed?" George could feel his anxiety mounting.

"The coroner told me. I asked him how she died. He thought someone had used a kitchen knife."

George went cold. He remembered the missing knife in his own house. He'd been frightened when Detective Reynolds had told him that Regina Bonaventure had been stabbed, but now he was terrified.

"What was your dream about?" He needed to change the subject.

"My dream?"

"You told me that you had a dream you wanted to tell me about."

"Yes. It was another weird dream."

"Tell me about it."

"It was about a dog. I was being chased by a dog. I was running across this field of tall grass and bushes, and this big dog was chasing me. A Collie or a Spaniel because he had long hair. He was sick or something, maybe rabid, because he was foaming at the mouth. He chased me to the edge of a cliff, above the ocean. There was nowhere to run. Then the scene suddenly switched, the way that it happens in dreams. I was lying in a ditch in the field and the dog was sitting in a tree, the dog that had been chasing me and four or five other dogs just like him, sitting on different branches. I stared at them and I couldn't move. I wanted to crawl out of the ditch and run away, but I couldn't move, my legs were paralyzed, just as in the other dreams. Then I woke up."

George recognized the dream. The dogs sitting in the tree were from Freud's case of "The Wolfman," a classic case of castration anxiety, seen by Freud when the patient was an adult, after having had a childhood history of animal phobia and then later manic- depressive illness as an adult. "Where did you read about that dream?" he asked.

"What do you mean?"

"That dream is right out of Freud. It's one of his most famous cases, called, 'The Wolfman' "

"It was my dream. I don't know about Freud's cases." Lucas didn't sound defensive.

"It's too much of a coincidence. You don't just dream one of Freud's most famous dreams for no reason. You must have read about it."

Lucas hesitated. "Perhaps I did. Maybe I glanced at one or two of Regina's books on psychology. In fact, I *do* remember seeing a picture of these dogs in a tree in one of the books. I remember it bothered me. I became angry with Regina for having a book like that in the house."

"So you saw the picture of the dogs sitting in the tree—they were wolves, incidentally—and it bothered you. What did it make you feel like?"

"Panicky. It reminded me of that dream of the man with the saw, the one I told you about a couple of weeks ago. Do you think I remembered the picture and that's why it showed up in my dream? I'm sure what I saw in my dream was that same picture from the book."

What Lucas was saying was plausible, although the "Wolfman" dream symbolized castration to Freud's patient because of specific experiences in the man's childhood, such as seeing his parents have intercourse, which could well apply to Lucas. But the Wolfman's dream also was based on experiences which Lucas never could have had, since they were unique to some children's storybooks in late nineteenth century Russia, the home of Freud's patient. If Lucas had read anything about the case, not just looked at the picture, he knew that it involved castration anxiety. That, in itself, could have made the description of the dream and the accompanying picture frightening to him because it provoked his own castration fears. It was a tenuous connection, but Freud's own analyses of dreams thrived on such thin strands of associations. "It's possible that the picture in the book became connected in your preconscious mind, the part of your mind that manufactures your dreams, to your unconscious fears of castration... or death. How much did you read about Freud's case?"

"I don't remember reading anything, but I suppose I did. I wouldn't have been just looking at pictures in a book. I'm not a five-year-old child."

Five-year-old boys were exactly who developed castration anxiety. "And what about Freud's other books, *The Interpretation of Dreams*, for instance? You told me earlier that you hadn't read it. Perhaps you didn't remember accurately at the time. How about now? Do you remember reading it?"

Lucas shook his head. "I'm almost sure that I didn't. I told you, those books were Regina's. I may have looked at the one with the picture in it once, but after that, I was afraid to look at any of the others. Afraid that they might make me panicky like that one had."

"It's still a little murky, but your dreams are all related to castration fears. And so is your paralysis. It's no coincidence that the very symptom that you feel in your dreams is the one you have developed in your waking life. And each time it has been provoked by an experience of the death of someone close to you. Viewing your wife's body not only aroused your anxiety because of her, but it brought back memories of your brother's death, bringing on the same symptom you had experienced after viewing his body."

"Castration fears?"

"Young boys often get the idea that their father may be jealous of them. It makes them afraid that their fathers will cut off their penises. All of this is unconscious of course, which is why it comes out in dreams, not in waking thoughts."

"That's awfully hard to believe doc. It all sounds like a theory, not something real."

"That's because your unconscious mind is still erecting defenses against it. Unconsciously, your anxiety is related to a wish, as are your dreams. We haven't begun to discover what that wish is." It wasn't yet time to bring up the Oedipal wish behind Lucas' castration fear.

"A wish? But all my dreams are nightmares. They all bring on anxiety. How could I wish for that?"

"The anxiety is the fear that the wish will become manifested directly in your consciousness, even in your dream consciousness. Your mind is fighting against itself in your dreams."

"That's a lot to swallow."

"Of course it is. It's something that further analysis will reveal to you, but it may take a long time."

"I have lots of time, doctor."

*Unless either you or I go to jail*, George thought.

# Chapter 38

"Some of the soil in Regina Bonaventure's hair was from the cliff above Crystal Cove," Abe Reynolds said. "Some of the soil in the knife wounds was from there too." He looked across his desk at Ben Murphy, trying to decide how much he should tell the private detective. Murphy was a highly experienced investigator, famous for solving difficult cases, but Abe wasn't sure what his true agenda was. The old man was working for Regina Bonaventure's father, who seemed to have a thing against his son-in-law. Murphy could just be trying to find evidence against Lucas Bonaventure. It was hard not to have a bias when investigating a murder, but Abe knew that such biases often led one astray.

"So the body was moved," Murphy said. "Did the coroner know how long ago?"

"The condition of the soil where she was found indicated that it wasn't more than a week or so ago."

"About the time that the Collie dog was buried."

"Exactly," Reynolds answered. "So someone *might* have buried the woman's body at Crystal Cove, then two weeks later killed the dog and dug the woman up and put the dog in her place. Then he moved the woman's body to Banning Ranch, to the shrink's homesite."

"That's a lot of work and a lot of additional risk doing all that digging and carrying around a body. Why would someone do that?" Ben asked.

"The site at Banning Ranch was a lot safer place to put a body. They were going to dump more topsoil on the spot where her body was buried. If Doctor Farquhar hadn't been prowling around that night and started digging, and if someone hadn't alerted the police that there were car lights on the property at night so they went to investigate, then her body would never have been recovered. At Crystal Cove, it was just a matter of time before somebody's dog or kid dug around and found her."

Murphy nodded in agreement. "So who would have done that?"

"The shrink is the logical suspect. It was his property, and he was digging her up when our patrol car appeared on the scene."

Murphy nodded. "Absolutely. But why bury the body on his own homesite? There were several others nearby. And why go back and start digging up the body again, after he'd reburied it? And the dog that was in the grave at Crystal Cove was taken from Bonaventure's neighborhood. From his neighbor, actually."

Reynolds scowled. "You and Doctor Lin both think that Bonaventure killed his wife. But there's a lot more evidence pointing toward Doctor Farquhar."

"There's *some* evidence," Murphy corrected him, "and the doctor had no motive. From what the coroner said, there were almost a dozen knife wounds, all deep. Whoever killed Regina was very angry... angry at her. As far as we know, Doctor Farquhar didn't know that either Lucas or Regina Bonaventure even existed at the time that she disappeared."

Reynolds nodded, his expression glum. "That's what's got me stymied. I'm not going to charge someone who didn't even know the victim, especially, when, as you point out, it looks like a crime of passion."

"How about Bonaventure's and Farquhar's cars? Someone carried a dead body from Crystal Cove to Banning Ranch."

"Bonaventure's car was clean," Reynolds said. "We haven't checked the doctor's yet."

"Then I'll be going and leave you to your work, detective," Ben said, standing up. "Good hunting."

———  ———

The real estate office at Banning Ranch was open after having been closed for just one day while the Newport Beach police conducted their crime scene investigation on George and Madeline Farquhar's property. Ben Murphy pulled into the gravel parking lot in front of the building. He was dressed in a blue linen sport coat over a pair of grey, light wool slacks. He wore a pair of loafers with dark socks. His head was bare and his braid was tucked up in a bun. "I'm thinking of moving down here from Santa Barbara," he told the saleslady in the office. "I'll be selling my home up there and using my equity to buy something down here. I've got an ocean view, and I don't want to give that up, so this place looks promising. And it would be a while before my house up there sells, so I just want a lot for now. Something I can build on later.”

“You’ve come to the right place,” Doris Macready, the slightly overweight, middle-aged, blonde saleswoman told him. She stood back, ready to help, being careful not to be intrusive. “None of our lots will be ready for building before another three to six months. As you can see, we haven’t paved any streets or put in utilities yet. Does that fit your timetable?”

“Perfectly,” Ben answered.

“Would you like to take a tour of the property or sit down and talk about prices, terms, size requirements, that sort of thing?”

“How about a tour?”

“Certainly. I’m afraid we’ll have to take our jeep. The roads are a little rough.”

“Let’s do it.”

The picture in Ben’s head had been a serious underestimate of the property’s extent and diversity. The first thing he was shown was a sizeable acreage that was to become a hotel. Then he viewed the park that was the concession to the environmentalists who had objected to the land’s development. Finally, he was driven to the single-family homesites. Yellow crime scene tape surrounded the homesite owned by Doctor George Farquhar and his wife.

“What is this?” Ben asked, feigning alarm at the sight of yellow tape marked *crime scene—do not cross.*

“Uh… I’m not sure. I think they found some kind of evidence related to a crime in Newport Coast. That’s all I know. It really has nothing to do with Banning Ranch,” the woman stammered.

Ben could hardly blame her for not acknowledging the presence of the body of a murder victim on one of her property’s lots. The presence of the crime scene tape prevented him from examining the area where Regina Bonaventure’s body had been buried.

When they arrived back at the real estate center, the agent asked him to sign into the register where those who had taken a tour of the property had recorded their names and addresses, no doubt for purposes of receiving follow-up inquiries.

“I don’t see my friend, Lucas Bonaventure’s name here. He recommended your property to me. He said he’d taken a tour.”

“Not everyone records their names. But I remember Mr. Bonaventure. He did take a tour. I’m surprised he didn’t leave his name. He was very interested. Wanted to know who had already bought property here. He was very particular about who his neighbors would be. I guess that was why he told you about us. He wanted his friends to be his neighbors."

"Do you tell people who has made purchases of property?"

"If that's important to them. It's public record so we're not divulging anything."

"So that lot that is owned by Doctor Farquhar—the one with the crime scene tape around it—was something you told Mr. Bonaventure about?"

"Of course. He was particularly interested in that property. But how did you know that Doctor Farquhar owned that lot?" A note of suspicion had entered the real estate agent's voice.

"Lucky guess," Ben said. "Did Mr. Bonaventure buy a piece of land?"

"Not yet, but he seemed interested." She continued to smile at him, her suspicion having disappeared as she resumed the role of salesperson.

"When was the last time you heard from him?

"Oh, he only came once, about two weeks ago."

Ben nodded. "Thank you for your time."

# Chapter 39

It was a clear day and Santa Catalina Island was visible in the distance, across the gently rolling hills of Pacific View Cemetery. Ben Murphy watched as Bertram Knowles exited the back seat of his chauffeur-driven Lincoln and made his way across the lawn toward the tented area in front of his daughter's newly excavated grave. Knowles was a tall, square-faced, angular man, dressed in a black suit, his white-haired head bare. He wore sunglasses. He walked with a brisk stride, despite his seventy years.

"Ben…" Knowles said, extending his hand when he reached Murphy, who was standing between the gravesite and the drive that wound its way around the elegant grounds of the Newport Beach cemetery. Today, Murphy was also dressed in a dark suit, white shirt, and tie. His head was bare, with what was left of his white hair drawn back in a braid, and instead of his tennis shoes, he wore gleaming black oxfords. "Good of you to come," Knowles said.

"Of course I'd be here, Bert. I cared very much for Regina."

"Lucas here yet?" Knowles asked, looking around at the several dozen people, some already sitting under the canopy that had been erected in front of the grave, others standing around talking.

"I haven't seen him, but his car is here. I saw it parked over by the cemetery office. Maybe he's waiting for the minister since I haven't seen him either."

Bert Knowles removed his sunglasses and stared at Ben. "Lucas has guts being here at all, acting like the grieving husband when he's most likely Regina's murderer. Any new information, by the way?" Knowles' features made him look younger than his actual age. Ben knew that he took good care of himself: exercising, eating right. He suspected that the wealthy, retired oil magnate also had cosmetic surgery on his face. His skin around his mouth and chin seemed unusually tight.

"Only circumstantial stuff so far. The police checked out his car to see if there was any evidence of a body, either a dog or a human, having been transported in it but didn't find anything. Of course, he could have used another car. His company owns about five of them. The police are suspicious of the psychiatrist who found Regina's body."

Knowles scanned the crowd. "Who are all these people? I see one or two of Regina's old friends, but I don't recognize anyone else."

"She lived down here for a long time, Bert. Most of her friends were from here."

Knowles nodded. "I suppose so." He looked Ben in the eyes. "It's probably a blessing that Marge didn't live to see this day, when her only child was buried." He turned and gazed across the cemetery lawn. "Here comes Lucas, the bastard."

Ben followed his gaze. Lucas Bonaventure was walking across the lawn with two men, both of them dressed in black suits, as he was. Ben assumed that one was the funeral director and the other the minister who would conduct the graveside service.

Lucas walked with a cane and had a pronounced limp. When Lucas noticed his father-in-law, he said something to the two men with whom he was walking and headed toward Knowles and Ben.

As Lucas approached, he stuck out his hand. Knowles didn't respond. "Good to see you, Bert," Lucas said, searching his father-in-law's face as if to gauge his feeling.

"I'm not happy to be here, but Regina deserved a decent burial," Knowles said. "I would have rather buried her next to her mother in Santa Barbara."

"This is her home, Bert. This is where her friends are... and her family."

"I'm her family," Knowles said. He had put his sunglasses back on, but he still appeared to be staring at Lucas' face.

"So am I, and this cemetery has a view that's similar to the one from our house. I thought she would like it."

"It's a little late to be thinking about what she would like," Knowles said, then he turned and walked toward the seats under the canopy.

"Why's he so sore at me?" Lucas asked Ben, who was still standing there.

Ben shrugged. "Maybe he thinks you had something to do with Regina's death."

Lucas' features became rigid. "If he does, then it's because that's what you've told him. You're his investigator down here."

"I just told him that the police haven't ruled you out as a suspect. That's my job to tell him that."

"Your job is over now. Regina's body has been found. You can go back to Santa Barbara."

"I'm gonna stick around for a while. I want to see this through, see if there's anything I can do to help the police find Regina's killer." Ben stared Lucas in the face.

"Really?" Lucas said, his displeasure evident in his voice. "Aren't the police pretty sure that Doctor Farquhar had something to do with it. Regina was buried on his property and he was digging her up when the police found her."

"Yet you're still seeing him for therapy, even though you think he killed your wife?"

Lucas' eyes widened, as if Ben's words had caught him off guard. "I said the police suspected Doctor Farquhar, not that I did. He wouldn't have any reason to kill her."

"Precisely," Ben said, smiling. "So that leaves the question of who *did* kill Regina. That's what I intend to find out." He turned and headed for the seats where Bertram Knowles had already seated himself, then he saw Susan Lin standing at the back of the canopied area behind the seats. He walked over to her and she greeted him with a hug. Ben escorted her to where Knowles was sitting so that he could introduce the two of them to each other.

Lucas had been watching the private detective with interest. When he saw the young psychologist hug the old man, his face registered his surprise. He watched with a grim frown as Ben Murphy introduced Susan to Regina's father. Then he nodded ever so slightly, as if he had just come to a decision.

# Chapter 40

"I'm leaving you, George." Madeline stood in the doorway to the kitchen, her hands on her hips. Her expression was sad.

"What are you talking about?" George turned his head, his drink poised in front of his lips. He had been reading *The Denial of Death* by Ernest Becker, in order to refresh himself on the anthropologist's theory of death anxiety.

"At least that got your head out of your book," she continued, still standing in the doorway. Her expression of sadness had been replaced with one of anger. "We haven't got anything in common anymore George. And I can't depend on you."

"We have a lot in common. And what do you mean, you can't depend on me?"

"You're completely absorbed in that Bonaventure man. That's all you talk about, and I can tell that that's all you think about. And you've gotten yourself involved not only in treating the man but in his wife's death, and his secretary's death too."

George felt a sense of queasiness " I'm not involved in either of those women's deaths."

"You found both their bodies, George." She scowled at him.

"That was not my intention; you know that. I didn't know that Sherry Bennett would be dead when I went to meet her. And when I went to our property I had no idea that I'd find Mrs. Bonaventure's body. In fact, I didn't find it, the police did." He knew that he was not being truthful to his wife. He had gone to their lot at Banning Ranch specifically because Lucas' dream had told him that was where Regina Bonaventure was buried.

"Going to meet that secretary or going to our homesite and digging around in the dirt for a body are not part of doing psychoanalysis, and you know it, George. I don't know what they represent, but they're not part of treating a patient. And now the newspaper says the police regard you as a 'person of interest.' That isn't who I want to be married to."

"You're blaming me for things that aren't my fault." His drink was empty. He got up and walked past her into the kitchen and poured himself another. "Come into the living room and let's talk this out."

"I don't want to talk it out, George. I've made up my mind."

"With no discussion? All by yourself? And you're the one accusing me of not talking to you."

"I've found someone else." She had taken two steps into the living room and was standing stock still, staring at him as if to gauge his reaction. "I'm leaving you for someone else."

He felt as if the floor had dropped from beneath him. He took a large gulp from his drink. "Someone else? Who? When did this happen?"

"It doesn't matter who it is. I'm leaving you because of what we no longer have together; because of what you've become, especially since taking on this patient." She wasn't looking him in the eyes anymore.

"When did you start seeing someone else? Who is it?" He was starting to become angry.

"Don't raise your voice to me, George. I said it doesn't matter who it is, this is about us. But if you must know, it's Jack Kingsley."

"The writer? The one who belongs to the yacht club? The one who writes books you said you'd never read? That's the person you have more in common with than me?" He couldn't believe this was happening.

"Jack's very intellectual. He only writes thrillers in order to make money. He's very practical. Unlike you, George."

"And he's rich, White, no doubt lives in a bigger house than we do and right here in Newport Beach. He's the epitome of all the things you said you despised." He knew that, despite her protestations, his wife remained chronically anxious about finances. Now she appeared to have solved that problem.

"He has a lot of money, but that's not why I'm interested in him. He loves good literature. He loves to talk about it. He likes to be around sophisticated, literate people."

"And he thinks you're the perfect example of that." He hung his head. "Well he's right, you are. That was one of the reasons that I was attracted to you; I still am. But I thought we had that in common."

"Not for a long time. You're always trying to please your silly society of old men who haven't moved past their adolescent affair with Freudian theory and a bunch of awestruck young social workers who fawn after all of you in order to get admitted to your club. And now you've lost all perspective since you started seeing Lucas Bonaventure, who's probably a serial killer."

Had he lost perspective? He was almost afraid to step back and examine his own behavior. He knew that some of the things he'd done didn't make sense, even to him. Going to his property at Banning Ranch to look for Regina Bonaventure's body, for instance. And why was he continuing to see Lucas at all? Madeline was probably right about the man being a serial killer. Even worse, Lucas was either using George to construct a defense for himself based upon having a mental disorder, or he had tried to set George up as his wife's killer by making up a dream that led George to search for her body. Maybe he'd done both of those things. Yet George still saw him two times a week. But the man was truly neurotic, and something about Lucas' neurosis was intriguingly familiar to George, close to his own psychodynamics in some way. Something that wouldn't let him abandon Lucas.

"I'm just treating a patient. Lucas Bonaventure hasn't been accused of anything."

"Only because *you're* now the prime suspect in his wife's and his secretary's murders. Oh, George, you're lost and you don't even know it." The concern on her face turned into something cold and hostile. "But I'm not going down with you George. I need peace. I need protection from society so I can work. I thought that was what you could give me, but I was wrong. You're probably going to end up in jail. I don't intend to be around when that happens."

George knew he was defeated. "When are you planning on leaving?"

"I want to move out this weekend. Live on my own for a while. I might go somewhere with Jack, just to get away while all this about Regina Bonaventure is in the news."

"But maybe you're not leaving permanently?"

"I'm mixed up too, George. I need to leave now. I know that. I'll see how it feels being away from you."

"I love you, Madeline."

"I love you too, George. I hope you find yourself before you're completely ruined."

# Chapter 41

"Sure," Susan Lin answered him over the phone. "I'd love to have lunch again. We never did have that one we talked about before. I even promise I won't ask you about your therapy with Lucas Bonaventure, although I might share a little about him with you.

"If you'd like," George answered. "How about someplace casual? I'm embarrassed to ask you to an Asian restaurant. It might not be up to your standards."

"Casual is perfect! If this is purely social, I'll need to get back to work pretty quickly anyway," she laughed.

"Quick and close. How about the best deli this side of New York City?"

"Sounds great. I'm a sucker for a good Pastrami sandwich. Give me the address and I'll meet you there."

———   ———   ———

The "deli" that George had chosen was part of a wine shop next door to one of Newport Beach's most prestigious French restaurants, which did not open until evening for dinner. The sandwich shop attached to the wine store sold not only sandwiches on their own freshly baked baguettes but wine by the glass. George ordered their sandwiches and two glasses of wine. "I know you're on duty, but I remember that you had a beer at the Yard House."

"How can I argue with such a perfect memory?" Susan said, smiling across the table at him. Her expression became concerned. "You look tired."

"Working a lot. And Bonaventure has become a strain on me, what with me being involved in finding his wife's body." He took a sip of his wine. "And I'm having some domestic problems, I'm afraid."

Her concerned expression remained. "I'm sorry."

"My wife is a novelist; a quite good one. She's not enamored with my work. I'm afraid she thinks I should cut Lucas Bonaventure loose. She's convinced that treating someone who might be a murderer will ruin my reputation." Why was he telling her this? Was he using her friendliness as an excuse to vent his problems? "Sorry. I shouldn't be telling you these things."

"Your wife is certainly right that your relationship with Lucas Bonaventure has gotten you involved with things that wouldn't ordinarily be part of psychotherapy."

"I'm afraid it's made me a suspect with your police friends, particularly Detective Reynolds."

"You're not really a suspect. Other than being present when their bodies were found, there's nothing to link you to either victim."

George felt relieved. "Good. I'll accept your reassurance and now we can talk about something else."

She smiled at him. "Before we do that, I'd like you to meet someone. I took the liberty of telling him where we were having lunch today so that I could introduce you. He's been working on Regina Bonaventure's murder as a private investigator. He's quite astute. You might be interested in what he's found."

George was disappointed. He had expected that he would be alone with the young psychologist for the entire lunch. Did he not want to share her, or was he afraid he wouldn't get to tell her more of his personal problems?

Susan had turned to greet an old man, dressed very casually in jeans, an unbuttoned shirt with the sleeves rolled and a tee shirt underneath, sneakers and a baseball hat. She stood up and gave him a hug. George felt a momentary twinge of jealousy. "Ben Murphy, this is Doctor George Farquhar," she said, turning back to George.

George stood and held out his hand. "Pleased to meet you, Ben."

Murphy shook his hand then pulled out a chair at their table and sat.

"Are you hungry?" George asked. He had planned on picking up the tab for Susan, and he'd extended the offer to Murphy, mostly to be amicable.

"I'll get mine. Do you order here or at the counter?" Ben asked.

"At the counter," George said.

Murphy got up and strolled over to the counter. George could see that his white hair hung in a braided ponytail beneath his baseball cap.

"He's quite a famous lawman," Susan said. "...from Santa Barbara. Regina Bonaventure's father has hired him to carry out his own investigation on her murder."

"A famous lawman sounds like a sheriff from the old West."

"He was the Chief of Police in Santa Barbara for many years. A very good investigator. Even Abe Reynolds welcomed his help on the case."

Murphy returned to the table carrying a glass of red wine. "I talked them into giving me this right away," he said, with a mischievous grin. He took a slow sip, then smiled. "This is quite good." He set his glass down. "You're Lucas Bonaventure's psychiatrist?"

George nodded. "At least for the time being."

Murphy looked at him quizzically. "What do you mean?"

"I'm suspicious of Bonaventure, just as you both probably are, but I don't want to abandon a patient just because of my suspicions, which may be unfounded. That could change, of course."

"Did you know that Lucas knew that you owned that lot at Banning Ranch?" Murphy asked.

George couldn't conceal his surprise. "No, I didn't." He thought about Lucas' dream; how it gave such a detailed description of his wife's burial place that George was convinced it was his property. "How do you know that?"

"Yes, how do you know that?" Susan asked, her confusion showing on her face. "And does Abe Reynolds know?"

Their sandwiches had arrived and Murphy paused to take a bite of his turkey and cheese sandwich. "I haven't talked to Detective Reynolds yet," he said, turning to Susan. "The real estate agent on the property told me that Lucas had been there, that he had asked about who already owned property there."

"Lucas never told me that," George said, still looking puzzled.

"He never told us either," Susan said.

"What do you think it means?" George asked, although he had a very good idea what it meant. He looked first from Murphy then toward Susan.

""Lucas must have been setting you up," Susan said. "Although how he knew that you'd visit the property and find his wife's body, I can't tell you." She allowed her gaze to linger on George.

"I know how," George said. "But I can't tell either of you because of client confidentiality. But what I thought was just coincidence looks as if it was very deliberate."

"Always distrust a coincidence," Murphy said before taking another bite of his sandwich.

"What happens next?" George asked, looking at Susan Lin.

"I think you should keep seeing Bonaventure," Susan answered.

George was surprised. "Why? He appears to be using me. I'm now a suspect in Detective Reynolds's eyes because of my association with Lucas." He realized, with a start, that his wife had been right all along. He had been manipulated and didn't know it.

"You're in a better position than anyone else to get information from Bonaventure. I'm going to try to work on him to give us a release of information. I don't want to ask for a subpoena because that will scare him too much and he won't reveal a thing. But I think I can convince him that allowing us to talk to you can help him if he later needs to use an insanity defense. That's not true, but he may believe it."

"My job is to heal people, not to spy on them," George said, although he wondered if he was just saying it to give the impression that he had professional ethics. He wanted to prove that Lucas Bonaventure had killed his wife, and no doubt Sherry Bennett also, and he wanted to eliminate himself as a suspect.

"Then continue to heal him of whatever it is that ails him," Susan said. "Although if, as I suspect, he's a psychopath, I doubt you'll have much luck."

"If he's a psychopath, he's not *just* a psychopath," George replied. "He has some real issues to wrestle with." When he thought about Lucas' neurotic symptoms he was reminded of his own dissociative fugue states. He felt relieved that Ben Murphy had found evidence of Lucas' deliberate manipulations, making it more likely that Lucas had killed and buried his wife. George suddenly realized that he had been worried that *he* might have had something to do with Regina Bonaventure's death. Was that the source of the guilt that had plagued him each time he returned from one of his fugue states? But, of course, such a thought was ridiculous. George hadn't even known Regina Bonaventure.

"There are Farquhars in Santa Barbara," Ben Murphy said, interrupting George's thoughts. "Are you related to them?"

"I have a great uncle and his wife who live there," George answered. "My grandfather's younger brother's family." Suddenly he felt overwhelmed with anxiety.

Ben nodded. "They're friends of Bertram Knowles. I've met them once or twice. Very nice people. Beautiful house right next to Bert's. You ever visit them?"

He swallowed hard. He felt as if he might vomit. "A few times with my grandparents and then for a vacation from medical school. I took my wife up to visit once, right after we were married. I'm afraid, I've kind of lost touch in recent years."

"You might have met Regina. Your uncle is her father's neighbor."

"Really?" George said. His entire body felt leaden. "I wasn't aware of that. I don't recall having ever met either her or her father."

"Just another coincidence, I guess," Ben Murphy said, drily.

"Six degrees of separation," George said, laughing lightly. He felt himself sweating. He remembered that Ben Murphy didn't trust coincidences.

"Small world," Susan said. She looked at her watch. "Time for me to get back to work."

George looked at his own watch. "You're right. Me too." He didn't have a patient for another hour, but George didn't want to stay and talk with Ben Murphy.

Ben hadn't moved. "You two have more stringent schedules than I do," he said. "That wine was so good I'm going to stay here and have another glass. Might even buy a bottle to take home with me. That's the beauty of being retired. No schedule."

Susan was already standing. "I thought you were still working for Mr. Knowles."

"I am," Ben said, standing to give her a hug and shake George's hand. "But sitting and thinking is always a good plan in the middle of an investigation. And I've got a lot to think about."

# Chapter 42

George poured himself another gin and tonic. He had to do something to reduce his anxiety. He was at home, sitting in his den with boxes of old pictures open around him. Somewhere within his collection of old photographs, he knew there were pictures of himself at his uncle's house in Santa Barbara. He was hoping that seeing the old photos would jog his memory. Ben Murphy's mention of the proximity of his uncle's house to that of Bertram Knowles' house had unsettled him. Was it possible that he had known Regina Bonaventure? George had no recollection of such an acquaintance. Was this one more trick that his memory was playing on him? And if so, what else didn't George remember about his relationship with the dead woman?

Murphy's revelation had shaken his conviction that Lucas Bonaventure was his wife's killer. George was afraid that his flawed memory might be concealing one more candidate in Regina Bonaventure's death: George himself.

There it was! It was the sixth box that he had opened, filled with old photos from his childhood and youth, most of them taken at his great uncle's home in Santa Barbara.

George had not realized what a shy child he had been. At least that was how he appeared in the various photographs of him in his early years, hiding behind his mother's skirts, gazing at the ground, rather than into the camera, standing on the sidelines in a game of flag football that was being led by his father. George gazed at the picture of his father. Even now George felt intimidated by the images in front of him. His father looked strong, fit, and athletic in those pictures, which always seemed to catch him running or throwing a pass. George knew that the image was misleading. His father had died at the age of 51, a victim of an aneurysm that had been lurking in his brain since infancy. His father's heavy smoking and excessive use of alcohol, perhaps even his volatile temper, had contributed to the bursting of the paper-thin arterial wall, which would have given way eventually, no matter how he'd lived his life.

George put his father's pictures aside and continued to sift through the hundreds of others in the box. He was now looking at a batch taken during his later high school years, some even from his vacations from college, vacations often spent at his great uncle's, although George had somehow erased those memories from his mind. He felt his anxiety rising, as if he were about to stumble upon some great danger.

The young man George in the pictures was handsome, his head held proudly erect, his smile a practiced social one, and his eyes gazing directly into the camera's lens. Something had happened to the shy young boy of the earlier pictures. George knew exactly what had happened: the fugue states had begun, magically erasing the conflicts that had created that earlier, neurotically inhibited child. This new George was confident and gregarious. When something provoked the conflicts that had paralyzed him as a young child, he blacked out, carrying out some kind of activity—he was never sure what he had done during those periods—that allowed his mind to encapsulate the memory that had threatened to reignite the troubling conflict in his history and to consign it once again to his unconscious.

Suddenly he was paralyzed. In his hand was a small photograph, taken by whom he had no idea. He looked to be about age twenty and was dressed in a checked sport coat, a tie and a pair of light-colored slacks. He was smiling brightly into the camera. At his side was Regina Knowles.

George stared at the picture. How could he have forgotten? He and Regina had been close friends once. They had seen each other each summer when George was sent to his great uncle's home to spend his vacation. As children, they had learned to sail together, gone picnicking together.

And they had dated.

Not really dated, George now recalled. The photograph was from the annual summer dance put on by his uncle's yacht club. Neither George nor Regina had wanted to go with anyone else so they had decided to go together. There had been no romance involved in their decision. Both were in Santa Barbara for their college summer vacations. Neither was dating anyone, and it had just seemed easier and more fun to go to the dance together, rather than alone.

But the evening had not ended well.

George had had too much to drink; he remembered that much now that his memories of Regina were returning. Something had happened, something about which, even with his memories of Regina reinstated, he still had no recollection. He had apparently gone into one of his fugue states, for he had no memory of what he had done. All he knew was that he had acted "disgracefully," according to Regina when he was dropping her off at her father's estate. She hadn't seemed angry at the time, in fact, her assessment of his behavior was accompanied by her embarrassed laughter. "You are a naughty, naughty boy George and in my opinion, a perverted one," she told him, smiling at his mystified look of guilt. "I won't tell anyone about you, but I don't want to go out with you again," she added. "I'm still your friend, but my advice is that you should never get drunk. You simply can't control your behavior."

George had had no idea what she was talking about. Even with his memory of Regina restored, he still didn't. In fact, they had never seen one another again. Except, George realized, that perhaps they had. With his memories rushing back into his head, he remembered that several months ago he had seen someone who reminded him of Regina in a bar in Newport Beach. But his memory of the evening was interrupted by a fugue episode, the first of the present series, which he had been experiencing, and the first such episode in twenty years.

Why hadn't he remembered any of this when Lucas Bonaventure appeared in his office? Why hadn't the newspaper description of Bertram Knowles' daughter provoked a flood of recollections on his part, recollections of all those summers spent together, of their single date and its enigmatic ending, of his chance glimpse of her at a bar a few months ago? George had no answer, except that he had obviously prevented his conscious mind from accessing those memories. Beginning when? Was it only after Regina's disappearance that he no longer remembered knowing her, or had he wiped her memory from his own history from the time of their disastrous date? No, he had the distinct feeling that it was seeing her in that bar a few months earlier that had provoked his massive repression, because the incident, which even now was vague to him, had marked the return of his dissociative symptoms.

George breathed a little easier, or perhaps it was the effect of his third gin and tonic. He told himself that the fact that he had buried his memories of his childhood friendship with Regina Knowles, buried them because they reminded him of whatever "disgraceful" thing he had done when he was twenty years old, had nothing to do with her disappearance two months later. He realized that he had been worried that he might have killed her.

The realization brought back his anxiety and prompted him to pour himself another gin and tonic. Such a thought was ridiculous. He wasn't capable of murder. He wasn't a psychopath, not even a neurotic psychopath as Lucas no doubt was. His own training analyst had assured him that, despite his feeling of guilt after his dissociative episodes, he had surely done nothing wrong. He was simply a neurotic with a debilitating Oedipus complex and a resulting castration anxiety. Such people became artists, poets, sometimes nonfunctioning failures, but never murderers. If they were lucky enough to undergo psychoanalysis, they sublimated their unconscious conflicts into a respectable profession, such as medicine, and turned their private lives into a reenactment of their conflict regarding their mother.

And most importantly, he had had no contact with Regina except that one fleeting moment a few months ago in a bar... at least as far as he could remember.

# Chapter 43

"It must have been a great shock seeing your wife like that," Susan said, searching Lucas' face, trying to read the feelings behind his expressions. She glanced down at his leg. "You're still having trouble walking?" They were standing in the vestibule of his home; he was leaning on a cane.

He shrugged. "I can get by. What is this visit about? Do you have news about my wife's killer?"

"Maybe we could sit down somewhere."

He looked at her with a cold stare. "You can't just tell me what you want?"

"I'd rather have a conversation."

He shrugged and limped down the hallway. "We can go in the study." Without looking back, he turned and entered a room on the right side of the hallway.

Susan followed. The room was a small den, with a desk on one side of the room and a heavily padded leather desk chair facing it. Across the room was a long, black leather couch. There was a TV screen on one wall and the others were all lined with books.

Lucas had taken a seat in the chair and swiveled it around to face the couch. Susan sat down on the couch and let her gaze wander around the room. "This is where you work?" she asked.

He shook his head. "Not really. I do almost all my work at my office. Regina and I shared this room for reading and TV or if one of us just wanted to be alone.

"Did your wife like to be alone?"

"She liked to read. She came in here to read."

"How about you?"

He gazed at her with a blank stare. "How about me what?"

"Do you like to be alone? Do you come in here to read?"

"I don't read much. Sometimes I watched games in here when Regina didn't like the noise of the game on the family room TV."

Her gaze swept around the room. "There are a lot of psychology books."

Lucas heaved a sigh. "You and that private detective Murphy, you both want to know about the psychology books. They're Regina's. I've never read any of them."

"Not even the books by Freud? There are several of those. And you've chosen a psychoanalyst for your therapist."

"Is that supposed to mean something? I didn't know anything about Doctor Farquhar until I met him. Regina had mentioned his name once and I remembered it when I felt like I needed to talk to someone."

"Your wife knew Doctor Farquhar?" She tried to hide her shock. George had told her and Ben Murphy that he and Regina Bonaventure were unacquainted, even though George's uncle lived near Regina's father's house in Santa Barbara.

"She said she did. But that's all. She only mentioned him once. Said she saw him someplace and hadn't known he lived in Orange County."

"But she knew he was a psychiatrist?"

"I guess so. She must have said so because when I started looking for someone, I thought of him. Is this what you came to talk to me about?"

"In a way. I wondered what you thought about Doctor Farquhar finding your wife's body and how that has affected your relationship with him as your therapist."

"Why do you care about that?"

"Partly it's professional. I'm a psychologist and I wonder about those things. But I'm also working with the police and we've wondered about the coincidence of your therapist finding your wife's body on his property. We wonder what it means. Don't you?"

"Sure, I thought it was strange, but I guess he was just checking on his property and saw the grave and started digging. That's what he said."

"So you asked him about it."

"We talked about it."

"And the fact that your wife was buried on Doctor Farquhar's property? Does that seem strange to you?"

"It doesn't make much sense to me, but I don't know if I'd call it strange." His expression was bland.

"What did Doctor Farquhar say about it?"

"Haven't you asked him?"

"You withdrew his permission to talk to us, remember?"

He looked at her sharply. "So you don't talk to him anymore?"

"I didn't say that. We questioned him about finding your wife's body of course. We don't ask him about his sessions with you."

He nodded but said nothing.

"What do the doctors say about your leg?" Susan asked.

He looked at her with suspicion. "You mean Doctor Farquhar?"

"You must have seen some other doctor about it. Doctor Farquhar is a psychiatrist, not a neurologist."

"My leg will be fine."

"Do they know what caused the paralysis?"

"Why are you so worried?"

"I'm just curious, since it happened right there in the morgue when I was present. It seemed to be triggered by your seeing your wife."

He glared at her. "You shouldn't be worrying about me. Maybe worry about yourself a little."

She looked up sharply. "What do you mean?"

"You seem to enjoy poking into my business. You come to my house, you sit back like a princess in that chair and, then you act as if you're interested in my welfare. I'll bet you try to seduce Doctor Farquhar the same way."

"Do I seem as though I'm trying to seduce you?"

"You sure seem interested. Maybe that's just the way you are around men. If so, it can lead to trouble."

She felt a surge of anxiety, but she forced it down. She needed to find out what Lucas meant by his remark. "What kind of trouble?"

He was struggling to control his anger. "Men don't like to be toyed with. Women think they can act like they're interested in you, but they'd act the same way to any other man. It's asking for trouble. You're playing with fire."

"You said it again, about trouble. What kind of trouble?"

He stopped glaring at her and looked at the floor. "Just trouble." He looked up. "I think this interview is over." He struggled to his feet.

Susan stood. "OK, I'll go then." She felt relieved that the interview was over. She recognized what she had been feeling. It was fear.

# Chapter 44

George couldn't stop checking the clock. If he had another fugue episode he ought to be able to detect it by seeing that time had elapsed without his being aware of it. He'd barely been able to pay attention to his morning appointments. Thank God all three of his clients were in analysis and had been lying on the couch with their backs to him. He'd mumbled vague answers to their queries and asked almost no questions, but they hadn't seemed to notice.

Lucas Bonaventure would arrive in less than five minutes. George felt his anxiety rising. He needed to keep probing for the key to Lucas' psychological disorder. But the more he learned about his patient, the greater his own anxiety, as if it were his own unconscious terrors that were being exposed. There was a connection between his fugue states and Lucas. It was that connection that terrified him.

— — —

"Did you send that Chinese detective over to my house?" Lucas demanded as soon as he walked into George's office. He was still walking with the aid of a cane.

"Chinese detective? You mean Dr. Lin, the psychologist?"

Lucas waved his hand dismissively. "Whatever. You told her things about me."

"I told her some things before you rescinded your waiver, but not really very much. She visited you at your house?" George felt himself getting angry. Was it jealousy he was feeling?

Lucas looked around the office. "Can we get started? I need to talk to you and I'm more comfortable lying down."

"Then let's begin our session." George got up and took a seat in his chair behind the couch as Lucas took off his suit coat and lay down, staring at the ceiling.

"I dreamt about that Chinese cop," Lucas said.

"You dreamt what?" George was barely able to keep the anxiety from his voice.

"It was a sexual dream. Weird, because I don't even like the woman. But I guess her wiles worked on me."

"Her wiles?"

"You know. You've met her. She's a flirt, a common flirt. Odd for a cop, don't you think?"

George would never have said Susan was a flirt, not in terms of how she'd acted around him. Had she acted differently with Lucas? George could feel his stomach churning, as if he were being challenged. He wasn't sure he wanted to hear Lucas' dream about the psychologist. "She flirted with you?"

"Just like a lot of women do around men, but she was also trying to find out something."

"What do you think she was trying to find out?"

"Who knows? I know she thinks I killed Regina. She's been talking to the private detective that Bert Knowles hired, and *he* thinks I killed her." He raised his head and turned toward George. "Don't you want to hear my dream?" It seemed to George that he was smiling, even smirking.

"Of course; if you want to tell me, that is."

"I've told you all of the other dreams. I thought that was what you wanted to hear. Dreams are the 'royal road to a knowledge of the unconscious' isn't that what you people say?"

Lucas hadn't just paraphrased Freud's words from *The Interpretation of Dreams*; Lucas had quoted the text exactly. "Freud said that in his book on dreams. You said you hadn't read it."

"You're sounding like Doctor Lin. I guess you and she *do* talk." Lucas continued to stare at the ceiling, but George imagined that he was still smirking. Was he trying to get under George's skin?

"I told you that Doctor Lin and I don't talk anymore."

Lucas was quiet for a moment. "So do you want to hear my dream?"

Did he? The thought of hearing Lucas' sexual fantasies about Susan disturbed him, but he was curious. And aroused? He tried to push such thoughts out of his head. "Of course."

"I was at home in my own house, sitting in my study reading when I heard the door open. I remember feeling this great sense of relief, thinking that it was Regina returning home. But instead of coming into the study, she walked right past the doorway and down the hall to her bedroom."

"And it was Regina?"

"It felt like it, although I didn't get a clear view of her as she walked past the doorway. I called her, but she didn't stop. When I got up and looked down the hallway, she'd gone into the bedroom and closed the door."

"What were you feeling?"

"Like I said, relieved. I felt this sense of relief, as if a burden were off my shoulders. It was as if something I'd done wrong had been removed from my conscience."

"You felt as if something had been removed from your conscience?"

Lucas hesitated before answering. "I meant I felt relieved that she was alive."

"OK. So what happened next in the dream?"

"I followed Regina down the hall and stopped in front of the door. It was still closed. I could hear the shower going. I went into the room. There were clothes all around the floor. The bathroom door was open. I walked into the bathroom and I could see her outline in the shower." He stopped and lay silent for a period of seconds.

"What happened next?"

"That's when it got weird. Suddenly I was naked. I stepped into the shower and it wasn't Regina, it was Doctor Lin. She was naked with her back to me."

George could feel himself sweating. As soon as Lucas mentioned Susan naked, George felt aroused. He was tempted to close his eyes and imagine the scene in his own mind.

"I had an erection," Lucas said, interrupting George's thoughts. "I was standing behind her looking at her body. Then she turned around. She gave me a sexy look then reached down and rubbed my penis. I became even more aroused. We began to kiss, but that's when I woke up."

George felt his muscles relax. He realized he'd been tensing his shoulder muscles so much that they were beginning to hurt. "How did you feel when you woke up?"

"Excited, disappointed that the dream had ended. Then I became angry."

"Angry?"

"Regina was gone again. She was there in my dream and then she was replaced by that bitch. That bitch who'd spent the day showing off her body to me, causing me to dream about her."

"You think it's her fault you dreamed about her?"

"She did everything but jump in my lap when she was at my house. Of course, I was going to dream about her. She should know she's playing with fire. If she acts that way around other men, it's going to get her in big trouble."

George was alarmed by Lucas' words. They were too similar to what he'd said about his wife and Sherry Bennett. "What kind of trouble."

"Somebody's going to do more than dream about her. Then when she doesn't come across, she's gonna get hurt."

"So you see her as a tease."

"Exactly. That's exactly what she is, a tease. Like a lot of women who want to make men feel inadequate."

"Did you feel inadequate around her?"

"Me? No, of course not. I was angry that she was teasing me that way. I'm sure she went back to that little apartment she owns in Irvine and gloated about how smart she was. But I saw right through her."

"How do you know she owns an apartment in Irvine?" George's alarm was starting to turn to fear.

"I looked her up on the internet. I wanted to find out more about her, if she's a cop or a doctor. She pretended not to be a cop when she visited me, like she was just a concerned doctor, but she didn't fool me." His voice was angry, menacing.

"Why did she say she was visiting you if it wasn't police business?"

"To see how I was doing, if my leg was improving."

"And how is your leg?" George wanted to change the subject. His anxiety about Susan was becoming too difficult to control.

"It's coming along. I use the cane, but I can walk a ways without it. It's no problem."

"Have you had any thoughts about why you developed a paralysis after seeing your wife's body?" George was still trying to keep Lucas from talking about Susan Lin.

"You and Doctor Lin, you both want to know the same things."

"You didn't answer my question."

Lucas hung his head, as if he were defeated. "I don't know what happened to my leg. I think seeing Regina reminded me of my brother."

"And you think that had something to do with why your leg became paralyzed?"

Lucas looked up. "I don't know." His face was blank.

"Since you have the same symptom, the paralysis, in your dreams, I think we can try to figure out why it happens."

"You mean it's all in my head?"

"What do you think?"

"I really don't know. It just happens."

George put down his note pad. "Well, we'll see what we can find out in our next few sessions."

"Times up?" Lucas sounded as if he didn't want the session to end.

"I'm afraid so."

# Chapter 45

"You haven't been honest with us," Abe Reynolds said, his eyes narrowed as he gave George a long, angry stare.

George dragged his eyes away from Reynolds and looked at Susan Lin, sitting in the chair next to the detective on the other side of George's desk. She dropped her gaze. George thought she looked embarrassed. He remembered Lucas' dream of seeing her naked. He put the thought out of his head. "What are you talking about?" George asked, turning back to Reynolds.

"Lucas Bonaventure says his wife mentioned to him that you were a psychiatrist here, locally. He said she knew you and had even run into you recently. He also said that he told you that the day he made his first appointment with you."

George tried to subdue his rising panic. How much more did the detective know about George's relationship with Regina Bonaventure? What had Lucas told Susan when she visited his house? "It's silly, I guess, but it hadn't really registered with me that Mrs. Bonaventure was the girl who lived next door to my uncle in Santa Barbara. I barely knew her, of course. I had no idea that she had mentioned me to her husband."

"But he said that he told you that when he called to make an appointment," Reynolds said. He looked at George with an accusatory stare.

"My secretary makes all my appointments. I guess he told her but she certainly never told me."

Susan seemed to have overcome her embarrassment and was staring at George. She leaned forward. "Lucas said that you met his wife somewhere a few months ago."

"He told you that?" Was it really Susan who had learned about his relationship with Regina? George wondered. It must have been. But why had she referred to Bonaventure as "Lucas," almost as if they were intimate? His thoughts returned to Lucas' dream of Susan, naked in the shower. He was sweating; he tried to clear his mind.

"Yes," she answered. "And he said he'd told you that it was because of her that he chose you instead of another therapist."

"I told you that my secretary makes my appointments. He must have told her. Either he was mixed up about it or you are."

She looked irritated. "I'm not mixed up, Doctor Farquhar. Did you meet Regina Bonaventure a few months ago, as Lucas said?"

Why was Susan taking Lucas' side? Were she and Lucas colluding somehow? He dismissed the idea. He was becoming paranoid and even jealous. He looked at both Susan and Abe Reynolds. They were both waiting for his answer. "I don't recall meeting Mrs. Bonaventure at all. It sounds as if Lucas is trying to shift the suspicion for his wife's murder onto me, and you've fallen for him... I mean for his story." He was still sweating and getting mixed up. Was it because he wasn't sure if he was guilty? How could he be guilty? And of what?

"So how well did you know Regina Bonaventure when you were younger?" Reynolds asked. "I guess she would have been Regina Knowles back then."

"I didn't know her at all. I was aware that my uncle's neighbor had a daughter, but I don't even know if I ever met her. I was only an occasional visitor to my uncle's house in the summers, I didn't live there or go to school there."

"You never knew her as an adult?" Susan asked. She had gotten over her apparent irritation and had a friendly smile on her face.

He shook his head. "I'm sure I wouldn't even have recognized her if I met her. In fact, her picture was in the paper and it never rang a bell in my memory." That part of his story was at least true.

"And Lucas never mentioned that she said she knew you during his sessions?" Susan asked.

"Never." He was as curious as she was as to why Lucas wouldn't have mentioned this to him, unless George had blocked such discussion from his memory and from his session notes. He knew that he had indeed known Regina when he was younger, but perhaps Lucas didn't know that. Perhaps he was, in fact, just trying to shift suspicion onto George. George's thoughts were traveling in circles.

Reynolds looked over at his partner. "I think we've asked enough for now." He closed his notebook and stood.

Susan looked less eager to leave, but she also stood up. "Thank you for your time, Doctor Farquhar. We'll be in touch with you if we need more information."

Why was she being so formal, George wondered. He had thought they were becoming friends. Would there be no more lunches? No more talks about psychoanalysis? He felt a surge of panic. Was it abandonment that he was feeling? He stood and shook each of their hands without saying anything.

———  ———  ———

"Did you think he was lying?" Reynolds asked as he and Susan rode the elevator to the psychiatrist's building's lobby.

"I'd say he was confused. He seemed completely thrown off by finding out we knew he might have known Regina Bonaventure when they were younger. He seemed to genuinely not remember her."

"I can find out if he's lying," Reynolds said.

"How?"

"Ben Murphy. He's from Santa Barbara. Probably knew Farquhar's uncle as well as old man Knowles. He can do some investigating in Santa Barbara and tell us how well Farquhar and Knowles' daughter knew each other."

"Good idea," Susan answered. "Maybe I'll talk to Bonaventure again and press him a little harder on what he really knows about how well his wife knew Doctor Farquhar. He could be leading us down the garden path on this one, just as the doctor said, trying to shift the suspicion off of himself."

They'd reached the lobby. Reynolds held the glass doors of the building open as Susan stepped outside. "There's something fishy about this case and about the doctor," he said, as they headed across the parking lot. "Farquhar found Mrs. Bonaventure's body on his own property. He also was the one to find Bonaventure's secretary's body. That's too strange to be a coincidence. He's involved in this in some way. Whether he's the killer or not, I'm not sure."

Susan nodded. He was right. George Farquhar wasn't just an innocent bystander in these two murders. She remembered Ben Murphy's advice to never trust a coincidence.

# Chapter 46

"Why are you back?" Lucas Bonaventure stood in the doorway of his home, addressing Susan Lin, who was standing on his front porch.

"I'd like to talk to you about Doctor Farquhar and your wife."

"What about them?"

"If they knew each other."

"Come into the house."

"I'd rather talk out here. I just need a couple of answers." Susan remembered her discomfort last time she'd talked to Bonaventure. She wished she'd brought Abe Reynolds with her.

Lucas glanced up and down the street. "I don't want my neighbors seeing you here. Every time a cop comes here I'm sure the neighbors talk. If you want me to talk to you, you're going to have to come in."

She hesitated. Maybe a couple of minutes wouldn't hurt. "OK," she said. "I only need to ask you a few questions."

He stepped aside and allowed her to enter the house. "We can use the den again," he said.

Susan sat in the same chair she'd sat in before. When Lucas followed, leaning heavily on his cane as he limped along the hallway, he closed the door.

"Is there someone else in the house?" Susan asked. "

No, why?" Lucas took a seat in the chair opposite her.

"You closed the door."

"Habit," Lucas answered. "Does it bother you?"

She didn't want him to sense her anxiety. "No."

"So what do you want to know?" Lucas asked. His eyes were directed at her legs.

Susan tugged her skirt down. His gaze was making her nervous. "You said that your wife told you she'd run into Doctor Farquhar a few months ago. What else did she say about that encounter?"

He looked up at her face. "Not much. She just said she saw him in a restaurant. She was confused because she said he saw her too, even smiled at her, but then he got up and left without ever speaking to her."

"Where was this restaurant and when did this happen?"

"I don't know where. For all I know it was a bar, not a restaurant. Regina went to bars, but then you know that because that's where she went the night she was killed. It was maybe two or three months ago, I'm not sure."

"And did she say anything more about him? You said she told you he was a psychiatrist; how did she know that?"

"She said they knew each other from Santa Barbara. She hadn't known he was here in Orange County. She looked him up on the Internet and found out he was a shrink. She told me that they knew each other when they were young, as kids. He lived next door to her or something."

"Did you ever bring this up to Doctor Farquhar?"

"Only the day I called to make an appointment. I told him my wife had told me she knew him. He said he knew her, too. He said he was sorry for what happened to her, that she was missing."

"So you talked to him directly; not his secretary?" Either he was lying or George Farquhar was.

He shook his head. "I talked to him. He answered the phone when I called his office. I thought it was a little strange, but that was what happened."

"Did he ever mention knowing your wife again, during any of your sessions?"

"Never. Even when we talked about her, he never acted as if he knew her."

"Didn't you think that was strange?"

He shrugged. "I just thought shrinks weren't supposed to talk about themselves."

"You're right of course, but it seems strange to me."

"So why don't you ask him about it, instead of questioning me?"

"I'm talking to both of you about it."

"Playing both of us, huh?"

"What do you mean?"

"I guess you're trying to seduce both of us; to see which one of us breaks first." There was an aggressive edge to Lucas' voice.

"I'm not seducing anyone. What do you mean to see which one of you breaks first?" She was feeling more nervous.

"We're both suspects in Regina's murder; Sherry Bennett's too. You've got to pick one of us." He seemed to be leering at her.

"Do we? We haven't ruled out Danny Rosberg yet."

Lucas looked surprised. "Really? Even after the doc found both Regina's and Sherry's bodies? Sounds to me as if you've fallen for his line."

She just looked at him, saying nothing.

"How does the doctor feel about you visiting me? He seemed pretty jealous when I told him about our last meeting." Lucas was leaning toward her.

"Really?" She didn't like the way the conversation was going. It was time to leave.

"Don't try to tell me you don't know the effect you have on men."

"I'm interviewing you and Doctor Farquhar as part of a police investigation."

"You're still a woman. Don't tell me you don't keep that in mind during these interviews. You're not that innocent."

"I'm not sure why you're saying these things, Mr. Bonaventure, but I think it's time for me to leave." She started to get up.

"Right. You're sooo innocent. You know exactly what you're doing and you're gonna have to pay the price."

"Are you threatening me?"

Lucas smiled. "I'm just warning you. I'm trying to be helpful."

She was standing. "I'll be going," she said, glancing toward the closed door.

"So go." He waved his arm as if to dismiss her. "The door's not locked."

# Chapter 47

George Farquhar had been lying to Detective Reynolds and Doctor Lin; that much Ben Murphy knew for sure. Edmund Farquhar, George's uncle, despite being in his late-eighties, had not only remembered George visiting the Knowles' house next to his to play with Regina on several occasions, but he described Regina as George's closest childhood friend during his nephew's summer visits to Santa Barbara. Bert Knowles also remembered George as a friend of his daughter, both as a child and then as a young man. In fact, Bert had several photographs of Regina and George together. The last one was taken when they were both in their early twenties when George had escorted Regina to a dance or party, Bert could not remember which. Bert was sure that they were never a real couple, just good friends. He had not heard his daughter mention George in recent years.

So why had Doctor Farquhar lied? Of course, it shed new light on Regina's murder to find that the man who'd found her body had been an old friend and not someone who had never met her, but the situation was doubly suspicious because the psychiatrist had denied any connection to Regina when he'd talked to the police. Ben would have liked to interview Farquhar himself, but that would be overstepping his bounds and interfering with the police investigation. All he could do was report his findings to Abe Reynolds.

Before he called Reynolds, he was going to tell Susan Lin. Ben knew that Doctor Lin had an informal relationship with George Farquhar in addition to her investigative one. After all, the lunch at which Ben had been introduced to Doctor Farquhar was a casual meeting between the psychiatrist and Susan, ostensibly to discuss professional issues, since, at the time, Lucas had not waived his confidentiality rights with Farquhar. If Susan was planning on meeting with George again, knowing that he had lied to her could be crucial to using her meeting with him to learn more.

Susan Lin's condominium complex was on a busy street in Irvine but set well back from the curb with a greenspace and trees between the street and the building. Ben parked his car in a visitor's space in the small lot in front of the building. Residents' cars were parked overnight in the underground garage. From the address, Susan's apartment was on the second floor.

The stairs to the second floor were on the outside of the building, although they were covered. On the second floor they opened to an outside walkway along which was a string of apartments. Ben stepped from the stairway onto the landing, looking out at the parking lot, the grass and trees, and the street beyond. Susan's apartment was to his right. He paused to look down the length of the balcony. He'd thought he'd seen someone entering the stairway, just as he was exiting his car, but no one was in sight. He turned to walk along the balcony to Susan's apartment.

That was the last thing he remembered as a crushing blow landed on the back of his head. He cried out, then fell to the balcony floor, losing consciousness.

# Chapter 48

"So you're Terri," Susan said, putting out her hand to Ben Murphy's granddaughter. "How is he?" Terri had come from her grandfather's side in the emergency room of the Irvine Medical Center to greet Susan in the hospital waiting room. Susan had found Murphy unconscious on the balcony outside her apartment and called 911. She'd told the medics to call his granddaughter. Later, she had gotten dressed and driven to the hospital herself.

"The doctor said he'll be fine. He's got a nasty gash on the back of his head and he's still a little fuzzy, but he's awake and talkative. He wanted to see you. They're not going to discharge him for several more hours so they can make sure he doesn't have any symptoms of brain injury." She was leading Susan to the rooms where the emergency room patients were situated.

"How did you get here so soon?" Susan asked. "You couldn't have been in Santa Barbara."

"Gramps had been up there interviewing some people and he brought me back with him. I was at the hotel when they called my cell. It's only five minutes from here."

"What was he doing in Santa Barbara?" Susan asked, walking alongside her. "Was it about Regina Bonaventure's case?"

"I'll let him tell you," Terri said, stopping and sliding open the curtain to one of the rooms.

Ben was sitting up in bed, an IV inserted into the back of his left hand. Susan had expected to see his head wrapped in bandages, given the amount of blood there had been on the landing when she'd found him, but she could just see the tape from a bandage on the back of his head as he looked at her with a half-smile.

"You found me I guess," Ben said, his voice subdued and unsteady. "Thank you for calling the medics."

"I heard someone cry out and then I heard a thud. My apartment is the first one after the landing. I came out and there you were. You were still unconscious when they put you in the ambulance. I told them to call Terri. I hadn't realized she was here in Orange County."

He shifted his gaze toward his granddaughter and gave her a weak smile. "I'm still a little groggy, but I wanted to talk to you. I think whoever did this was waiting for you... or coming to visit you."

"Me?" Susan was shocked.

Ben sighed and closed his eyes for a minute, as though he were tired. "Whoever hit me was coming to your apartment. When I showed, up he was either afraid of being discovered or didn't want me to talk to you."

"Someone waiting outside my apartment? Who? Why?" Susan felt a cold chill.

Ben sighed. It looked as if it took a lot of effort for him to talk. "Doctor Farquhar and Lucas are the top two candidates. Farquhar wouldn't have wanted me to tell you what I learned in Santa Barbara. But he wouldn't have known I was coming to talk to you. He would have thought I'd go straight to Abe Reynolds. I don't know why Lucas would have been stalking you, but it just seems to me that it could have been him."

Susan had her suspicions as to why Lucas Bonaventure might stalk her. He seemed to be viewing her in the same category as his wife and his secretary: as a seducer who was courting trouble from men. "What did you find out about Doctor Farquhar and Mrs. Bonaventure?" she asked.

"I'll give you a full report—you and Abe Reynolds—when my head is completely clear, but I talked to Farquhar's uncle whose house is next to the Knowles' place and to Bert Knowles. Both of them remembered Farquhar and Regina being close friends from childhood until they were in college. Farquhar has been lying to you."

Susan was almost as shocked as she had been when Ben had told her that someone might be stalking her. She knew that she'd believed George when he'd said that he didn't know Regina or at least didn't remember her. She hadn't believed Bonaventure's story about his wife having met George at a bar a few months ago. Abe Reynolds had been more doubtful about Doctor Farquhar's story and it was his idea to ask Murphy to look into it. Abe had been right and she'd been wrong. What else had she been wrong about with regard to the psychiatrist?

"You look tired, Gramps," Terri said, interrupting Susan's thoughts.

"You can tell me all this later," Susan said, feeling guilty for making the aging detective talk so much when he was still recovering from the blow to his head.

Ben nodded. He closed his eyes, then opened them. "I'm supposed to stay awake if I can," he said. "But maybe I won't think so much for awhile." He looked over at Susan. "I mostly wanted you to know that someone was there at your apartment—the person who did this to me—and you need to take precautions."

Susan nodded. She felt a wave of gratitude toward the old man in the hospital bed. "I don't carry a weapon, but I'll let Abe know and he can tell me what to do. I'm sure that the Irvine Police are investigating the area. I'll talk to Detective Jensen from the Irvine PD. He's the one investigating Sherry Bennett's murder. My apartment is in his jurisdiction and this may be connected to his case."

Ben nodded again and closed his eyes, then reopened them. He smiled. "I'll rest for a while, then when I'm out I'll come and talk to you and Reynolds."

Susan smiled back. "Thank you, Ben. And thank you for your concern. Get well."

# Chapter 49

"I need to talk to you," Susan Lin told George over the phone.

"Shall we do lunch?" he offered, trying to sound cheerful, although the psychologist's voice sounded ominous and, since he had lied both to her and to Detective Reynolds about knowing Regina Bonaventure, he had been waiting for a call from either of them. His uncle had called to tell him that the private detective, Ben Murphy, had been inquiring about George and Regina Knowles, and his uncle had told Murphy all about their friendship. No doubt Murphy had talked to the Newport Beach police.

"This is police business." Her voice was flat, without emotion.

"So do you want me to come to you or do you want to come here?"

"I'll come to your office."

———  ———  ———

"You're alone? No Detective Reynolds?" George felt relieved. Perhaps Susan's visit was as much social as official.

"I wanted to give you a chance to explain yourself to me before I involved Detective Reynolds."

"Explain myself?'

Susan stared at him from across his desk. "You told us that you didn't know Regina Bonaventure."

"Or that I didn't remember knowing her."

She frowned. "What is that supposed to mean?"

He hesitated. There was no way he could explain the repression of his memory of Regina to Susan without sounding either mentally ill or as if he were lying. "It was a long time ago."

"Ben Murphy talked to your uncle and to Regina's father. Both of them remembered you and she as having a close relationship that lasted until you were in college."

He nodded. "My uncle told me that Murphy had talked to him." He glanced around the room, as if looking for something to help him explain himself. "All I can say is that I didn't remember knowing her."

She continued to frown at him. "You know that it makes you a suspect in Regina's murder, both the fact of you knowing her and that you lied about it."

"It wasn't a lie."

She shook her head. "I wish you would be honest with me."

He looked back at her without answering.

"Somebody was at my apartment, stalking me or something. Whoever it was attacked Ben Murphy when he came to see me."

George felt a chill. "Someone was stalking you? Attacked Murphy?" He was starting to perspire. He felt nauseous.

"Ben's in the hospital. He said he thought someone was at my apartment house watching me, or waiting for him."

George's anxiety was almost overwhelming. "And you think it was me?"

"I never said that. But was it?"

"Of course not. Why would I do that?" George knew that he had thought about visiting her apartment. Was that out of curiosity or was it to make sure that Lucas wasn't stalking her? Had he been there and not known it? He wasn't sure of anything anymore.

She shook her head. "I have no idea. I don't really think it was you, which means either that Ben is wrong, and it had nothing to do with me, or else it was the person Ben suspects, which is Lucas Bonaventure."

George felt his anxiety spike. Lucas knew where Susan lived. Lately, he'd been talking about Susan and using the same terms he'd used when he talked about his wife or Sherry Bennett. Had he begun to stalk Susan, just as he'd stalked Sherry? Or was George just trying to shift the blame from himself? He didn't trust his own thought processes anymore.

"I can't talk about Lucas," George said. He was legally permitted, in fact, required, to warn Susan if his patient had made a clear threat concerning her, but Lucas hadn't. George was torn between his professional ethics and his fear for Susan's safety. "What are you going to do in case someone *is* stalking you?" he asked.

"Is Lucas capable of doing that?" she asked him.

George wasn't sure how to answer. "He's a murder suspect. Sherry Bennett said he'd stalked her."

"And had he?"

"She was sure of it." He didn't mention that he had followed Sherry himself and seen Lucas following her.

She stared at him, as if she had hoped he'd say more. "I'm sure Abe Reynolds will want to talk to you. Are you sure there isn't anything more you can tell me about your relationship with Regina Bonaventure?"

The truth was that he remembered most of his relationship with Regina now that he had seen the picture of them together. But to admit that would imply that he had lied before. And he still knew nothing about his having seen her recently or even if he'd only seen her once. Whatever mechanism had suppressed his memory of their relationship was still fogging his recent recollections. There was no way he could explain that to Susan. "I've told you everything I know."

She stood. "I'm going to tell all of this to Abe Reynolds. He's going to want to talk to you."

George just nodded. He didn't know what to say.

# Chapter 50

"Why did you interview Farquhar without me?" Abe Reynolds asked, his face red with anger. "And you told him that Ben Murphy already found out that he and Mrs. Bonaventure were old friends?" He stared at her accusingly.

"I thought he might be more open if he just talked to me," Susan answered. "I was wrong."

"So he's still lying, even to you."

She nodded.

Reynolds took a deep breath and settled further into his chair. "Ok, that was a dumb move on your part, but that's water under the bridge. I'm putting my money on the doctor as the one who whacked Murphy on the head, hoping he could get rid of him before he talked to us."

"Ben Murphy doesn't think so. He thinks it was someone stalking me, someone who recognized him, someone related to this case. He thinks it might have been Bonaventure."

"Why would Bonaventure stalk you? Why would he go after you or attack Murphy for that matter? Only Farquhar wanted Murphy silenced. Murphy knew Farquhar was lying and now we do too. I think it's enough to haul the good doctor in."

"Arrest him?"

"At least grill him. He found Mrs. Bonaventure's body, he lied about knowing her, and he probably assaulted Murphy to keep him quiet. If we bring him in and start questioning him, I bet we can make him talk. If you ask me, he's Mrs. Bonaventure's killer; maybe the Bennett woman's also."

Susan was silent. She still couldn't believe Doctor Farquhar was a killer, but she had to admit that the circumstantial evidence against him was growing. "If you think that's the best thing to do," she said.

Reynolds pursed his lips. "I don't know if it's the best thing to do, but we need to do something to shake up the doctor so he'll talk to us. He's involved in this one way or another."

"You can handle it. I want to stay on Doctor Farquhar's good side in case he doesn't talk. If he trusts me, he may eventually confide in me. Meanwhile, I'm going to do a little more investigating of Bonaventure; show my neighbors his photo and find out if anyone has seen him hanging around my apartment house."

"Be careful. I don't want you visiting either Farquhar or Bonaventure by yourself again. You're not a cop and one of them is dangerous. You need to be careful."

"Don't worry. I won't take any chances."

———    ———    ———

Madeline would be furious. Detective Reynolds and a uniformed policeman had come to George's office and escorted him out of the building. Then he'd been driven to the Newport Beach police station. At least they hadn't handcuffed him. Mrs. Schrempf had certainly noticed that he'd left with the two policemen. By now the news would be all over his building. Pretty soon it would be in the papers.

"You can clear all this up pretty quickly if you level with us, doctor," Detective Reynolds said. The room in which the two of them were seated reminded George of those he had seen on TV. One side of the room had a one-way window. He wondered if Susan Lin was on the other side of the window.

"I don't know what you think I can clear up," George said. He hadn't called a lawyer yet, partly because the only lawyers he knew were Michael Steele, who had an office in his building and Tom Cooper, who was his neighbor. He was embarrassed to let either of them know what had happened to him.

"Why did you lie about knowing Regina Bonaventure?"

"I didn't lie, I just forgot." He knew that his answer wouldn't satisfy the detective any more than it had satisfied Susan.

"Forgot? Your uncle in Santa Barbara remembered, and Mrs. Bonaventure's father remembered. Both of them said that you and she were friends for years. How could you have forgotten?"

George was sweating. There was nothing he could tell Reynolds that made any sense. Maybe he needed to tell the truth. He wondered if they were going to hold him in jail just because he'd lied to them about knowing Regina. His thoughts jumped to Susan. He was sure that Lucas was stalking her. "Why isn't Doctor Lin here?"

"That's not your worry, doctor. She's got other things to do. Besides she already talked to you and you didn't tell her anything."

"She's in danger."

"What are you talking about?"

"Someone is stalking her."

Reynolds frowned. "That someone is you. At least it was you waiting outside her apartment so Murphy couldn't tell her what he found out in Santa Barbara."

"I didn't even know he went to Santa Barbara. Why would I wait outside of her apartment for Murphy?"

"Because your uncle told you that Murphy had talked to him about you and Mrs. Bonaventure, and you knew that Murphy would tell us unless you stopped him."

George debated lying, but he knew they could just ask his uncle and find out the truth. "I knew that Murphy had talked to my uncle about Regina and me, but that wouldn't make me go after Murphy. Besides, why would I be outside of Susan's—Doctor Lin's—apartment? How would I know that Murphy was going to go there?"

"You tell me."

"I don't know why Murphy was attacked, but I'm pretty sure Lucas Bonaventure has stalked Doctor Lin, and he probably still is. That's why she's in danger." George was feeling desperate. While Reynolds was focusing on him, Lucas could be going after Susan Lin.

"What makes you think that Bonaventure has been stalking Doctor Lin?"

George needed to break confidentiality and tell Reynolds about Lucas' fixation on Susan. "Bonaventure has been obsessed with Doctor Lin lately, just as he was obsessed with his secretary, Sherry Bennett, whom he also stalked." He looked straight at Reynolds. "And Sherry Bennett was murdered."

"And her body was discovered by you, just as you discovered Mrs. Bonaventure's body. You're trying to distract me, doctor. You still haven't answered my question about why you lied about knowing Regina Bonaventure." Reynolds stared at him, the detective's face drawn into a scowl.

George felt desperate. He had to make Reynolds understand that Susan's life was at risk. "I've got this problem, detective. I block things out sometimes. I can't remember whole episodes of my life. I've had the problem off and on for years. For some reason, I blocked out knowing Regina Knowles, that is, Regina Bonaventure. When I said I didn't know her, I was telling you the truth about what I remembered. Later, I realized I was wrong. I found a picture of us together and remembered that we had been friends from childhood."

"Did you tell Doctor Lin that?"

He looked down at the table. "No. I was embarrassed to tell her. I thought she'd think I was crazy."

"So why are you telling me now?"

"Because Doctor Lin is in danger and you have to stop thinking I did something wrong and start protecting her from Lucas Bonaventure." His voice had become shrill.

Reynolds nodded, though he still looked skeptical. "OK, I'll make sure Doctor Lin is under department protection. Just as soon as you tell me what you know."

George felt some relief, although he still worried about Susan. "I knew Regina Knowles when we were both kids. My uncle's house in Santa Barbara was next to hers. I stayed with my uncle almost every summer from the time I was about eight years old. Regina and I played together. We saw each other in summers all the way through high school. The last time I saw her was when I came to my uncle's house the summer after my sophomore year in college."

"You didn't visit your uncle after that?"

"A few times, but I didn't see Regina." George hadn't mentioned the incident that had signaled the end of their friendship. He still didn't remember what had happened. It was Regina who had stopped their seeing each other.

"And you didn't tell us any of this until now because you didn't remember that you knew her?" Reynolds' tone was sarcastic.

"Yes."

"And you say you don't remember whole periods of our life?"

He looked down at the floor. He really didn't want to have to explain his fugue states to the detective. Reynolds would just think that it meant that George could have killed either Regina or Sherry Bennett, or both, and not remember it. The thought made George's heart race. What if it were true?

Reynolds leaned forward. "Don't zone out on me, doctor. I asked you a question. Do you not remember whole periods of your life? Is this some kind of mental problem you have?"

George looked up. "It's a problem I used to have. It went away after I had treatment for it. The only time it's come back is with regard to Regina Knowles, and this time it was different. I just forgot all of my interactions with her when I was younger."

"So you don't 'blank out' and do things you're not aware of."

"No." George looked the detective in the eye, mustering his staunchest look of confidence.

"But that *did* happen in the past? You'd do things you didn't remember you'd done, later?"

George nodded. He was afraid he was sounding like a deranged killer who didn't remember his crimes. "Only I never did anything dramatic. I just didn't remember periods of time, maybe a few minutes, maybe a few hours. No one else could tell. I just went about my usual activities." What he'd said wasn't exactly true, since he never knew what he'd done during his fugue states, but he was trying to dampen Reynolds' curiosity.

Reynolds shook his head. "Sounds wacky to me." He heaved a sigh. "I'm going to let you go for now. I think you're holding back, but we haven't got enough to charge you with Mrs. Bonaventure's murder, and Sherry Bennett is Irvine's business." He gave George a steely stare. "This doesn't mean we're going to stop looking. You know more than you're telling us, doctor. I'm not sure if you killed either of those women, but you know a lot more than you're saying."

George felt a wave of relief. It was almost unbelievable to him that he was being released. Now he could warn Susan Lin. "So I'm free to leave? Right now?"

"Take a walk," Reynolds answered.

# Chapter 51

None of Susan's neighbors had seen Lucas Bonaventure or George Farquhar near her apartment house. Most of them were still at work, but among those at home, most of them were aware of Ben Murphy's mugging outside her apartment. They were frightened and eager to help but knew nothing.

She went to her apartment and fixed herself a cup of tea. Abe would still be interviewing George Farquhar, and it was probably better that she let him do it by himself. She didn't want to sabotage her relationship with the psychoanalyst completely. As she waited for her tea to steep, her cell phone rang. It was Lucas Bonaventure.

"I hope it's OK to call you directly. Your number was on your card," Lucas said. He sounded apologetic

"Certainly. What can I help you with?" She was trying to keep her tone neutral. She didn't want him accusing her of leading him on again.

"My wife knew Doctor Farquhar a lot better than I thought," he said.

"What do you mean?"

"I found messages and pictures. They were quite the friends. Behind my back even."

Susan was shaken. "You mean recently? Not just when they were younger?"

"Now, this year. He sent her texts… romantic texts."

Susan's shoulders sagged. Doctor Farquhar had lied to her. "Can you bring them into the station and show them to me and Detective Reynolds?"

"Not really. My leg has gotten worse. I can barely move it at all. Besides, I want to give her phone directly to you. I don't trust Detective Reynolds. He wants to pin Regina's murder on me. I'm only going to put this evidence directly in your hands."

Susan felt a momentary panic. She didn't want to return to Bonaventure's house.

"I'll come over with Detective Reynolds. You can give the phone to both of us."

"Just you. You need to read the texts first, see the pictures to verify that they exist. Then you can give them to Reynolds or whoever you want to give them to."

"You can give them to me when I come with Detective Reynolds. I'll look at them first, and then turn them over to him. You can watch me do it. That's the only way it's going to happen I'm afraid."

Lucas was quiet. "OK," he finally said. "Just knock and then walk in. It'll be unlocked. I can't get down the hallway so easily. I'll be in the den. You remember where that is."

# Chapter 52

He needed to do something to protect Susan. If he'd ever thought that his imagination had exaggerated the peril she was in, learning that Ben Murphy had been mugged by someone who'd been lurking outside of her apartment was enough to convince him that the danger to Susan was real. He was sure that Lucas was behind the attack on Murphy and he was just as sure that Lucas' real target was Susan. But what could he do about it?

He was standing outside the Newport Beach police station. His own office was less than a mile away. He walked back.

"Big mistake by the police," he said to Mrs. Schrempf, who was trying to avoid looking at him. *She's probably embarrassed that she told everyone in the building that I was arrested,* he thought to himself.

He sat at his desk and called Lucas.

"Did I miss an appointment?" Lucas asked. He sounded suspicious.

"No. Are you at home?" George wasn't sure what he was going to say to Lucas, but he wanted to make sure he wasn't out somewhere stalking Susan.

"What do you mean am I at home? What are you calling about?" Lucas was becoming irritated.

"I want you to come in for an extra appointment. The police have been questioning me, and they're pressuring me to talk to them about you."

"You told me that everything I said to you was confidential. I rescinded my waiver of confidentiality, remember?"

"Of course. I... I just thought maybe we should talk about it," George stammered. He just wanted to keep Lucas within his sight, but he couldn't say that.

"I'll talk to them myself," Lucas answered. "Doctor Lin is coming to talk to me again."

George felt a wave of panic. "Coming to your house?"

"She's supposed to be here right now."

"What for?"

"How should I know? I guess she just can't stay away from me. Say, what's up anyway? You sound worried. You're not worried about that poor little police doctor are you?" His tone was sarcastic.

"Of course not," George answered. He was embarrassed but he was also afraid. Why on earth would Susan come to Lucas' house? Didn't Reynolds warn her that she was in danger? "Call me after you talk to her. Let me know that you told her that you weren't waiving confidentiality."

"You mean let you know that she's safe? What are you afraid of Doctor Farquhar? What have you got going for that Chinese chick?"

George hung up. Lucas was taunting him. He wished he had a drink right now. He felt as if he had to do something, but he was paralyzed. The thought made him check his legs, to make sure both of them still moved. What was he doing? Paralysis was Lucas' symptom, not his. And what about his fear for Susan's safety, was that real or was he taking on Lucas' pathology, disguising his anger and jealousy as protective worry, just as Lucas had done with Sherry Bennett?

He couldn't just sit and obsess. He got out of his chair and headed for the door.

# Chapter 53

"Mr. Bonaventure?" Abe Reynolds called. He and Susan Lin had let themselves into the house, just as Lucas had instructed them to do. They were standing in the vestibule just inside the front door.

"In the den," Lucas shouted.

Lucas was sitting behind his desk. A polished black cane leaned against the wall. "Thanks for coming. Sorry, I didn't get up to greet you. My leg seems to have gotten worse." His face was serious and he looked tense.

"Doctor Lin said you have some evidence for us," Reynolds said. His voice was flat. His eyes showed his suspicion.

"Have a seat," Lucas motioned toward the couch. "No, wait a minute. I need to get Regina's cell phone. It's in the bedroom. Detective, can you come with me?" He started to get up.

"You want me to get it? You said you have trouble walking."

"I can walk that far. It's on this floor." Lucas struggled to his feet and reached over and picked up his cane. He leaned heavily on it as he slowly limped out of the room. Detective Reynolds followed him.

A few minutes later, Lucas returned. He sat down behind the desk.

"Where's Detective Reynolds?" Susan asked.

"He's fiddling with Regina's phone. He said he wanted to check some things out. He's checking the drawers in her dressing table and some pictures she'd printed out."

"There really were pictures?"

Lucas smiled. "Of course, I told you there were. Surprised at your doctor, doctor? He's not the innocent egghead that he seems to be. Sounds like you were taken in a much as I was."

"You seem happy," Susan said.

"I'm amused."

"Amused?"

"You and the doctor seemed to have a thing going. I guess I was wrong about who seduced whom. He played you I guess."

They were interrupted by the front doorbell.

"That's probably your doctor now," Lucas said.

"Doctor Farquhar? Why would he be here?"

"Just a guess," Lucas said, still smiling. "Do you mind getting it for me?"

—— —— ——

The road up to Lucas' house had seemed strangely familiar. George had a vague sense of the Newport Coast area—he'd passed it many times traveling along PCH—but he had no recollection of ever visiting the Bonaventure residence. He felt an involuntary shudder as he passed the shopping center at the bottom of the hill. He ignored the feeling and kept driving. The road twisted and turned. As he turned a corner, he had a momentary image of a large dog standing in the middle of the street. He swerved, but then it was gone. His mind was playing tricks on him.

Lucas' home was a large ranch style house, all one story, although it sat on the side of the hill and may have had a second story below the first on the side away from the street. A black Ford with official Newport Beach plates was in the driveway. Was that Susan's car? For some reason, he thought she drove a Prius. Why did he think that? He'd never seen her car, had he? He parked his car.

He was surprised when Susan answered the door.

"What are you doing here?" she asked.

"Lucas told me you were coming to see him. I was worried," George answered. "Why are you answering the door?"

"Mr. Bonaventure is having trouble walking. He asked me to answer the door for him." She stepped aside and let him in. "He's in his den." She turned and walked down the hallway. George followed.

"Here to rescue Doctor Lin?" Lucas said as Susan and George entered the den.

"You came here by yourself?" George asked Susan, ignoring Lucas.

"Detective Reynolds is in the bedroom, checking out Lucas' wife's cell phone."

George sat down. "What do you mean her cell phone?" He felt sick.

"Your texts, doctor. And the pictures you sent her," Lucas said.

Had he? George had no memory of texting Regina. And what kind of pictures would he have sent her? Had George blocked out even more than he'd thought he had? "I didn't text Regina," he said weakly. He was addressing Susan.

Susan stared at him. Her disappointment showed on her face. "You lied before," she said. "Detective Reynolds said you admitted knowing Mrs. Bonaventure, knowing her quite well."

He nodded. "But that was years ago. I haven't seen her for years."

"She told me you ran into each other in a bar," Lucas said. His smile had been replaced by a scowl.

"I thought I saw her in a bar a few months ago, but we didn't even talk. I certainly didn't send her any text messages."

"You texted her the night she went missing," Lucas said savagely. "That very night!"

"That's impossible," George answered. He was getting dizzy.

"Lucas says the text messages are all on her cell phone," Susan said coldly. "You've admitted you saw her in a bar. Can't you just tell the truth?"

He couldn't admit what he didn't remember. "I'm telling you everything I remember. I have this problem with my memory…" How was he going to explain things to Susan?

"I'm the patient, Doctor Farquhar," Lucas said. He face was twisted in a sneer. "You're sounding as if it's you with the mental problem."

Susan continued to stare at him, her face expressionless.

"Why do you have her cell phone?" George asked Lucas.

"Don't try to change the subject," Lucas said, scowling. "How well did you know my wife?"

George turned to Susan. "No, really. Why would Lucas have Regina's cell phone? She was buried without even her clothes on. None of her possessions were found, were they?"

Susan looked over at Lucas. "No, they weren't. How *do* you have her cell phone?" she asked.

"I guess she left it at home."

"You said there was a text on it from me, from that night," George said.

"The phone was in her bedroom. Maybe you texted her before she left the house, or she never received the text."

"I want to see the cell phone," Susan said. "I don't know why Abe hasn't brought it in here."

"I told you, he's searching the bedroom," Lucas answered. He reached for his cane. "Let's all go look at the cell phone, shall we? It's the only way to prove what's true."

Lucas struggled to his feet and George and Susan followed him as he hobbled down the hallway, leaning heavily on his cane. The door to the bedroom was closed. Lucas stepped aside. "You first, he said to the two of them."

Detective Reynolds was lying on the floor. Susan ran to him. She knelt down. "He's alive."

George whirled around. Lucas was standing in the doorway with a gun in his hand. "The Detective was kind enough to loan me his gun."

Susan looked up. "What's going on? Abe's got blood all over the back of his head."

"The detective didn't believe me," Lucas said. "I'm afraid I had to hit him." He had entered the bedroom. He walked normally, without the aid of the cane, which he'd let fall to the floor.

"He needs a doctor," Susan said. She stood up. "Stop this while you can, Mr. Bonaventure. You haven't killed anyone yet. Turn yourself in."

"Haven't I?" Lucas asked.

"He killed Regina and Sherry Bennett!" George said. Despite Lucas's gun pointed at him and Susan, he felt immense relief. He hadn't been sure that he hadn't done the killings himself.

"But the cell phone, doctor?" Lucas said. "What about the cell phone?"

George's feeling of dread was back. "You mean there *is* a cell phone?"

Lucas was pacing back and forth. There was no sign of his limp. "Of course there's a cell phone, complete with your messages to Regina."

Susan looked over at George. "Where is this cell phone?"

Lucas reached in his pocket. "I had it with me all the time." He threw it over to Susan, who caught it in midair. "Go to the text messages, look for Doctor Farquhar's name."

Susan scrolled through the texts on the phone. She began reading. "You *did* text her," she said, looking at George accusingly.

"What did I say?" George asked. He still didn't remember anything.

"You wanted to meet her. She didn't reply."

"That's all?"

Susan was bent over the phone. "There was only one set of messages. You asked her to meet. Said you'd seen her in a bar." She scrolled more. "That was it."

"They were carrying on an affair," Lucas said. The look he directed at George was vicious. "She was cheating on me."

George was still confused. Even when Susan had read the text message, he couldn't remember sending it.

"Do you have any other evidence?" Susan asked, staring at Lucas.

"I don't need more evidence. I didn't need more with Sherry either. Both Regina and Sherry were shopping for men. They made that clear. The doctor was an eager buyer."

"That's not true," George said. "I was never interested in Sherry or Regina. We were just old friends."

"And how about the doctor here?" Lucas said, waving the gun at Susan. "Her seduction worked just like Regina's and Sherry's had. You fell for her the same way." He looked back at George. "Now you both have to pay for toying with me like that."

"This cell phone is no evidence of anything," Susan said in disgust. She threw the phone toward Lucas. It fell short and skittered across the floor to Lucas' feet. He bent to pick it up.

George leaped for the cane on the floor. It was closer to him than to Lucas. He managed to get his hand on it before Lucas, who was still bent over, saw what he was doing. George brought the cane down on Lucas' wrist. The gun fell to the ground. George dived toward Lucas and tackled him around the waist. They both fell to the ground. Lucas was stronger and heavier; he rolled on top of George.

A shot rang out. "Stop it," Susan shouted. She was pointing the gun at both of them. Plaster was falling from the ceiling where she'd shot a hole in it.

Lucas rolled off of George. He stood up, his hands in the air. George struggled to his feet and backed away. Susan still had the gun pointed at Lucas. "Call 911," she told George. "Tell them officer down."

# Chapter 54

"How is Detective Reynolds doing?" George asked, looking at Susan from across their table at the Fig and Olive, one of Newport Beach's nicest restaurants. They each had a glass of wine and were waiting for their orders.

"He's recovering. He got a nasty blow on the back of the head, apparently from Lucas' cane, which has a metal tip, but he only suffered a mild concussion, and he should be out of the hospital later today or tomorrow."

"And Lucas?"

"He's behind bars. He's charged with both his wife's and Sherry Bennett's murders and the attempted murder of you and me, as well as assaulting a police officer. They found his wife's clothing, with her blood on it, in that same bedroom. They also found the gloves he used when he killed both women, or it looks as if they're the same gloves. They had traces of blood and they're looking for fibers from the rope he used to kill Sherry Bennett. But anyway, he's confessed to everything."

George nodded. "He must have taken Regina's cell phone after he killed her." He took a long drink of his wine.

"He was hoping to use that text message to implicate you in his wife's death. He may have opened it after he killed her. She may not even have seen it, since she didn't answer, although it was sent weeks before she went missing."

He looked across at Susan without saying anything.

"You still don't remember sending that text, do you?"

George took another sip. He looked around for the waiter, hoping to be interrupted by the arrival of food. Talking about his dissociative amnesia was still something that embarrassed him. "I only have a vague memory of having met her in a bar and not speaking to her. I don't even remember leaving the bar that night."

The waiter finally arrived and they busied themselves with their food before Susan spoke again. "How long have you had such dissociative symptoms?"

George put down his fork. "They started in early adolescence, then they stopped after I had my training analysis. So far as I know, they never returned until that night when I saw Regina in the bar." He took another long drink of his wine.

"Why do you think they came back?"

"Regina and I went out in college once. We went to a dance over summer vacation. I was still having fugue states now and then. I drank too much and apparently misbehaved during a fugue state. I don't remember what I did, but Regina objected to it. It upset both of us and we never saw each other again until that night in the bar. I guess that brought the memory back and provoked enough defenses against it to put me into a dissociative state. Then I blocked out having known Regina at all until I saw a picture of us together. It was taken the night we had that awful date."

She looked at him quizzically. "Have you had other fugue episodes since then?"

He felt anxious. He reached for his glass of wine and saw that it was empty. He looked around for the waiter. "I'm going to need another glass of wine to talk about this."

Susan looked concerned. "Really?"

"Really."

When the waiter had brought him another glass of wine, George took a long sip then shut his eyes for a moment. "OK," he said, opening his eyes. "I had three more fugue episodes that I'm aware of. The first one was when I scheduled Lucas for his first appointment. My secretary was out and I made the appointment myself, but I don't remember doing so."

Susan took a sip of her own wine and nodded. "So Bonaventure was telling the truth about you scheduling his appointment yourself."

George nodded. "The second time was when I went to meet Sherry Bennett that night when she called me from the parking garage. From the time I entered the parking garage until the time I found myself trying to remove the rope from her neck, I have no memory."

Susan's eyes widened in surprise. "You blacked out that whole time?"

"Not blacked out. I drove to her car and got out and tried to save her, but I don't remember doing so."

"You said there were three episodes."

"The third time was when I went to my property and dug up Regina's body. Lucas had told me about a dream in which he described what sounded like my homesite at Banning Ranch. He said that in his dream he saw Regina buried there. I was curious, but when I got there and saw this mound of dirt, I blanked out. The next thing I knew I was digging in the dirt and her body was coming up."

"My God," Susan said.

"I thought I might have murdered them," George said, taking another drink.

"But you didn't. Lucas has admitted killing those women and he tried to kill us, and they've found the evidence in his house."

George hung his head and nodded. He looked up. "Didn't you wonder about me, yourself?"

Susan shook her head. "I was shocked that you had lied to me, but I never believed you were the killer." She gazed at him. "Abe thought it was you, I think." Her expression became puzzled. "What about Lucas? Has he got a neurosis or was he making all of his symptoms up?"

George smiled. It was the first time since the beginning of their lunch. "That's my one big disappointment. I'll never be able to complete Lucas' therapy. I still think he has a real neurosis. He was fixated on Sherry Bennett as a substitute for his wife. And most of his dreams were real. He may have copied some from his wife's books, but not all of them. Somehow, though, maybe after he saw the text from me on his wife's cell phone, he decided to pin the murders on me. I'm not sure if he had that in mind when he scheduled his first appointment, but after I saw Sherry Bennett, I think the idea crystallized in his mind, or maybe after I found her dead and he knew that I could easily become a suspect. I'll never know exactly."

"What about his paralysis?"

"I think that was real. I mean you saw its onset yourself in the morgue. But obviously, it had remitted before we saw him that last time. His leg was fully functional when he pulled Reynolds' gun on us."

Susan gazed across the table at him. "You saved both Abe and me by disarming Bonaventure. That was very brave of you. If you hadn't done that, we wouldn't be sitting here today talking about this."

"Thank you, but you probably think that all this talk about neurosis and dream analysis is just psychoanalytic mumbo jumbo. I'm glad I got to tell you about it though, especially about my own symptoms. I hope it doesn't make you think that all analysts are just in the business because they're neurotic themselves."

She looked up at him, a broad smile on her face. "Not at all. I'm just thinking that maybe I need to learn more about psychoanalysis. I didn't really believe in unconscious motivation or the unconscious for that matter, but you're living proof that it exists."

"So my own pathology is what may convince you that I've been right?"

She raised her eyebrows. "Maybe. Understanding you is going to be a challenge Doctor Farquhar and I think I'm going to need all the help I can get."

"You mean this relationship is going to continue?" he asked, a look of surprise on his face.

"I think so, doctor."

"Then you should start calling me George."

# Note from the Author

Word-of-mouth is crucial for any author to succeed. If you enjoyed the book, please leave a review online—anywhere you are able. Even if it's just a sentence or two. It would make all the difference and would be very much appreciated.

Thanks!
Casey

# About the Author

Casey Dorman was the editor and publisher of *Lost Coast Review,* a print and online literary review. He has authored numerous articles on psychology and neuroscience and is the author of more than ten novels, including the bestselling mysteries, *I, Carlos* and *Murder in Nirvana.* He lives with his wife in Southern California.

Thank you so much for reading one of our **Crime Fiction** novels.
If you enjoyed the experience, please check out our recommended
title for your next great read!

*Caught in a Web* by Joseph Lewis

"This important, nail-biting crime thriller about MS-13 sets the
bar very high. One of the year's best thrillers."
*-BEST THRILLERS*

View other Black Rose Writing titles at
www.blackrosewriting.com/books and use promo code
**PRINT** to receive a **20% discount** when purchasing.